Praise for the Sara Browne Series ...

"LaRochelle's Sara Browne series is a winning group of tales filled with vibrant characters, a compelling storyline, and a sweet sexy romance." —The Prairies Book Review

"Tricia LaRochelle understands what makes an effective romance story work. She doesn't just offer a girl-meets-boy setup. What she assembles is an interesting pair of characters with flaws that make them distinct, relatable, and utterly human. She handles Sara's traumatic past with sensitivity and keen attention to its emotional and psychological components, which makes Sara a convincing and fascinating case study in PTSD." —Readers' Favorite

"LaRochelle writes like a pro and delivers a profoundly entertaining romance story with genuinely flawed characters and a deftly handled plot with explosive moments. The prose is dazzling, the first-person narrative voice is expertly executed, and the dialogues sparkle from page to page." —The Book Commentary

Bleeding Heart

A Holiday Romance

Sara Browne Series Book 4

Tricia T. LaRochelle

Manufactured in the United States of America

Copyright © 2023 by Tricia T. LaRochelle

ISBN 979-8-9861756-9-0 (ebook)

ISBN 979-8-9909107–0-6 (paperback)

All rights reserved

Published by Flaming Heart Press, United States of America

Distributed by Ingram Book Group

Cover design by Damonza

 Created with Vellum

I dedicate this book to Hattie and Hannah, two women who bring joy to my life during the holidays and every other day of the year.

Bleeding Heart

Chapter One

"Try not to kill yourself tonight, babe." From my peripheral, I saw Scott's smirk and rolled my eyes. It was the same thing he'd said this morning after I tripped over the edge of the kitchen mat and nearly broke my neck. Sitting at the breakfast table, Scott had just sipped his coffee and shook his head. I'm about to give him a snarky reply when a voice pulls my attention to the front of the room.

"Okay, class, now that we're all here and in position, let's begin with our standing deep breathing pose. Breathing is called Pranayama, the yoga practice of breath, the *prana-shakti* or life energies. It will improve detoxification to the organs and heighten mental relaxation and blood flow." Tanya, our yoga instructor with short, black curly hair, followed her speech with several breathing exercises that both Scott and I practiced from the back of the room. I knew what to do, but Scott didn't, who struggled at first with the sequence. Feet together, hands interlocked underneath the chin, head leaning back—all while focusing on your breath—it was a lot to take in.

Our fearless leader, however, stood barefoot on her yoga

mat at the front of the room, doing the exercise to perfection, her gaze washing over each of her students for accuracy. Her gray yoga pants and black tank top hugged her lean body, which wasn't so much packed with muscles as toned in a healthier and more wholesome sort of way. Tanya reminded me of a twenty-something version of Halle Berry. Skin flawless, she didn't strike me as someone who wore much makeup, either.

"That's right," she said as she homed in on a woman two rows in front of me who was slightly off with her timing but was trying to correct herself. Scott seemed to have it down now, so she didn't focus on him. When it came to exercise, he was definitely gifted. Unlike his klutz of a wife.

"You're doing great. Keep filling those lungs and connecting with your internal sense of awareness. Calm that nervous system." Tanya stopped her pose momentarily while the rest of us continued. She tipped her chin at something behind me through the glass barrier that separated the yoga studio from the reception. First a grin and then a wink told me she must've been addressing her wife, Andie, who often sat at the reception desk, greeting customers and working on her laptop. Andie was also attractive. Her short, wispy blond hair and fair complexion complemented her pale blue eyes. They were both natural beauties, really, which I was sure Scott had noticed when we arrived.

"You are all doing fantastic." And soon, Tanya was back in position.

Tanya and Andie owned this yoga studio called The Shape of You and planned on expanding to include a juice bar soon— or as soon as they could get the space next door ready after the small sandwich shop had sold it to them last month. I knew this because they talked about it often with their students, even offering samples of some of the juices they planned to sell. The one with apple, cucumber, ginger, celery, and lemon was my favorite.

I liked Tanya, striking up a few conversations on my way in and out of class. I even considered inviting her and Andie over for a drink sometime or maybe dinner. Making new friends wasn't my thing, but I was trying to get better at it. No one could replace my college suitemate and BFF, Amy, but there were times when I missed having someone to chat with over a cup of tea or a glass of wine. I had friends at work, but it wasn't the same thing. It was hard to let your hair down with workmates who saw you professionally on a daily basis.

Amy now lived in Richmond, Virginia, where her new hubby, Luke, played guitar in a band, and I lived in Scott's hometown of Phoenixville, Pennsylvania. Four-and-a-half hours did little to hinder the closeness of our bond, and we saw each other as often as we could. Plus, there was always texting and FaceTime.

"Breathing allows you to focus on the here and now. Put everything else out of your mind. Let your body talk to you ..."

About twenty people had shown up for hot yoga tonight, more than I was used to seeing, diminishing the small room shamelessly. And the powerfully built blond man looming next to me, only added to the feeling of confinement. He sure was nice to look at, though. Two mirrored walls, running adjacent to one another, did their best to expand our perception of the room while lavender essential oils calmed the air and the mind —*my* mind, anyway.

Tonight's class was a little different from the ones I'd been attending these past few months, mainly because of the number and the fact that Scott had decided to join. Always willing to accept a physical challenge, he had jumped at the chance when I'd brought it up to him earlier. It was late afternoon Thursday when he had just arrived home from the architecture firm where he worked, wearing a casual, olive-green button-down, complemented by a pair of slim-fit beige pants and oxford loafers on his feet. He looked like a male model, the fabric embracing his body as though it appreciated his beauty as much as I did.

I was already dressed for yoga, which he noticed right away. Those puppy dog eyes of his told me he had other plans for us—*cuddle-time* plans.

After he snagged a beer from the fridge, he pulled his laptop out of his briefcase and placed it on the breakfast bar. "Skip class tonight, babe. It's just yoga. I can give you a better workout here than anyone there can do."

Spending time with Scott was always at the top of my list, but after we'd decked the house both inside and out last weekend for the holidays and cleaned everything top to bottom afterward, my lower back was in need of some serious stretching. I had been doing a lot of lifting at work as well. Not addressing it now could result in a pulled muscle or worse. I'd been down that road before. Wasn't going there again. Not if I could help it. I didn't want to spend the holidays in pain.

Scott wiggled his eyebrows as he sat at the counter, swiveling on his stool. "I promise you my workout will be a lot more fun."

I imagined the type of workout Scott was referring to and my cheeks flushed at the thought. *Would there ever come a day that this man couldn't make me blush?*

"That's *very* tempting, but I need to stretch my back out." With my palms braced against my lower back, I arched into the stiffness of my body. "You know, it's not as easy as you think. Why don't you come and see for yourself? It's only an hour. And then we can have a late dinner and our fun time afterward." *That is, if I can stay awake that long,* I thought to myself with skepticism. I approached the sink, where I filled my stainless-steel water bottle and yawned from a long day with my four special-needs middle schoolers. Those kids rocked my world but wore me out at the same time.

I expected Scott to decline my invitation. I was certain yoga wasn't his thing. To my surprise, he perked right up. Once he finished the quick email he said he had to send, he slapped his laptop closed and rose to his feet. "You know what? A bunch of sweaty women wearing skimpy clothes and turning themselves into a pretzel. I'd be down for that on a Thursday night."

Concerned he might lose interest, I refrained from telling him that both men and women attended, most with regular bodies and some a tad more *regular* than others, Tanya and Andie excluded. "We aren't supermodels," I said with a playful huff as I screwed the lid on my water bottle. "It's not an aerobic workout or weight training like you're used to. It's more stretching and holding poses, but you'd be surprised how hard it can be and how much it tones your muscles." I spoke as I pulled my yoga mat out from the hall closet, set my bag on a chair in the breakfast nook, and went to packing it up for class, my water bottle sliding into the side pocket.

Scott came up from behind me and waited while I finished organizing. His musky scent reached out to my senses, drawing me in.

Once I had plunked my yoga mat and tote filled with a small towel, a change of clothes, and my water bottle onto the breakfast counter, he spun me around, his arms lassoing my waist. He snuggled me into his hunky body, smile dazzling the way it always did when he had something sweet to say. "And just so you know, *they* may not be supermodels, but you could put any supermodel to shame in my book." His lips, all soft and supple, landed on mine, offering several succulent kisses that trailed down the side of my neck, his breath warm against my ear. "Anytime you want to walk the runway, I'll be ready and waiting, babe. I'll even buy the lingerie." He nestled his hips slowly into mine, telling me just how *ready* he was. "I love to watch you move." Excitement swirled in his voice and eyes.

On many occasions, I'd danced for Scott, and I'd even surprised him with a striptease every now and then. Was he now expecting me to stroll around the house like a runway model in nothing but a teddy or a thong? I giggled to myself, knowing I'd do just about anything this gorgeous man asked of me—mainly because he would *always* make it worth my while.

And *that* thought pumped moist heat through my lower half, enough that I mentally had to shake myself out of the sexual stupor he was determined to put me in. Lately, he'd been a tad more needy than usual, but I understood why.

Our fall schedules had been busy. I spent my weeknights grading classwork or setting up projects to test my students for comprehension and fine motor skills. Teaching special-needs children required enormous amounts of paperwork and proof of their testing ability. Scott had his job at the architecture firm, but he was also working toward opening his own business, something his father had said he'd back when the time was right, but only if Scott proved it would be a successful venture.

Scott had landed his first official job right after we were married, but he still had another year-and-a-half of work experience to go under a licensed architect, who turned out to be his boss, Ben, before he could take the ARE exam and venture out on his own. And he was working furiously on all of that. Ultimately, he wanted to design buildings, but he also wanted to design eco-friendly homes that could sustain dangerous weather. He'd spent the better part of a year slaving over a model home that he planned to use to sell more. Our home.

Even before we were able to move in, we lived on-site, the land gifted to us by his parents, in a small camper that Scott's cousin had lent us temporarily. It was exciting to watch our new home take form, each phase providing something new. We had power and water in our camper, but I jumped up and down like a child with a new toy when we finally had a breaker box and plumbing in the house. The main floor anyway.

The first floor of our four-thousand-square-foot house was mostly done, but studs, insulation, plumbing, and electrical wires ran rampant on the upper floor. Scott worked a forty-hour week at the firm and then spent most of his evenings and weekends finishing our house. Electricians, plumbers, and inspectors, everyone had their own deadlines.

He'd often come to bed after I had dozed off. As if that wasn't enough, he was also helping his father with computer work at the car dealership that Mr. Williams owned in town. At least his dad paid him for his time, which our new house greedily took and spent like a Real Housewife of some place or another. Add in holiday gatherings, and we hadn't had much time for intimacy as of late. And what intimacy we did have was short and to the point—not the attentive lovemaking his vibrant blue eyes were telling me they desired now.

"Why are you home so early?" I asked, noticing the time. The sun hadn't even dropped below the horizon yet.

Scott shrugged. "Because the boss closed up early. He asked everyone out for a holiday drink."

I touched his arm. "How come you didn't go?"

With eyes so blue you could take a swim in them, he gave me that look again, the one determined to knock down all my defenses. His fingers touched my cheek, his voice going all soft and fuzzy. "Because I wanted to spend time with *you*. We're not gonna get much of a chance after tonight."

He was right. His sister, Kelsey, was coming over tomorrow night to introduce us to her new beau. His name was Stuart, and from what she'd told me, he was quite dreamy with big brown eyes and a nice bod. I'd prepped appetizers and bought plenty of wine, beer, and drink mixers for the occasion. The weekend was also booked with a Saturday brunch at Scott's parents' house before we all gathered in their enormous living room to trim their tree. After that, we'd set out on the Phoenixville annual Holiday Lights Run, followed by homemade pizzas and plenty of drinks back at the Williamses' home. These people knew how to party, and we planned to spend the night. The next morning, I offered to help Scott's mom make trays and trays of Christmas cookies (mostly for their customers, the local food bank, and some of her board member friends) while we all watched football. Sunday nights were all about getting ready for the workweek: making meals, doing laundry, and cleaning the house. That left tonight and only tonight free for *extracurriculars*.

I groaned internally. There were moments when I could understand Captain Hook's need to destroy all the clocks in *Peter Pan*, although I didn't have a crocodile set on vengeance. My enemy was time, or lack thereof.

Scott snuggled me closer for a hug. "I miss my *she-beast*." He'd even unpacked the nickname, reserved for special moments or convincing. "All I want to do is kiss every inch of your gorgeous body." His need pushed against me again, making my decision to attend yoga even more difficult.

If it wasn't for my darn back ...

I gave him a light shove and giggled while shaking my head. "You have a one-track mind, my love."

Scott stood there dumbfounded, feigning outrage. "What do you expect?" He flung one arm out before he placed a hand indignantly against his chest, all burly and beautiful. "It's not *my* fault. You're the one who's so damn hot." He lowered his brow and stared up at me in a do-I-need-to-state-the-obvious sort of way, the edges of his smile curling upward. "Are you sure I can't talk you into skipping class?" There went his lower lip.

I shook my head. He was a brat, but he was a cute brat.

Not sure how to follow up his *extremely* tempting offer with something non-offensive, I simply sighed. "But I'm already dressed for class, handsome." I lifted up on my tiptoes and placed a light kiss on his cheek, my lips prickling against his five-o'clock stubble. "And I've gotta leave in about"—I grabbed my phone off the breakfast bar—"seven minutes, so if you're coming, you better get ready."

Scott stood back and placed both hands on his hips, his tone less than enthused. "Well, I guess if I want to spend time with my wife, I have no other choice." He darted off, while I returned his unopened beer to the fridge.

Back in class, a few of the women—some younger, some middle-aged—kept glancing over at Scott as though their eyes couldn't help themselves. Especially when Scott bent over to stretch the backs of his legs. I was sure they weren't used to seeing a gorgeous six-foot-three blond, graced with muscles— one who dominated the space around him—in our humble little yoga class. There may have been a time when it bothered me that women *and* men enjoyed the sight of my husband so much, but not anymore. He was gorgeous, so who was I to say otherwise? Plus, he was mine, and that would never change.

As class continued, what did change, however, were the sounds coming out of one woman's butt. And she was right in front of us. I mean, this woman was playing a tune all her own.

Each new stretch encouraged another flatulent encore from the woman with wavy brown hair gathered into a ponytail, and a pear-shaped physique. *Thank God that's not me.* Yoga had a way of doing this to people.

Tanya tried her best to help. "Flatulence is expected during these classes as you stretch out your body and release gases stored in your intestinal tract. Don't be embarrassed if it happens."

If it happens? This woman was playing a tuba out of her backside. And how weird that Scott just happened to be here to witness it all. He kept glancing over, his eyes bursting with humor. This wasn't a bunch of hot cheerleaders or volleyball champs, looking sexy, as he had predicted, which made the whole experience even more amusing *and* awkward.

Another stretch prompted yet another fart. At least I didn't detect any foul odor, none that reached my nose.

Did someone from across the room just toot as well? Geez. I was sure it was a man this time. *What is happening?* This was a first for me. And for Scott, too, whose shoulders were starting to rattle in my periphery.

He's going to lose it. And if he loses it, I'm next. Think of something sad ... think of something sad ...

Thrrrrrppp flew through the air once again. If the woman was embarrassed, she didn't show it. And good for her. *Men fart all the time*, I reasoned to myself in support.

Why I thought bringing Scott to my yoga class was a good idea was beyond me. I was sure I'd never hear the end of this one.

After class, we hydrated, changed into our spare clothes, put on sneakers, wrapped ourselves in thick coats, and headed out the door as fast as our feet would carry us. Cuddle time awaited.

The minute we were outside, the Pennsylvania wind reminded me it was early December, the winter chill ready to keep us company for the next several months.

I pointed toward the vacant space next door, its floor-to-ceiling windows covered in sheets of brown paper. "You know, Tanya and Andie bought the space next door. They're expanding and adding a juice bar. You should see if they need any help designing it." I fished my keys from my bag. "Would Ben mind if you took on side jobs?"

Scott stopped and gazed over at the darkened building. "Well, I might be able to talk Ben into supervising the project since I'm not licensed yet. He's well aware that I'm working toward my license and my own business. I can offer to do the work after hours and on weekends so it doesn't interfere with my clients."

From what I'd seen and what Scott had shared, Ben saw potential in my husband and allowed him to work fairly independently. Ben just had to look over and sign off on the jobs when the time came.

Scott stared some more, his wheels turning, his hand rubbing his chin in a thoughtful way. "That's a good idea. I'll talk to Ben and then call them and set up an appointment." He touched my shoulder. "Thanks, babe." As we turned toward my car and began walking again, his expression changed to a jokier one. "Hey, what the hell was the deal with that woman in front of us?"

I knew he was going to ask me about her. I glanced back to make sure we were alone or at least that the flatulent woman wasn't within earshot.

"Did she have a burrito or something beforehand? Maybe Mexican wasn't the best idea before yoga. Is it like this all the time? Man, I thought dudes farted a lot. That woman could win a contest. She sounded like a goddamn racecar." Fog danced around Scott's lips as he ranted with a playful lilt in his voice.

We strolled over to my Subaru SUV, where I opened the back door and placed my tote on the back seat. Scott did the same on the opposite side of the car.

We climbed inside.

"I heard someone else let one rip on the other side of the

room. You women got rotten innards." Scott nudged my shoulder and chuckled, clearly enjoying himself. "Not too lady-like. And I thought you farted a lot."

I started the vehicle and cranked the heater to high. And then I huffed, trying to be serious. "First of all, I think the other side of the room came from a man. And second, I hardly ever fart, mister!" I slapped him on the arm.

Scott's mouth dropped open, his face beaming with delight. "I'm sorry to break it to you, babe, but you fart all the time. In your sleep. I just never told you about it before." He puffed his chest out and lifted his chin. "Because I'm a gentleman."

I flung my mouth open, my eyes wide with feigned outrage. "I do not fart in my sleep."

Oh my God did *that* make Scott laugh. He was practically doubled over. "Yes, you do, but you don't fart like the yoga queen . . . . She farts more than my college soccer coach did, and I thought he was the worst . . . . I can't imagine the two of them in the same room . . . . No one would be able to hear themselves think . . . . That is if everyone didn't pass out from the fumes, first."

I angled my head, my expression deadpan. "You bout done?" I tried my best not to crack a smile.

Scott hooked his hand around my far shoulder and tugged me closer for a kiss. "Oh, I'm just getting' started, babe . . . . You know why they call it hot yoga?" He only waited a millisecond before he answered his own question. "From all the hot gas floating around the room . . . . You think cars are bad for global warming, hot yoga's worse . . . . Hot yoga? They oughta call it fart yoga."

Okay, so that one was funny, and I giggled against my better judgment. "I get the picture, smart aleck. You didn't like the class." I shifted the car into drive and steered toward the parking lot exit, the heater blasting lukewarm air throughout the small cabin.

"Oh, I wouldn't say I didn't like the class. It was funny as shit." He gazed out the window as we passed by various shops and houses all twinkling with Christmas lights. Manicured bushes and leafless trees stood ground in the frozen medians providing the perfect canvas for more gleeful illumination. Every lamppost wore wreaths like necklaces while swags of lights swung across the streets from above, their tiny white dots reflecting off my windshield. As I drove along, I took it all in.

I loved this time of year and how everything sparkled with joy.

Scott glanced over, the darkness inside the car doing little to obscure his inquisitive eyes. "Hey, what was that pose called where you bend over with your legs fully apart?"

I proceeded through a traffic light, then navigated a right turn toward the direction of our house. I scratched my ear. "I don't know. Some standing, stretch leg pose, why?" I knew the answer but had to ask anyway.

"After we shower at home, you can try that one naked, and I'll stand right behind you. I've got something to give you that might just make it more fun. And then we can have a nice relaxing dinner, sound good?"

"Fun for you? Or fun for me?" My inner thighs quivered at the images playing out in my mind's eye.

A broad smile stretched across his gorgeous face. "Well, fun for both of us, babe." Then he *pffted* through his lips. "I'm no amateur." He quirked his brow, his face all disgusted with *how could you even doubt that?*

I flipped the blinker for another right turn, trying not to hyperventilate. "Sounds like you've got it all planned out."

Face forward, Scott nodded slowly. "You know it, babe. I've got just what you want."

I decided to tease him back for a change. "Okay, I'll do my best not to fart on you."

Scott looked at me in horror, his lower jaw practically ricocheting off his lap. "Sara Williams, I'm shocked. This class is turning you into Amy." My BFF never minced words, not like I always did.

A pause followed, and then we both burst out laughing. Nearly six years later, Scott could still make me laugh, and swoon, and feel just about any emotion along the spectrum. Best of all, he made me feel safe and happy. I adored this man. We held hands for the remainder of the drive home.

* * *

The next morning, I sat at my desk waiting for my students to return from gym class. I had just eaten my lunch and gotten caught up on a few emails and announcements for the week. With nothing pressing to do, I revisited that pose that Scott had requested from the night before—the one that still made me shudder inside sixteen hours later. With my back to him and my legs fully apart, my butt in his face, Scott went to work. He'd positioned me at the foot of our bed, pillows galore for me to lean into. Then he used his fingers and tongue to stimulate every fold of my female flesh before gliding his generous erection inside the warmth of my body. Even though I was on the pill, he wore a condom, which he often did to minimize the mess. The sensations I experienced were almost too much to bear, and I began moaning. When his hands weren't holding my hips firmly, they were stimulating my nipples, adding to the intensity of it all.

"You are so fucking hot, babe. I love your tight ass and your wet pussy." Scott continued to thrust into me from behind. "You feel incredible."

When I climaxed, I screamed as though I was possessed. And then Scott did the same, only with a lot more baritone in *his* voice. We both fell onto our king-sized bed and just lay there, our lungs catching pockets of needed oxygen.

"That was great." Scott rolled onto his side and ran a hand down my chest and stomach, the pads of his fingers igniting a shiver.

My nerve endings felt like a million points of light, all pulsating with sexual pleasure that were having a hard time returning to normal.

"I've missed this. But it was worth the wait." He smiled that satisfied smile he got when utterly fulfilled. "I love you."

Mouth dry, I turned toward him, in awe of what he could do to me with his rugged body. "I love you too. How much time do you need before another round?" My newfound hunger brewed, and I had to satisfy it. Either that or lose my mind.

Scott lifted his head, his eyes filled with surprise. "Really? My little she-beast is up for another round?"

I flung my leg over his hips. "Oh, yeah, handsome. Go wash up, and when you get back, I'm going to use my mouth to—"

"Mrs. Williams. We're back."

Huh? What? I had to snap my brain into focus as a skinny little blond boy named Daryl, also known as speed demon, came running into the classroom, his cheeks flushed, my para-professional, Giselle, on his heels. "We played dodgeball," he said with squeaky excitement. "And I won."

Trying to settle my pulse, I glanced up at Giselle with trepidation. According to my lungs, I'd just run a mile. "I hope it wasn't as violent as the other students play. Dodgeball can be pretty intense." I kept my voice even, hoping no one noticed my flustered disposition.

In her mid-twenties (a year older than me) and studying to be a teacher herself, Giselle waved a consolatory hand my way, seemingly unfazed by me or my question. "Nah, the game was geared for our class. It was all good." She set her tote down on her designated table and brushed some lint off her light-pink tunic, which complemented her dark skin tone and silky black hair.

I liked Giselle. She hadn't finished college quite yet. She had taken a couple of years off after high school to travel abroad and tour certain areas of the US. This internship was part of the program she was enrolled in now. I knew my time with her was coming to an end, but I appreciated her good nature and her willingness to help me whenever I needed it.

She'd even stayed late one afternoon to help me decorate my classroom right before Thanksgiving break. Since all four of our students celebrated Christmas, we designed our door to look like a fireplace with pinkish-red bricks and a roaring fire made of yellow-and-orange craft paper. The kids made their own paper stockings, which hung proudly from the two-dimensional mantle. In the corner stood a small imitation tree waiting for our Secret Santa gift exchange, along with a few other games on the day before winter break would begin. I also had a holiday movie for them and a short comprehension test afterward. I tried to make everything a lesson if I could.

As Giselle stood at the doorway, keeping an eye out for our other three students, Annabelle, Walker, and Trina came rushing past her.

"Can we have our snacks now, Mrs. Williams?" Trina, my petite student with short, blond hair asked with a hopeful spark in her greenish-blue eyes.

"Sure." I stood. "Go ahead and grab your snacks and sit at your desks for snack time. But wash your hands first. Knowing the drill, my students made their way to the bathroom to scrub up. Thankfully, they never seemed to mind.

"I'll continue reading our first Magic Tree House book,

Dinosaurs Before Dark." I made my way to the story corner where a cushy carpet covered the floor, and a small bookcase displayed our class selections. With book in hand, I dragged a stool to the front of the room. "Do you all remember where we left off?" This was always a good way to see how much they had retained from a previous reading.

But before anyone could answer me, my walkie-talkie crackled to life on my desk. I lifted my index finger. "Hold that thought. I'll be right back."

Oblivious, the students opened their respective snacks and drinks, chatting with each other about the dodgeball game while I grabbed my walkie-talkie. Giselle hovered near the students in case anyone needed help opening a chip bag or a juice box.

I lifted the walkie-talkie close to my ear and heard what sounded like Principal Robbins say, "Lockdown. This is not a drill. Code 3. Shelter in Place. Follow protocol." My heart leapt into my throat. Code 3 meant there was a possible threat on campus!

Holy crap!

Chapter Two

From within my desk, my cell phone, which remained on vibrate, blew up a moment later. I pulled open the drawer and scanned the warning texts from the school as well. Another protocol. There was no chance I'd misunderstood, though I'd held onto that hope for a brief moment.

Trying to ignore my racing heart, I grabbed my lockdown binder and flung it open to the procedural page. "Giselle, can you read to the students for me?" I rushed over and handed her the book, trying to stay calm.

"What's going on?" she mumbled, one of her hands half-covering her mouth.

"Lockdown, Code 3. We need to shelter in place."

Giselle nodded, her expression doing its best to stay in control. She sat on the stool and continued my line of questioning from our last read. "Does anyone remember where the Magic Tree House came from?"

Two eager hands flew up.

Back at my desk, I focused on the job at hand. Step one: I quickly approached our door and checked that it was locked.

Step two: I covered the small window on the door with the laminated paper provided. Step three. I drew the blinds. I continued to dart around the room with a purpose in mind. At least the students weren't near any windows, which was step four.

"Mrs. Williams, why are you covering the windows?" My inquisitive Daryl asked, causing the other three to take notice.

Giselle paused her reading lesson, her eyes also curious.

"Well, remember how we practiced what to do if we have a fire, bad weather, or if someone comes on campus that isn't supposed to be here?"

Four heads nodded as Daryl said, "Yeah. Are we practicing now?" He was so innocent and kind. I loved these kids.

I had to think about my answer. While I wanted to keep them safe, I didn't want to freak them out. Trina had Down syndrome. The other three had autism, some of them like Daryl with heightened sensitivity and nervous systems. When stressed, he could spiral and *had* when situations grew unpredictable or chaotic. Like when we experienced our first fire drill. I had to take him aside and practice breathing exercises, assuring him there was no fire, which helped. Annabelle had a tendency to pull her hair out in similar circumstances. Loud noises were their nemesis. *Guns are loud, and so are screaming students and teachers running for their lives.* I tried to settle my nerves. *You are their best line of defense.* I felt so vulnerable and protective at the same time.

I swallowed the hardness of the situation. "For the moment, that is what I'm doing. But I will keep you posted as I learn more." I gazed over at Giselle who was now standing with the book in her hands. "Why don't you all go sit on the carpet in the story time corner. You can even bring your snacks this time, and Miss Giselle will read the next chapter to you. Trina, it's okay if you want to take your pillow with you. It will be like a picnic." I smiled and clapped my hands together, hoping to generate enthusiasm. I only allowed snacks at their desks, mainly to keep the mess to a minimum. I'd learned that lesson right away. This would be a treat for them, and I hoped they'd see it that way.

"Yay," Walker said as he grabbed his drink and small package of crackers to take with him. "I want to sit by Miss Giselle." He rushed over to a spot next to the white rocking chair in the story corner, the remaining three following in his footsteps.

For the next half hour, I stood near the windows, my trusty walkie-talkie clipped to my waistband, and my senses on high alert. I pretended to be straightening various folders and paperwork nearby. The problem was our classroom faced the baseball and football fields out back. I had no idea what was going on in the parking lot or out front—or in the rest of the school for that matter. Every now and then, an officer would walk by, scaring the daylights out of me, but I kept myself in check. Harry, our school resource officer, even made an appearance. No one had their gun drawn. They were merely looking around. *That's a good sign, right?*

The kids remained away from the windows and, hopefully, out of harm's way. So far, everything was running smoothly. Once Giselle finished her chapter, she encouraged a discussion and Q&A afterward. These kids loved to talk, so that worked.

Images of a lone gunman barreling down the hallways, hysteria in his midst, stormed my thoughts. I envisioned diving over the students to keep them safe, glass shattering, the smell of gunpowder and fear engulfing the air. Blood spattering the walls.

PTSD was a tricky demon in my life—one that liked to rear up when situations warranted. I had a past riddled with trauma, but I also had to stay in control. I was their teacher, their protector, and I took that job seriously. Before I entered this profession, I had thought about the what-ifs in my line of work. Who hadn't, given the tragic stories dominating the news outlets and social media? But thinking about a situation and being faced with one was a very different experience. *You aren't faced with anything yet. Don't jump to conclusions. Just breathe.*

While I received updates to stay put on my two-way, I used my cell to try and find out what was going on. I checked a few news outlets to no avail. *Maybe the story is too new?* Or maybe I was checking in the wrong places.

And then a text came rolling in, startling me to the point that I almost dropped my phone. It was Scott.

Are you okay? I just saw on the news that an inmate escaped from Faulkner State Correctional Institution, which is only about five miles away from you. He's in for murder and considered VERY dangerous. Is the school aware of this?

Me: *I wondered what had happened. Yes, they are aware. Someone suspicious was spotted on the school grounds. The police are here searching now.*

Scott: *Fuck. I'm coming there.*

Me: *We're in lockdown, so if you come, you won't get in.*

Scott: *I don't care. I'll wait wherever they tell me. Are they going to release the students?*

I glanced over at Giselle who was still engaged with the kids, everyone smiling and laughing. *So far, so good.*

Me: *IDK. I haven't had any updates yet. We are in lockdown. And they are searching the grounds and probably the school too. That's all I know for now.*

Scott: *Be safe. I love you, babe. Don't take any chances. Stay in your classroom. I'll be there soon.*

Just don't do anything stupid and get yourself killed. The thought made me nauseous. Scott had grown into a rather level-headed adult, but when it came to his family and his loved ones, he was as fierce as a lion protecting his pride.

Me: *I won't, and I will. Love you too.*

My breath hitched every time I thought about the possibilities of this day. *Please, God, don't let the escapee be here. Let this be a better-safe-than-sorry situation.*

Another half hour passed, and the kids were getting restless. Walker and his nervous bladder had peed twice now in our private bathroom, and everyone else wanted to know why we had to keep the room so dark. I had turned off the lights, knowing there was enough natural light to read or play games, but this wasn't our normal day. Not by a long shot. At least we weren't in the hallways, trying to sit against the walls quietly with several hundred other students, like we'd be doing with a weather drill. This time, we were isolated, which came with its own set of pros and cons.

The last update I received only repeated that there had been a possible sighting of an unauthorized person on campus. The authorities were checking the grounds and the surrounding area. Nothing new.

I was trying to come up with a way to better explain what was happening, when my two-way radio crackled to life again.

"Hello? This is Mrs. Williams in Room 14." I listened as our school counselor spoke this time.

"Hey, Sara. I need to follow protocol. Bear with me," she said. "Can you tell me the names of all the occupants in your classroom at this time?"

"Yes, my students are all here. Annabelle Smith, Walker James, Trina Palatino, and Daryl Morgenstern. My paraprofessional is also here, Giselle Sharma." I listened for more instructions.

By now, my students were all standing, along with Giselle, watching my every move. Trying to keep my expression positive, I had a new appreciation for flight attendants and their nervous passengers. "Everybody stay where you are."

"I'm relieved to say that the authorities have checked and cleared the campus, and the parents have been notified of our status."

I exhaled what felt like a breath the size of a hot air balloon, my body trying not to slump.

"Students who have been preapproved will leave on the buses in the loop. Several officers are out there on standby. This is just a precaution to make the students feel safer. Your students will ride home with their parents, who are all here with me in the counseling office. An officer will be coming to your door momentarily to escort your students out of the building. You may unlock your door after they've identified themselves to you. Again, this is just a precaution."

My phone also flashed a new message about the shortened schedule.

"Got it. Thank you. We'll be ready." I set my radio down. "Class. That was our school counselor, Mrs. Baker. I have some good news." I clasped my hands in front of my chest again. "You are all going home early. And your parents are already here to pick you up. Gather your things, and don't forget your laptops."

The small group made a beeline for the door.

I raised my palms. "Wait. You can't go quite yet. You need to get your backpacks ready and your coats and mittens on."

Each student moved with remarkable speed, not one of them grabbing the essential item I had just mentioned.

"And don't forget your laptops." I often felt like a broken record these days.

Soon, a knock sounded from the door, which was a good thing considering the students were growing impatient knowing their parents were waiting for them.

After identifying herself and showing me her badge through the small window on the door, a female officer with short brown hair and a kind face, entered our classroom.

She smiled. "Hey, guys"—she quirked a brow—"and gals. I hope you're all having a good day." She spoke like a mother or someone with experience with the younger generation.

Even still, my students were a bit timid at first, their eyes wary of her uniform, equipped with handcuffs and a gun.

"My name is Officer Elsa Boucher." She beamed a smile. "And I'll be walking you out to greet your parents."

"Elsa from *Frozen*?" Annabelle asked, her eyes livelier.

Officer Elsa bent over to bring her line of vision closer to Annabelle's, who was all of five-feet tall and ninety pounds soaking wet. "I do have the same name as Elsa from *Frozen*. And my daughter also loves that movie." She straightened her posture. "Are you all ready to go meet your parents?" Elsa gazed over at me, and I nodded as I helped Walker finish getting his backpack over his shoulders.

"Yes, they are all ready to go." My gaze swept over my students. "Stay with Officer Elsa everyone, and be good students for her, okay?"

Daryl nodded in his usual spirited manner.

"Okay, let's go." Elsa opened the door. "So, tell me, do you all like the movie *Frozen*?"

Walker rolled his eyes. "That movie is for babies ... and girls." He said it as though it was a crime against humanity. As he strolled out the door, he told Elsa about all the movies that boys liked, *Transformers* being at the top of his list.

Daryl agreed with him, but Annabelle had a few choice words on the subject. "*Frozen* is not for babies. My big sister likes it, and so do I. We're not babies."

An argument ensued, one that my ears followed all the way down the hallway until they were out of sight and earshot.

I returned to my room. "You should go, too, Giselle. Sounds like the grounds have all been searched and are safe."

Giselle approached her winter-white fleece coat, which hung waiting for her from a hook on the wall. "What about you?" She laced her pashmina scarf around her neck.

"I'm not far behind you. I just want to get some stuff together in case we need to work remotely at the beginning of next week, and then I'll close everything up."

I'd only worked remotely with my students once before when we had a power outage due to a windstorm last September. But knowing it was a possibility, especially in these times, I had spent last summer preparing for such a circumstance. My online platform came with links for students to access assignments, and I had a daily Zoom link on my home page, so we could do attendance and discuss the assignments for the day. My computer guru of a husband had helped me set it all up. I had even practiced how to use it with both the students and their parents during our open house last August.

The unexpected power outage proved that we had a few kinks in our system, but I was confident we'd do better this time (if it turned out there was a *this time*). At least, I had all of my students in one place, unlike regular education teachers who had multiple classes *and* subjects. I knew of a few who really struggled with this new format.

"So, what happened again?"

I explained to Giselle everything I knew.

"Jesus. I hope they find him soon. Where is Faulkner Prison, anyway? It must be nearby."

I nodded. "Yeah, it's only like five miles from here. It's down off Route 460, over near the soap factory."

Giselle had just laced her arms through her coat and pulled her long hair out from beneath the collar. She grabbed her bag and things. "Where?"

"It's about five miles north of here. It's kind of hard to explain. There isn't much around that area. Pretty rural."

"Oh. Well, I'm glad I live on the south side, then." She released a nervous chuckle as she approached the door, her tote bag and purse draped over her shoulder.

She may have lived on the south side of town, but Scott and I didn't. Our house was located on the west side of Phoenixville. We were farther away from the prison than the middle school was, but not by much. Maybe an extra few miles. I wasn't sure exactly, but knew it wasn't too far. Scott and I had driven out to the northern areas a few times to walk some of the trails that he loved.

Among running and weight training, Scott also loved to hike and explore. He had brought me to all sorts of locations as a result. No surprise that on our first date, Scott had taken me hiking into the Blue Ridge Mountains of Virginia. I was a freshman at Commonwealth University in Charlottesville, and he was a junior. On a beautiful mountain top with a panoramic view that was nothing short of awe-inspiring, he blessed me with my very first kiss. Even though I hadn't quite grasped the concept at the time, I had already fallen for him.

"Okay, well, have a nice weekend. And stay safe out there." Giselle placed her hand on the door casing distracting me from my thoughts. "Let's keep in touch by text if either of us hears anything."

"Sounds good, Giselle. I'm sure the school will do the same. Have a nice weekend."

After she left, I stood in the center of the room for a brief moment and gazed at all the student artwork, calendars, and the bins filled with learning toys. A large map adorned one wall where we acquainted ourselves with various locations around the world.

I'd only known these particular students for about four

months now, but I had already grown to love each and every one of them. I'd spent my first year after college substitute teaching, which was hectic, but gave me a chance to see which schools I liked, and which ones I wanted to avoid. Valley Park Middle School was like a dream come true. A short distance from home, the location was perfect, but what struck me the most was how supportive the staff were to each other and their students. "No one gets belittled at Valley Park Middle" was scrolled across the high wall of the cafeteria for all to see as students came and went. And they meant it too. Bullying was *not* tolerated.

Not only did I adore the students and the staff at this school, but I took pride in my classroom as well and the way my kids had influenced every inch of this space. What warmed my heart the most was the "Who am I?" section. Each of the students had brought in photos and facts about themselves that we tacked up together. Walker loved dogs and anything pertaining to Transformers. Trina played basketball at the YMCA and adored her cat, Mittens. Annabelle played piano and loved to read. And Daryl was our athlete with enough energy to play multiple sports every season. Giselle was from India and liked to run marathons. These people were amazing and equally unique.

All at once, the scary moments of the day shook me as if the ground itself had moved beneath my feet. I realized what we could have lost here. How devastated our families would have been if things had gone a different way, mine included.

I approached the corkboard, where my "Who am I?" section remained tacked in place. And there at the center of my world, my wedding photo hung proudly, two newlyweds in love and blossoming with smiles. The top button of his white shirt unfastened, and with his sleeves rolled up a few inches, Scott leaned into my back, his arms laced around my waist, his smile devastatingly beautiful. His soft caramel curls shimmered in the afternoon sun.

If I lost him. Or if he lost me ...

A throat cleared, right before knuckles wrapped against the metal casing. I looked up as Scott emerged through the doorway.

Unexpectedly, I teared up as he rushed into my arms.

"Oh, babe. Are you okay?" His voice nurturing, he kissed my forehead and cheek. "I was so worried."

I angled my head back to get a better look at the love of my life. "Yeah, for a few minutes it got kind of scary. But I'm okay now that you're here."

Chapter Three

Kelsey and her new man, Stuart, came by for drinks and appetizers that evening. Of course, Scott wasted no time offering a tour of his new baby, otherwise known as our house.

As Kelsey and Stuart removed their coats and boots, their eyes widened, taking in the foyer. And believe me, there was a lot to take in. Beige marble floors reflected the light emanating from the French-scrolled wrought iron chandelier hanging prominently from the two-story-high ceiling. The effect was glassy and dazzling. A round mahogany table stood at its center to collect the day's mail or car keys in need of a temporary home. Anchoring the right side of this impressive room, a staircase decorated with iron balusters continued the French theme as they took flight to the second floor, sealed tight with sheets of plywood. Eventually, a small balcony would peer down at us from above. Scott hadn't gotten that far yet. And we could have a lengthy wait on our hands, given our finances. I decided that one floor was more than enough for us right now.

In the meantime, the more modest staircase leading from

the kitchen to the second floor would suffice. He even installed a door at the top to keep the chill out and to provide a sound barrier when he was working late.

I hung their coats in the hall closet, hidden beneath the stairway, before we made our way through the house, Scott making sure to point out the coffered ceilings complementing the main floor and the picture-frame molding paying tribute to our formal dining room. White marble with soft streaks of gray (handpicked by Scott), embellished our counters, offset nicely by the melancholic shades of black marble that made up the enormous island—one side serving as a breakfast bar—standing slightly elevated and large enough to fit six stools. With white designer cabinets—some lighted with glass door insets—Scott didn't skimp on much of anything when designing this house. It was more than we could afford but somehow we'd managed.

To add my personal touch, I chose muted earth tones in shades of brown, green, beige, and gray for the interior walls, along with window dressings designed to enhance the feeling of style and home.

I loved watching him boast about the angles and the functionality of the rooms. "These floors are eastern hemlock," he said as we strolled down a wide hallway bridging the formal dining room from the formal living room. "I found them in an old church being remodeled and restored them."

"Good work, little brother. Every time I come here it looks even nicer," Kelsey said with a nod of approval.

Scott exchanged a wide smile with his big sister.

By the time we'd shuffled past our his-and-her walk-in closets, our marble fireplace with a detailed wood mantel, and had reached our master bath, more specifically the shower—one that could fit an entire family inside of it—Stuart's mouth was starting to gape open, his eyes taking in the custom tile and multiple showerheads.

"Check this out." Scott opened the top drawer of a vanity where two outlets and two charging stations sat ready to power a hairdryer or a cell phone at a moment's notice.

"Man, this place is unbelievable." Stuart's eyes widened, his head turning in every direction. "I may never leave."

I winked at Scott whose shoulders rose with pride. He slapped Stuart on the shoulder. "We've got a finished guestroom on the main floor if you two want to stay over."

The invitation made not only Stuart's cheeks flush, but Kelsey's as well. It was a little soon to be making those sorts of plans, I thought to myself. Was this their second or third date? *Have they even slept together yet?* That question rolled around in my head as we strolled back toward the kitchen.

"Once I get the upstairs finished, we'll have three more bedrooms." Scott draped his arm over my shoulders. "Gotta have enough room for those babies Sara is gonna give me." He jostled my shoulders. "Right, babe?"

I slid my arm along his lower back, all firm and muscular. "We'll see. I may need a few more years to think about that, first." Considering July twenty-eighth would be my twenty-fourth birthday, I didn't see the urgency. Plus, I kind of liked being spoiled by my man for a few more years yet.

"Copy that. I'm in no hurry, either. It's gonna take some time to afford anyway, right?"

I nodded. *Good, we're in agreement.* We'd discussed the issue a few times, but it was always nice to confirm that we were still on the same page.

He kissed the side of my head and whispered in my ear, "We'll just have fun practicing." My husband's left dimple winked at me, my heart ramping up with the possibilities of future "practice sessions."

We drew near a door that remained closed halfway down the hallway.

"Is that door to the basement, or do you have a crawl space?" Stuart asked.

"Full basement." Scott stopped and opened the door, a musty smell rising up with a splash of sawdust chasing it. "But it's not finished yet. I plan to make it into a media room at some point. And a workout room." He closed the door. "Maybe even get a pool table." Scott's eyes glazed over the way they always did when he was envisioning something spectacular.

His dream spanned years down the road, but if you didn't reach for the stars, how would you ever get there?

Stuart took Kelsey's hand as the four of us approached the kitchen, the savory scent of mozzarella and bacon wafting from the oven that I had turned off to allow my appetizers to stay warm. My stomach rumbled with anticipation. "I've got our drinks covered, Kelsey. Let me just get the food out." I opened one of the double-oven doors, my nose embracing the tasty aromas.

"Can I help?" Kelsey leaned over the breakfast bar in my direction.

I waved her off. "Nah, it's already done. I just have to pull it all out." With oven mitts covering my hands, I placed a large tray of bruschetta bread on the breakfast bar, along with another tray of bacon-wrapped dates with sprinkles of gorgonzola cheese. A generous bowl of tortilla chips kept two smaller bowls containing guacamole and fresh salsa company near a small stack of appetizer plates, paper napkins with Christmas designs, and forks.

"Beer, Stuart?" Scott beelined for the oversized fridge, its door a perfect match to the cabinets.

"Sure." Having already let go of Kelsey's hand, Stuart stood by the breakfast bar. "So, what is this house, like in the millions?"

Scott cracked two beers open and handed one of them to

Stuart before taking a quick sip himself and smacking his lips. "That's a fair question. But, nah. You'd be surprised where you can find deals when you work in the industry." His gaze glided over the interior once again. It reminded me of a father overflowing with adoration for his child. "I want this house to be a model of the possibilities. Let my customers see what options they have available to them. The heating system is top-of-the-line, and I may add solar panels at some point. The electrical and insulation are meant to cost less and to last long. It's got smart technology and a generator in case we lose power. I didn't spare on anything, although I did find good deals."

Kelsey smirked. "You're starting to sound like that old man in *Jurassic Park*"—she mimicked the actor's tone—"'I spared no expense.'" She walked over and jabbed Scott in the ribs.

Scott blew out his lips. "Yeah, right, Kelse. Like you don't constantly brag about your new BMW that dad helped you get."

Owning a car dealership, Mr. Williams had connections all over town. He'd struck a deal with the owner of the BMW place in exchange for a great deal on two fully loaded Jeep Cherokees that went to the other man's family. Of course, Mr. Williams wasn't thrilled that Kelsey didn't want a domestically made car from his shop, but Theo knew his daughter when she got her heart set on something. Kelsey wasn't pushy, but she was strong-willed. So was Scott. Their stubborn streak ran like greyhounds on a racetrack in this family.

Kelsey stuck her tongue out at him as she found a seat next to mine near the food. It appeared that neither one of them had outgrown their sibling rivalry.

"I'll stop picking on you, little brother, when you build me a house like this one." She lifted her chin in a hoity-toity manner.

Scott raised both eyebrows, his beer a few inches from his

lips, his reply loaded with sarcasm. "Can I finish this one first, please?"

Kelsey shrugged one shoulder. "I suppose."

Rather enjoying their playful banter, I touched Kelsey's arm as I sampled some bruschetta bread, mozzarella cheese providing a magic carpet of *delicious* for the tangy bruschetta sauce on top. My mouth was in heaven. "I bought the ingredients for cosmos. Want one?" Licking my fingers, I stood from my chair. "I also have wine if you prefer it."

Kelsey's eyes brightened. "Oh, cosmo, for sure." She followed me over to the butler pantry, where a selection of liquors and mixers displayed their possibilities, including a pair of martini glasses waiting to be filled.

The pink mixture sloshed against the glass as I handed Kelsey her drink. "Let's eat. I'm still starving."

"You don't have to ask me twice," she said, taking a refreshing sip of her drink as we returned to our seats moments later.

As we savored our drinks and munched on our food, the conversation shifted from the house to more pressing issues: the man who had escaped from the maximum security prison.

"That dude, Randy Meyers, was in for killing his girlfriend and her parents, you know," Stuart said as he leaned against our breakfast bar, staying close to Kelsey. He sipped on a beer and crunched on some chips. "Happened two years ago. What the hell is going on with our prisons lately? It seems like there are escapees all the time."

Is that true? My nervous system ramped up like the engine of a 747 ready to take off.

In close proximity to Stuart, Scott shook his head. "No idea. But you're right, he definitely sounds violent. The only other prisoner I know of who escaped recently was from a minimum-security prison, if I'm not mistaken." Scott pulled from his beer. "I get your point, though."

Stuart nodded. "I watched a documentary recently about how the Pennsylvania prisons are in dire need of upgrading." He lifted his brow. "If violent criminals are now escaping from maximum security prisons, someone better do something about it soon."

"I wonder if there's any updates about it on the news. Maybe they caught him already." Scott found the remote on the counter over by the toaster and clicked on the small TV mounted high on the wall in the corner of our breakfast nook. A commercial ran about some sort of medication or another, an elderly woman playing with what appeared to be her grand-kids. More commercials flashed on the screen before the station returned to *Jeopardy*, which we all zoned out on until a "Breaking News" alert interrupted the end of the show.

"Looks like they're having a press conference." I swiveled my stool to face the TV. Kelsey did the same as Scott turned the volume up.

A man with broad shoulders and cropped, gray hair, spoke. "Good evening. My name is Lieutenant Frank Driscoll of the Pennsylvania State Police." Colorful patches adorning the arms and chest of his gray uniform, the lieutenant went on to explain who else was standing behind him on the podium, including the District Attorney, a US Marshall, and someone he referred to as an FBI ASAC.

"What's ASAC mean?"

Scott paused the TV. "Assistant Special Agent in Charge." He held the remote up, his eyes waiting to see if I had any more questions.

I raised a palm. "Sorry. Go ahead."

Scott winked at me and hit play, allowing Frank Driscoll to continue.

"I regret to inform you that we have not apprehended Randy Meyers at this time." In the top right-hand corner of the TV screen, an image of a white man with stringy black hair and angry brown eyes—a Gothic cross tattooed at one of his temples—glared at us, wearing that distinctive orange jumpsuit. I assumed anyway. All I could see was the collar and the white T-shirt hidden beneath. He had eyes that had seen a lot in his life, and none of it good. If I saw this man on the street, prison or no prison, I'd turn and head in the opposite direction. Even his jaw looked angry, clenched and unforgiving. Ready to take a bite out of a world that had betrayed him. Again, PTSD was narrating his story for me.

"I guess that answers one question," Scott said, his gaze glued to the TV.

"Because of this, our investigation has taken a change in direction. We have moved from a containment model to one that utilizes a variety of investigators that has proven successful for us in the past. We continue to receive tips from the public, which we are following up on." He cleared his throat. "The public can expect to see a significant increase in police presence within Phoenixville and the surrounding areas. There is no need to be alarmed when you see this. If a threat arises, we will use the reverse 911 system to notify residents." He went on to warn anyone who may possibly assist Randy Meyers and promised to prosecute them to the full extent of the law.

Does Randy have friends nearby? The thought sent a shiver up my spine.

"We ask residents of Phoenixville and in the surrounding areas to please secure homes, outbuildings, and vehicles as best you can. We have one report of Meyers attempting to steal a Ford pickup truck from a civilian but was unsuccessful. The event took place upon his escape from the Faulkner State Correctional Institution." He encouraged anyone with information about Randy Meyers to contact their tip line, and reminded us all that there was a significant reward for anyone who helped bring Randy to justice. "Before I take questions, I want to remind the public that Randy Meyers is a dangerous criminal who has been convicted of the brutal murder of his girlfriend and her parents. If you see Randy, do not engage. Call the authorities and let us handle it. Finally, we request that all outdoor celebrations, outdoor sports, and the Holiday Lights Run be postponed until further notice." He stared into the camera, his eyes firm. "We have the resources, and I can assure you, he *will* be caught. I have no doubt about that. Okay, now I will take your questions." He lifted his gaze away from the camera and over the gaggle of reporters in his midst.

Scott muted the TV just as the entourage shouted questions from multiple locations around the room, cameras flashing away.

For a second or two, we all just stared into space, our minds absorbing these details. At least my mind was. "Wow, that's a lot to take in," I finally said. "Hon, when do you think we can get that alarm system working on the second floor?"

Feeling safe was a big deal for me. And it had been that way since surviving a horrible car accident when I was twelve. The one that killed my parents and left me orphaned.

With compassion in his loving blue eyes, Scott set his beer down and approached. Standing between my legs, he wrapped his big, strong arms around my shoulders and kissed my forehead. "I'll get it done soon, babe. Don't worry. The first floor is secure, I just need to get Barry to finish some wiring upstairs. He's booked solid right now with everyone trying to get projects done before the holidays." He ran his hands up and down my back causing my stool to swivel from the motion. "Randy's not gonna come here. He's probably hiding out somewhere in the woods."

I gazed up at my loving husband, who knew very well how much security and safety meant to me. "Yeah, but we have a lot of land here. And what about the barn?"

Another reason Scott took so long to complete the first floor of our house, and hadn't finished the second floor yet, which would require much more time to finish, was because he was also remodeling and upgrading an old post-and-beam barn that sat on our property. Scott's great-great-grandfather had bought oodles of land in this area many moons ago for farming. And when Scott's father deeded a portion of that land to us right before our wedding as a gift, the only remnant of that lost era was a barn that stood awkwardly and crookedly on our twenty-five acres, about a quarter of a mile down our curved driveway.

I loved barns. Probably because I had an aunt on my mother's side who lived in Vermont when I was young. She had since passed away. A couple of times, my parents brought me to their farm, populated with a fair amount of milking cows, pigs, and a whole coop of chickens. Aunt Eva would take me with her to gather hay for the cows, which they stored in the upper floor of their enormous barn. I'd stand in the center of the loft and stare up at the vaulted ceiling, a few pinpricks of light sending streams onto the hay below. Maybe it was the extremely high ceilings or maybe it was the raw nature of the structure, but there was something inspiring about that space that I could never quite describe. So when Scott decided to remodel our barn, I was thrilled to have something like that on our property. Knowing the structure had a past only made it feel more like a treasure to me.

Holes pocked the roof of our barn, while decay weathered the walls and the foundation. It had no windows, just square gaps where glass used to reflect the trees and the sky outside.

Regardless, Scott saw its usefulness right away. "If I can secure the foundation and beams, I can remodel it," he'd said.

"I'll talk to Ben about it. I could put my office in the front and use the large area to store building materials." Scott continued to think out loud. "Ben knows a guy who does roofs . . . . I bet Ben would hook me up if I comped him some work on the side . . . . Ben was just mentioning a lake house he's interested in buying and remodeling . . . . I'll work on it with him for free . . . . I'm sure we can use the same lines for power and plumbing that we'll need for the house." All sorts of ideas ignited in Scott's eyes. Within no time, he was a man on a mission, and before long, the barn had a sturdy foundation, a new roof, and the possibility for much more.

Late last summer, he'd hired someone to install the over-sized windows, which cost more than our budget allowed, even with Scott sourcing some of his products from salvage companies. It took some effort, but I convinced him to let me donate money from my inheritance. He'd already used his, bequeathed from his grandfather.

"This is *our* barn and house, right? Not just yours. And I want to contribute!"

"I won't have you funding *my* projects, babe. Your parents gave you that money. It's yours." Scott paced our camper, his weight making the small trailer sway back and forth.

I corrected him with a firm voice. "No, it's *ours*. We're a family. It's not my money, and it's not your money. It's our money."

He shook his head, defiant. "I'm not letting you use your inheritance. And that's the end of it." His tight expression told me he wasn't playing around. "I'll get a loan."

I was flabbergasted. "You'll get a loan? You already have a loan. A big one for the house and the barn. That makes zero sense." I made a zero symbol with my thumb and forefinger right in his face before I crossed my arms over my chest, my mouth twitching with irritation. What was the big deal? He was making me feel left out of his life, and I didn't like it much.

"You can get mad at me if you want to, but I'm not budging on this, Sara." He stormed out of our camper to go for a run, returning an hour later soaked with sweat and no closer to compromise.

We'd shared everything in our lives, why was he being so stubborn? And if he wouldn't let me help him out, how would I feel about ever asking him for help in return? This was a road I'd prefer not travel.

The following night, I tried again to no avail. I caught him sitting in front of his laptop exploring interest rates, when I lost it.

"This is ridiculous. I have plenty of money—"

"I said no, Sara!" Scott flew to his feet. "I don't want to discuss this any further. Let it go!"

I gritted my teeth together. He was as stubborn as a mule. "Fine. If you won't let me help you, you may as well build a bunk in that barn for yourself, cause that's where you'll be sleeping." I remembered how a summer storm was pushing through that night and how the ozone wasn't the only thing riled in our little camper.

It took three days of no cuddles or physical affection of any kind, really, for his resolve to crumble. I paid for the windows and made him agree to let me help him with the heating system, which he installed the following month. I was on a roll.

Scott rested his chin over my head, returning my thoughts to the moment. "The garage door on the back is automatic. All I have to do is lock up the front and side doors. I can take care of that over the weekend. Now that they're postponing the Holiday Lights Run, I'll have to check with Mom and Dad and see if they still want us to come over."

"Oh, yeah," Kelsey said from her stool. "Good point. I'm

kind of bummed that they postponed it, but I guess they don't want a bunch of people outside at night, jogging all over town." She grabbed her cell from the counter in front of her. "I'll text Mom and see what she wants to do."

* * *

As it turned out, we decided to continue with the brunch at Scott's parents' house. Everyone had a job to do. Kelsey and I helped my mother-in-law, Beth, bake a coffee cake, along with a large pan of cinnamon rolls. After that, I chopped the potatoes for the home fries before I cooked and seasoned them while Scott made his renowned sausage egg casserole and sweet potato hash. Mr. Williams took charge of the waffle bar, equipped with fresh strawberries, blueberries, and plenty of whipped cream. Kelsey helped her mother set the table and prepare the serving dishes.

Stuart arrived mid-morning to a kitchen bustling with activity. After he kissed Kelsey hello, he looked around at us worker bees. "What can I do to help?" he asked.

Mr. Williams guided him over to the fridge. "We're down a pot. Know how to make coffee?"

Stuart nodded. "Yes, sir, I do."

Mr. Williams wiped his hands on his "Kiss the Cook" apron. "Good. We need some." He grabbed a bag of coffee from the freezer and led Stuart to a less crowded section of their spacious kitchen where a commercial-sized coffee maker created its own private haven. "When you finish with this"—he handed Stuart the bag of coffee—"pour it into this urn." He patted the stainless-steel urn that looked like it belonged in a dining room at The Four Seasons, chaffing burner included. "Then grab the mugs from that cabinet"—he pointed in the direction of an upper cabinet where an assortment of mugs formed shapes through the small stained-glass window—"Use the fancy mugs. You can put them by the coffee urn." He placed his hand on Stuart's shoulder and smiled. "Thanks, Stuart. Appreciate the help." He made his way back to his waffle station.

We enjoyed a feast in the formal dining room, the ginormous mahogany buffet with a marble top, a traffic jam of dishes both hot and cold. An assortment of juices filled crystal pitchers at the center of the table, their matching crystal juice glasses providing joyful comfort at the head of each place setting. Glass chargers with gold beading brought the table to another level of luxury. Dimming the lights, Beth even lit tapers, casting a warm glow across the room. It was a brisk, cloudy day, making the space feel even cozier.

Wrapped around the good silverware, white cloth napkins offset the red damask taffeta tablecloth. To avoid an abundance of clutter in the room, the coffee remained in the kitchen, which kept the waffle station from becoming too lonely.

I stood at the head of the buffet where elegant plates with a burgundy-and-gold rim stacked high. "I feel like I'm at a fancy restaurant." I inhaled the succulent goodies in front of me.

Scott nudged me with his elbow. "Well, get going, woman. I'm hungry." He leaned over and kissed my cheek, telling me he wasn't serious, but *hurry up he was hungry.*

It wasn't long before we were all seated and filling our faces.

"Any updates about Randy Meyers?" Scott asked, diving into his egg casserole first.

"Not that I'm aware of," Beth said. "He sounds like a dreadful man." Scott's mom sipped her juice before taking another bite of her waffle. "How could anyone do that to their loved ones?"

"There is no shortage of crazy in this country," Scott's

father said with conviction, his head bent over his plate. "Damn prisons need to keep these people locked up where they belong."

"I heard that he tried to break into someone's shed, but I haven't seen anything on the news about it." Beth's eyes showed concern. "You better make sure you keep your showroom and your lot secured, Theo."

Scott's mom thought like I did.

Theo glanced over at her. "Already taken care of. Got cameras all over that lot. He comes there, and we'll know about it."

Beth sighed regretfully. "I guess we all need to be careful. And what a tough time of year for this. Everyone is out shopping and attending parties."

"I know," I said as I picked up my mug of hot tea, my fingers warming against the ceramic. "Scott and I were going hiking on the Perkiomen Trail next weekend, but that's off now." I turned to Scott who had taken his last bite of casserole. "Right, honey?" I didn't want to head north for any reason. Again, my cautious side was rearing up.

Scott wiped his mouth and sat back in his chair. His eyes softened on me, his hand finding my shoulder. "We can go in the spring. It would be prettier then, anyway." His hand slid down my arm in a comforting sort of way. "Sound good?" Then he leaned into his coffee cake, giving it his full attention.

I nodded and placed my hand on his muscular thigh. "Yes. I like that idea."

Seeming oblivious to the conversation, Kelsey and Stuart exchanged a few glances and smiles. Kelsey even stole a strawberry from Stuart's plate, chewing on it with a seductive flair.

I looked away, feeling like I was paying way too much attention to their private moment. I was happy for Scott's sister.

She'd had trouble with relationships in the past, and I hoped Stuart would be a good match for her.

As she chewed her next bite, Beth's eyes brightened. "You did a superb job on these waffles, Theo." Her tongue reached out and mopped up a small droplet of strawberry juice from the edge of her lower lip.

With his usual controlled demeanor, Scott's father drank from his coffee mug. "Always aim to please, my dear."

"Oh, and thank you again for the maple syrup, Sara. It's yummy. What do you call it?" From across the table, Beth gazed over at me.

"Liquid gold." I smiled and took a generous bite of my home fries. "My dad used to put it on practically everything." I smiled remembering how nothing was off-limits when it came to his *liquid gold*, which he bought locally from a few of his favorite sellers. He even put maple syrup on his sandwiches.

Scott took my hand from under the table. "I don't blame him. It's good stuff." He smacked his lips after swallowing his own bite of waffles. Scott was inhaling everything on his plate. Nothing new, the man had a hearty appetite. And for more things than just food. I flushed at the thought.

"Will you get to see your uncle again soon?" Mrs. Williams asked as she enjoyed more of her orange juice.

I wiped my mouth with my cloth napkin, the fabric soft against my lips. "I hope so. I haven't heard from him lately, but I know he's been busy working on his land."

My Uncle Aidan, the closest thing I would ever have to my father, lived in Lahinch, Ireland, where my dad had grown up. In fact, my dad had bequeathed me a sizable portion of that same land that bordered my uncle's property. The picturesque countryside led to a cliff overlooking the Atlantic Ocean and a modest beach with a cave. I shuddered, my blood turning to ice from the memory of the brisk water and that cave I had explored with Scott.

"Oh, what's he doing with his land?" Beth leaned slightly forward, her forearms rested on the table, her eyes engaged in our conversation.

"I think he's trying to clear a few areas and see what he can do with it. He leased one section to a man who needed room to graze his sheep. He lives just up the road in a house that used to be abandoned, but he bought the place and is fixing it up. The land around the house is too dense with scrub for his sheep, so he's leasing a portion of Uncle Aidan's cleared land until he can get his own pasture up and running." I thought about my uncle and how much I missed him, which wasn't always the case. Uncle Aidan wasn't what you'd call a stand-up guy when I had first met him. In fact, he was more of a swindler, but when Scott and I flew to Ireland right after our college graduation over a year-and-a-half ago to see him and check out the land, circumstances changed for us all. It wasn't the best trip in the world but, thankfully, things turned out okay, and my relationship with my uncle had been strong ever since.

"How is Abigail and the rest of your family?"

About to take a sip of my juice, I held the glass near my lips. "Good. They're still coming for Christmas, so you'll get to see them soon." I couldn't wait to see my bonus mom and my family. I was counting the days.

"I look forward to that. And Mel must be getting big by now."

I smiled. "She sure is. The older she gets, the more inquisitive she becomes. I can't imagine what she'll be when she grows up." I took a sip of juice, the tangy orange bursting on my tongue, fond thoughts of my little sister dancing through my mind.

That was all Beth asked me regarding my family, and soon,

we were all stuffed and clearing the table, except for Scott and his father, who had run out to Lowe's to get locks for our barn. Since work needed to be done at our place, the plan was to have our pizza there instead of here. After we trimmed the tree, of course.

The drinks would remain at a minimum since everyone wanted to be at home for the night. Randy had subdued our plans, but he hadn't canceled them entirely.

Wearing Santa hats and with Nat King Cole serenading us from the surround-sound speakers hidden within the walls, the six of us unwrapped ornaments covered in tissue paper and hung them on the enormous Douglas fir playing a starring role in the Williamses' large but cozy family room. Flames danced and swayed from the roaring fireplace, citrus and pine infusing the air with the tree's balsam goodness. Lighted imitation garland, thick with pinecones and berries draped lazily across the windows, their counterpart embracing candlesticks and two nutcrackers atop the large mantel.

"Isn't that cute." Stuart grinned at Kelsey, a round ornament covered in stars made from glitter glue, resting in his hand. "You were only two when you made this one. Aw."

Kelsey met his grin with one of her own, a bashful shrug implying her modesty.

"I love all of these ornaments. They're precious. And they still look so good. You've done an excellent job preserving them, Beth." Holding a small wooden Santa head that Scott had painted when he was eight, according to the writing on the back, I lifted up on my tiptoes to fill a vacant spot on the tree.

As I hung each decoration that Scott or Kelsey had made when they were little, I ran careful fingers over all the imperfections that made them distinct. I thought about the future when Scott and I would be doing this with our own kids. When it came to children, Scott had all the patience in the world. Add in his fun-loving energy, and they flocked to him, which was probably why my little sister, Mel, who was past her toddler years and was now in kindergarten, preferred Scott over all of us, including her mom. I smiled at the memory of Scott passed out on Abigail's couch after a long summer day of fun, Mel tucked under his arm, her eyes sealed shut, her mouth hanging open with fatigue, Scott's doing the same. How had I been so lucky to find a man who still made my knees wobble at the sight of him, and who I knew would always put our children's best interests ahead of his own? I glanced up at the ceiling to thank my guardian angels, otherwise known as my mother and father, for what I believed was their part in our match made from heaven.

Stuart looked down at his phone. "Hey, I just got a notification on my phone that says Randy may have stolen a rifle from someone's truck. According to this article, the man had a gun rack mounted on the back window."

We all stopped working, my body tensing.

"Where did this happen?" Scott came up beside me, his eyes shadowed with concern.

Stuart stared at his phone, his fingers swiping this way and that. "Just says that he may have stolen the rifle. Doesn't say much else." His eyes widened. "Oh, wait. It says near Reeves Park."

Beth's hand flew to her chest. "But that's only a few miles away."

Chapter Four

"I love these wreaths that you hung on your cupboards, Sara," Beth said as she touched the soft, plastic pine needles with her fingers and her eyes approving. "I'll have to try that for next year. It really makes your kitchen look festive."

We had all gathered at my house to make homemade pizzas while Scott and his father worked on installing locks to two of our barn doors. Stuart had left to check on his parents across town. We were all pretty freaked out about Randy's theft, which now made him an armed escapee. In fact, Scott's parents considered staying home, but their house had a state-of-the-art security system, *and* they lived in a gated community. They also had cameras covering the front and back of their house. Their neighborhood watch was already monitoring the area. All bases covered.

For me, it was nice to distance myself from that part of town, not that we were very far away, either. Aside from the man having a gun (I hoped without bullets), the theft proved that for the time being, Randy was still here. I had hoped Scott was right and he was hiding out in the wilderness somewhere. I imagined the Allegheny Mountains, which ran along the western border of the state.

Beth cleared her throat, interrupting my ruminations.

"Thank you. I'm glad you like them. My mom used to put them up like that." I enjoyed the extra splash of color from the small wreaths, each dangling from a piece of wide tartan ribbon that matched the bows resting at the bottom of each arrangement. I even attached a few imitation berries with wire to heighten the color scheme. Growing up in Vermont this time of year, my mom had our country kitchen brimming with festive flair, from the miniature wreaths that hung like mine from the natural wood of her cupboard doors to lighted garland running across the top of the cupboards, reminding me of a thick caterpillar. She even had a small lantern hanging from the kitchen window, a tea light flickering at its heart.

Last year, my house was a work-in-progress. Not much decorating took place. So, I was thrilled to be able to go a little crazy with it this season.

"What did you attach the tartan ribbon to?" Distracting me again from my thoughts, Beth opened one cupboard to find her answer. "Oh, I see, you used those Command Strips. Very smart."

"That was Scott's idea." I gazed out the picture window of our breakfast nook at Scott and his father, who stood bent over the barn door approximately one hundred yards away. If it were spring or summer, vegetation and leaves would obscure my view, but with the trees now barren for a few more months yet, winter had granted me a clear view. Calculating time already lost and the days so short, I hoped they would be able to finish before sunset. Images of Randy holed up in our barn gave me the heebie-jeebies, his dark eyes aimed on destruction.

"Kelse, hand me that ball of dough." Wearing a red apron,

Beth utilized the large island to roll out her pizza dough, several round pizza pans stacked at the ready, while I opened the mason jars for the homemade sauce and chopped the onions, garlic, and peppers. Kelsey worked on cutting up the ham, barbecue chicken, and bacon. We'd already taken out the pepperoni and cooked the brown-sugar-and-maple sausage that filled the room with delectable aromas.

Having worked at a pizza restaurant all through her college years, Beth was a master with the dough, which she molded perfectly to each pan with just the right height of crust. The final touch? She basted the crust with garlic infused olive oil that complemented its mouthwatering flavor.

Our options for the night consisted of barbecue chicken pizza, ham and pineapple, veggie lovers, and meat lovers. Needless to say, my kitchen had transformed into a pizza joint, the ingredients, both cooked and raw, making me drool.

The Christmas glow drifting in from our eight-foot-tall imitation Christmas tree, standing guard in the family room next door, called out to me. I loved Christmas lights and their ability to soften the walls and areas around them. Of course, you could put Christmas lights on a pile of junk, and I would find it festive.

Once Kelsey was finished with her duties, she wandered over. "So, what do you think of Stuart?" With her chin lowered slightly, she gazed up at me with timid eyes.

I was flattered she cared what I thought. "I like him. He's cute too."

Kelsey's entire face brightened as if my opinion had lifted a burden off her shoulders. "I know, right?" She gave me a light shove. "Not too shabby." She giggled. "It was nice of him to go check on his parents as well."

"I agree," Beth said with a nod, flour creeping over her hands and forearms, a few splatters on her cheeks. "So, tell us.

How do *you* feel about him?" Kelsey's mom kept her eyes on her work, but something told me she was paying a lot more attention to her daughter than she let on. "Has he done anything that would be considered a deal breaker yet? Or should we send out the wedding invitations?" She giggled to herself.

"Oh, Mom." Kelsey waved her mother off with a daughterly whine. "Don't start."

Beth smirked and then shrugged. "What? I was only kidding. Don't be so sensitive. He seems like a nice young man. I was just curious how you feel about him."

I tried not to smile. So typical, the relationship between mother and daughter. How I envied that. And then I thought about Abigail, remembering that I owed her a phone call. They were all coming for Christmas, and I was thrilled about that. My little sister, Mel (short for Melinda named after my natural mother), in my house on Christmas morning, her eyes dazzled by what Santa had brought her, gave me goosebumps every time I thought about it.

"Sara, am I wrong to ask what she thinks about her new boyfriend? Didn't your mother—" All at once, the fun-loving mood in the room took a nosedive. First Beth looked away and then Kelsey's gaze dropped to the floor, both of them going silent. They acted as if Beth had just stepped onto a verbal landmine.

Beth's chin sunk, her shoulders dropping. "I'm so sorry, Sara. I wasn't thinking."

What? And then it dawned on me. I smiled at them both as I continued to chop away, realizing the onions were probably making my eyes water too. *Not helping matters.* My mother had been gone for well over a decade now. And, yes, I missed her every day, but I had learned to accept that loss. It took years, but I was in a good place now. Abigail—my biological mother's best friend—and my stepfather, Joel, had done a pretty good job filling the void. *And* I had a little sister. I was truly blessed.

I attempted to satisfy an itch on my cheek with the back of my wrist, careful not to touch my eyes with my onion-laced fingers. "No worries. It's totally fine. I was too young to discuss boys before my mother died but, yes, Abigail has definitely grilled me many times about Scott. Especially at the beginning of our relationship." I wasn't kidding, either. When I'd first met Scott freshman year of college, Abigail was less than trusting of him or any man, really, who could capture my heart so quickly. Even though I was in a good place *now*, I wasn't back then. We'd had a few *discussions* on the subject, some downright intense. But just like with my Uncle Aidan, things had worked out for the best, and Abigail grew to love Scott dearly. He was her son-in-law, after all. And as she always reminded me, *He certainly is cute.*

Kelsey lowered her guard, her tone more accommodating. "Okay, okay. Yes, I like him. And he's hot." She wagged a finger at her mother. "But that's all I'm sayin' on the subject, *Mother*. I don't want to jinx it." Her voice carried no anger, just playful bantering, the way it always did between these two.

Beth kneaded her dough, the words "Fine, fine, just asking a question" rolling out from under her tongue.

"Stuart wants to take me to the opera in Philly. I think I'm going to buy a dress, but I thought I'd ask you first if you happen to have one I could wear. You know, save a few bucks?"

Since Kelsey and I were about the same size, I understood her reasoning.

"Well, I've only got one gown fancy enough for something like that." I thought about the crab apple red chiffon gown hiding in a dress bag at the back of my walk-in. The one with a long slit up the leg and halter top with an exposed back. The one that fit me perfectly. The one I bought freshman year of college for a holiday party, hosted by Scott's fraternity. And the one I never got to wear because of unforeseen circumstances. Scott never even saw it, although he'd bought a matching tie after he'd pried the color out of me all those years ago.

Kelsey placed her hand on my forearm, and I realized I had stopped chopping. "Are you okay? Did I say something wrong?" Her brow lowered with concern.

"Oh, no. Sorry. I bought a special dress back when I was a freshman for a holiday party that Scott was going to take me to." I sighed. "I just never got the chance to wear it." My eyes stared off.

"I'm sorry, dear," Beth said, halting her work. "I know that was a very difficult time for you both."

A tear ran down my cheek unbidden before I refocused my eyes and wiped it away with the back of my wrist again. "It's just that I never got to go to a prom, and that dress was my way of making up for it."

"You never went to prom?" Kelsey kept studying me with her eyes. "Did you get to wear the dress another time?"

I shook my head. "Scott's never even seen it."

A few moments of silence drifted around the room until Kelsey made a face. "Well, that sucks."

For a moment, she sounded just like my BFF Amy, known for her take-no-prisoners attitude and colorful language.

"Yeah, well ..." I redirected my thoughts. "I'm almost done with the veggies, Beth."

* * *

After everyone had left for the evening, we'd secured the barn and cleaned the kitchen, leaving a bunch of leftover pizza packaged in the fridge. There was plenty for Scott's family and ours to enjoy for lunches all week. Scott and I sat on the sofa watching *How the Grinch Stole Christmas*, starring Jim Carrey. I'd loved this movie since I was a kid.

Scott chuckled when Jim Carrey played his answering machine, mainly the recording threatening to "hunt you down and gut you like a fish" if you left a message, followed by "If you'd like to fax me, press the star key." He cracked up some more.

I rested the back of my head against his shoulder, his arm draped around my neck. And then I gazed back at him. "You gotta cute laugh. You know that?" Stretching my neck, I kissed his chin.

Scott gave me a bashful glance. "It's Jim Carrey. He brings it out of me." Then he wiggled his fingers into my side, more precisely my tickle spot. "Then again, you crack me up all the time too."

Trying not to lose my composure, I forced a serious face, several uncomfortable chuckles steamrolling their way up my throat. "Don't you dare!" I hated what was coming next, so I grabbed his hand to stop him from another agonizing tickle fight. The one he *always* won. "I mean it, Scott. Stop it!"

His eyes shined with mischievous thoughts. "Oh, yeah? You don't want me to tickle you?" His hands went crazy, rendering me helpless.

I squealed. "No! Don't be a brat! If you don't stop right now, I'm going to pee all over you. I mean it!" I wiggled. I squirmed. I tried to slide off the couch onto the floor. "Please, no. Come on, Scott." And then I thought of something that just might help. "Ow. You're hurting me!"

Scott ripped his hands away and stared in horror. "I'm so sorry, babe. I didn't mean to be so rough." He looked mortified; his hands not sure where to go next.

Keeping my face sullen, I rose to my feet and headed for the bathroom, my bladder on borrowed time.

"Sara, are you okay?"

I waited to answer, adding to his fears. And then, when I had reached the edge of the family room, I gazed back at him and grinned like the Grinch himself, minus the termites crawling through my teeth. "Gotcha." After that, I ran like the wind, slamming into the guest bathroom and locking the door. I expected him to rattle the door or knock loudly, but he didn't.

By the time I emerged, my bladder empty, it seemed Scott had lost his playfulness. Instead, he stood in the center of the family room, his brow furrowed, his gaze directed at his phone.

"What's wrong?" I stood beside him, trying to see what he was looking at. "Is there something new about Randy?"

"Nope." His eyes lit up as he tossed his cell phone onto the couch. "But I got you over here, didn't I?" Naughtiness laced his words. "Now you're in for it."

"Huh? No way!" I made it two steps before he grabbed me and slung me over his shoulder like I was a sack of potatoes.

"For being such a pest and making me feel so bad, you're gonna make it up to me now." He carried me into the bedroom where he tickled me in a whole new sort of way. This time, we wrestled a little before making love, our spirits in the mood for something a little spicier. Of course, Scott made sure he wasn't hurting me when he had my arms up over my head, his mouth suckling my breasts. At one point, I had *him* on his back, with his arms over his head. It was comical, really, given the size of him. He obviously let me do it.

"Don't move." I told him in a commanding voice as I licked his neck and chest, my hair cascading down his torso. "If you move, I win." Challenge set, I went to work arousing him with my tongue and hands, anything to get him to squirm. And he almost made it too. *Almost.* When he practically bent the wrought iron spindle of our headboard, I knew he was close. That was when he decided to return the love ...

* * *

Scott turned on the fireplace, filling the room with added warmth, the orange-and-yellow embers decorating the walls and furniture with its dancing light. As we lay in each other's arms, his mouth right next to my ear, he spoke in a tender voice. "First of all, thank you for that."

I released a satisfied breath and hugged his head from behind me. "You're very welcome, handsome."

"Second, Kelse said you had a sad moment in the kitchen earlier when you were all making pizzas." He lifted his face away so he could get a better view of me. "She said it had something to do with that dress you bought freshman year." He blinked, his lashes long enough to make models envious. "I'd forgotten about that dress. And I guess I also forgot that you never went to prom." He kissed my shoulder with tender lips. "Why don't I take you out for a fancy dinner over the holidays and you can wear that dress. I'll make sure I find a place fitting." He smirked. "I have to admit, I'd love to see it on you."

I tried to wave him off. "It's fine. You don't have to do that. I'll wear it someday." My voice sounded less than convinced. What was it about that dress that bothered me so much? Was it the turmoil of my freshman year? Or was it the fact that I was about to turn twenty-four in six months and hadn't been to a party fancy enough for a dress like that one? Even my wedding dress didn't compare to that level of elegance. At one point or another, a girl dreamed of being a princess, didn't we? Was that it? Was it princess envy? Or was it the fact that for six years after my parents had died, I closed myself off from the world, missing out on all the things that most girls experienced. I hadn't even kissed a boy until I met Scott. And I was eighteen at the time. Yup, a late bloomer for sure. I hissed a little under my breath.

Scott snuggled into me. "I hate that you never went to prom. And I hate that you lost your parents so young. It would make me happy to take you out for an extravagant dinner." He took a strand of my blond hair and ran it between his fingers. "Let me see if I can get us a reservation someplace nice. I'll check Philly. It's only an hour away, and it would be nice to get out of town for a night."

I closed my eyes, enjoying his warm embrace. "Given the time of year, I bet everywhere is booked." I yawned.

"If that's true, we'll go for a Valentine's Day dinner, then." He yawned, too, and then rolled over. "I'm gonna go turn everything off. I'm beat." He swung his feet over the side of the bed while I got up to brush my teeth.

"Want some help?" I paused.

"Nah, I got it, gorgeous."

* * *

I awoke to the light of the moon filtering in through the plantation blinds, our room quiet as a mouse. The measure of Scott's breathing told me he was out cold. I turned over to face my clock, which flashed 2:33 a.m. with its neon-blue digits. Why was I awake? A dry mouth answered me. Thirst. I did eat a lot of pizza, and I did have two cosmos. I sat up, trying to rouse my mind enough to head to the bathroom to get some water.

All at once, a noise came out of nowhere. *What was that?*

I froze. Was it the wind hitting the house? The forecast had called for high winds, the enemy of outdoor Christmas decorations. Plus, this house was new, and I needed to get acquainted with its creaks and gentle moans. A nearby oak cast its shadowy branches across my window, and I found myself imagining it waving hello.

I lowered my feet to the floor and stood, my body suddenly cold. After making love, I often slept naked next to Scott, but in the winter, my shoulders had a way of chilling the rest of my body. Realizing this, I shuffled over to my closet and grabbed a nightshirt and pants made of brushed cotton.

Another sound came from ... upstairs? I gazed at the ceiling. Was it a scrape or ...? I struggled to process.

And then *bang*.

My heart practically leaped out of my chest.

Okay, that wasn't the wind. And that wasn't a tree, either, unless one was coming through our second floor right now. I crept over to Scott and shook his shoulders. "Scott, I heard a noise upstairs." Terror engulfed my senses, making it difficult to breathe.

All I could think was *is it Randy?*

Chapter Five

Scott gasped a few times, his lungs trying to promote consciousness. "Sara, what are you doing?" He squinted up at me as he lifted his head a few inches off the pillow. "Did you have a nightmare?"

I leaned over him. "No. I heard a noise upstairs."

He let his head drop. "Sara. Go back to bed. It's just the wind."

And then another *bang* vibrated through the ceiling, causing Scott to spring up, his back now stiff as a board. Even his eyes were wide open. He gazed up at the ceiling as my heart palpated. My stomach shot into my throat.

Once again, I feared it might be Randy. And he was armed. Was he going to shoot us? Our house sat on twenty-five acres of land, no neighbors in sight. Suddenly, I wished we lived in a city. Not that that would be any safer. My thoughts were spinning out of control.

Mouth dry as dust, I tried to speak. "Do you think it's Randy?"

Without answering me, Scott leapt out of bed, threw on a

T-shirt and a pair of sweatpants and then opened the bottom drawer to his nightstand. In the drawer sat a pistol that he retrieved. A clip full of bullets came a moment later.

I knew he had a gun. He practiced with it every now and then at the gun range. I just didn't know he kept it so close to our bed.

"Stay here. I'm gonna check it out," he said with the barrel of his gun aimed toward the floor.

Wait here? For you to get killed? "No, I'm coming with you," I whisper-shouted. I stood behind him, my hands gripping his waist.

"Don't be stupid. Grab your cell phone and get ready to call 911. If I don't come back in—"

"No! I'm going with you." I refused to relent. I did grab my cell phone from my nightstand, however, as Scott hissed at me, clearly frustrated.

Didn't matter, I wasn't staying behind while the love of my life was dealing with God knew what. He was stubborn? Well, so was I.

"Damn it, woman."

I circled around the foot of the bed to face him. "After everything we've been through, Scott Williams, do you seriously think I'm going to let you go this alone? Have you met me?" I wedged my hand on my hip for impact and stared him down. He knew better than to push me on this. At least, I hoped he did.

"Fine. Stay behind me, then."

Together we crept down the hallway like the cast of Mystery Incorporated and toward the kitchen where the ominous back stairwell awaited.

LED nightlights throughout our large house cast spheres of illumination across the floor, enough so we could navigate without running into walls or furniture. And then we reached the kitchen, where everything remained in its place. The scent of old pizza hung in the air, garlic winning the strongest vote.

Outside our breakfast nook window, the reflection of the moon shined bright, and for a moment, I feared it would give us away. *That's silly. He's upstairs, not in the kitchen. Or is he?* My imagination threatened to play tricks. Shadows of trees in the distance stretched long and frightening across our frozen lawn, a patchwork of snow and brown grass.

"Is the upstairs door locked?" I asked, my body now shivering with fear, my feet practically walking on Scott's heels.

"I can't remember. Now be quiet." Scott put a finger to his lips to reinforce his message. His other hand remained poised, holding the gun.

If my heart could have beat any harder, it would have literally punched Scott in the back. My stomach was clenched so tight, I feared I'd barf.

We reached the foot of the stairs, and I gulped. One step and then two ...

Could Randy hear us coming? Did the carpet runner help soften our footfalls? What was waiting on the other side of that dreaded door? Whatever it was, could Scott react to it in time? I was driving myself insane, my insides rattling like the fenders of an old, rusted-out car.

With each step, our bare feet struggled to remain silent. When we reached the top, Scott tried the handle. Unlocked. He glanced down at me, one step below him, his expression hard to read.

Why hadn't we locked it? *Because Scott is up here all the time working, you idiot.* I held a hand over my mouth to slow my breathing. I'd been scared before. Heck, I'd been downright terrified in the past. Didn't matter. I'd never get used to this.

A knock came from the other side of the door. And then a

scrape. Or a slide. My ears couldn't tell which. *Is he up against the door now?*

Scott crept the door open, but it stopped short. He tried it again.

Ajar only a few inches, the door remained stubbornly closed. Something or someone was blocking it from the other side.

"We should back up against the wall. What if he shoots through the door?" I kept an iron grip on the waistband of Scott's pants.

Scott gazed down at me again. "Stand back." He removed my hold from his waist and handed me the gun. "Safety's off. Point it at that door, and if anyone other than me comes out, shoot!"

The gun felt heavy in my hand and now slippery since I was sweating like crazy. "Why?" I'd shot his gun a few times when he'd set up some targets out back, but I wasn't prepared for this. *Can I shoot another human being?* I wasn't sure. "What are you going to do?"

He didn't bother answering. Instead, he descended two steps and then ran like a linebacker into the door, thrusting it open.

Something smashed while other items scattered.

I couldn't tell whether my heart had stopped or it was beating out of my chest. The scent of fresh wood and dust slid past my nose, darkness awaiting. I pointed the gun upward, my hand tremoring so badly, I had to use two.

Another noise startled the life out of me. I almost fell down the stairs. In an instant, Scott was gone, swallowed into the shadows.

I was alone.

And then I thought about losing him for the second time in two days. Pushing my fears, the weight of an elephant, aside

I stormed up those stairs. As I sprinted through the doorway, an incandescent work light switched on, bringing everything into view, including my husband who stood on the other side of the floor, unharmed. I lowered the gun's muzzle toward the floor.

"It looks like those boards fell over across the door and wedged themselves between those studs over there." He pointed at an unfinished wall where one board leaned haphazardly and another one lay split in half on the floor below.

And then I felt it. A breeze. A strong breeze that whistled. "Where is that air coming from?" I shivered.

Both of our eyes followed the moving air to its source, which appeared to be an open window in one of the soon-to-be guest bedrooms. My gaze drifted downward, where more boards lay disorganized on the floor. It was the floor right above our bedroom.

Remorse washed over Scott's face. "I haven't been up here since the story about Randy broke. I guess I forgot to close the window. The wind must've blown those boards over. That's what we heard."

I tried not to be angry. "How could you forget something like that?" I turned my head in every direction, realizing the advantage of studded walls with no sheetrock. Every room exposed itself to my viewpoint. And unless my eyes were deceiving me, no one was up here. Other than a bunch of unfinished materials, Scott, and myself.

"I told you I haven't been up here since then. He just escaped yesterday afternoon. And it's not like Randy can shoot webs from his hands and climb thirty-foot walls." He went to the window to close it. "I was trying to air it out up here. It can get pretty dusty. And I was planning on closing it. I just forgot."

"Yeah, but he could have climbed up on the porch roof." I was still shivering, partially from the cold and partially from the adrenaline rush. "If he'd gotten up here, he could have easily come downstairs."

Scott locked the window and approached me, taking the gun from my hand. After putting the safety on, he stuffed it in the back waistband of his pants. "You're all turned around, babe. The porch is on the front of the house. This window faces the back."

"Are the windows on the front locked?" I rushed over to discover they weren't. "We need to be more careful, Scott. He's a violent criminal." I locked one window and then two, Scott doing the same. We had a large house, and there were a lot of windows spanning across the unfinished second floor. I gazed up at the moon, showering our front lawn in reflective light again, and searched for movement. In the distance, the barn stood tall, a barrier against the winter wind swirling around its formidable walls.

"Are the windows in the barn locked?"

Scott's exhale told me he was losing patience. "Yes, my dad and I locked them. And we installed the locks for the doors. Tomorrow, I'm putting up a motion-detector light"—he fanned his hands out—"and if you want, I'll put in a security system." He rubbed his eyes and mumbled. "I probably should put one in anyway with all the materials I plan to have stored in there." He tilted his head. "Okay?" His tone carried an edge, one influenced by fatigue.

My resolve melted away like butter on a hot stove. "I just ... I mean." I struggled to form my words and my thoughts.

Standing close, Scott kept me under his watchful eye. "What?"

Tears stung my eyes. I hugged my waist for comfort. "I worry that you and I are always going to have horrible things happen to us. And what if, someday, one of those horrible things ..." I couldn't say the words. They hurt my heart too much to speak out loud. All the counseling I'd been through couldn't seem to stop my insecure mind from going to places that would be the end of him or me. If we were cats, what life would we be on by now?

Two big, strong arms enveloped my shoulders, Scott's chest providing a landing strip for my tears and my cheek. His breath rustled the messy hair on the top of my head. "Nothing is going to happen."

I inched myself back. "But—"

"Sara." Scott brushed my hair over my shoulders, his hands soothing and strong. He bent his head closer to pin my gaze. "Listen to me, nothing is going to happen. I understand why you're scared." For a few seconds, he didn't blink. "I'll be more careful. I promise. We're good. We have a security system, and I'll try to get it linked up here as soon as I can." He held my face in his hands. He held my heart too. "We're safe. I promise you that."

* * *

With Randy now wandering around the area armed, the Phoenixville school system switched over to remote learning for the foreseeable future, or at least until Randy was apprehended or showed evidence he'd vacated the area. The alerts came through on Sunday, my department chair calling to make sure I had everything I needed to perform my duties.

More details about the theft emerged. Randy stole a hunting rifle that was stored on a gun rack in a Phoenixville resident's pickup truck. He also stole a box of bullets from the man's glove compartment. It was the perfect time of year for Randy to do this. Depending on what people hunted around here, the season could linger until mid-January. Meaning, guns were everywhere. Still, the owner of the truck should have been more careful considering there was a dangerous criminal in our midst.

Scott asked his boss if it would be okay for him to also work remotely from home. Even though I told him not to (that I'd be fine), the mishaps of the previous night didn't quite set his mind at ease. The following night, I woke up screaming, which only reinforced his decision.

With bloodshot eyes, Scott did his best to calm my racing heart. It was like we were thrust back into my freshman year. If there was ever a silver lining in this situation, it was the reminder of how patient and supportive my husband could be. He understood the triggers going off in my head like fireworks on the Fourth of July, and he did his best to tamp them down.

Normally, Scott stopped off at the gym to get an early workout before heading to the office. But after I had kept him up most of last night, he just skipped *that* workout altogether.

"Remember that counselor you saw back at Commonwealth University?" Scott gazed skyward, his droopy eyes searching for an answer.

"Dr. Zeller," I said to help his memory along.

He had made me a cup of tea, which I sipped at our breakfast table while Scott devoured an egg sandwich that I had made for him to start his Monday morning. He also needed a full pot of coffee to revitalize his tired brain.

"You still have her number, right?"

I nodded and sipped some more tea, the warm citrusy ginger and sweet cinnamon sending a cozy sensation down my throat. From my restless night, I also needed the caffeine boost. "You think I should call her?"

Scott took my hand from across the table. "I do. Couldn't hurt. She may have some good advice to help you over this ... hurdle."

I knew he was right; he usually was when it came to my

health and well-being. "Okay, I will." I planned to make the call over my lunch break.

While Scott worked in his office in the barn, I set up my laptop in my office, taking residence at the back corner of our house. Equipped with a floor-to-ceiling bookcase and an L-shaped desk, the room provided me with ample amounts of workspace. A warm shade of olive coated the walls, embellished by two prominent pieces of artwork from a local artist, one titled *Summer Cottage*, and the other *Winter Wonderland*. A thick wool rug with detailed borders, set in earth tones and muted flowery patterns at its center, brought warmth to the room and a nice cushion for my feet.

Moody clouds outside my window cluttered the chilly sky, concealing the vibrant blue abyss scheduled for another day. Two tall oaks stood center ground within our yard, ready to provide shade whenever Mother Nature blessed them with their springtime leaves.

Scott planned to put a rope swing on the tallest oak someday, and I imagined him pushing me while my feet kicked up in the air. A procession of evergreens running along the edge of our property line swayed as wind currents pushed their way through aggressively.

I powered up my laptop and clicked on the link that would bring me to my students. It was great to see their faces again, their smiles as bright and beautiful as a diamond in the sun. After I took attendance, we discussed the assignments for the day.

"I posted two short stories on my page for you to read and then take the multiple-choice test afterward, okay? After that, we will have a science lesson. And this afternoon, we'll practice math."

Four squares dotted the landscape of my computer screen, and within those four squares, my students nodded back at me.

"Once you complete the reading assignment, click on the submit button. After that, I've uploaded a presentation in PowerPoint for you to watch about caterpillars. We will meet back here at eleven o'clock to discuss the video, and then I want you to do an interactive exercise about the stages of growth." I smiled at those adorable faces. "Sound good?" More nods. "Any questions?"

Daryl raised his hand.

"Yes, Daryl?'

"Where are you?"

"Well, I'm at home in my office." I picked up my laptop and moved it around the room to show them my space, more importantly a corkboard where I had just pinned up photos of each of them, somehow knowing there would be a need for it. "See? And I have you all here with me." I returned to my seat.

"When can we go back to school?" Daryl's inquisitive eyes peered out at me.

"Hopefully soon. Why? Do you miss school that much?"

He nodded with abandon, which made me giggle and feel flattered at the same time. Daryl's mom appeared in the upper-right section of the square. "He just wants to play dodgeball again." Mrs. Morgenstern smirked as she rustled Daryl's hair and disappeared out of view.

Trina's cat, with her black fur feet, which looked like mittens against the rest of her white fur, hopped onto Trina's lap. "Mrs. Williams?" she asked as she petted the furry critter. "This is Mittens."

I waved. "Hello, Mittens. Nice to meet you."

"Mrs. Williams?" Trina asked again.

"Yes?"

"My mom said a bad man ran away from prison. When Mittens went out last night, I was worried the bad man would find her. Do you think he would hurt Mittens?" Just like

Daryl's mom, this time Trina's mom appeared in the upper left side of the screen. "I already told you that he won't come after Mittens. The police are out there looking for him, and they will find him soon."

"Yes, your mom is right, Trina. I couldn't have said it better myself." I waited for more questions. "Okay, unless there are more questions, you can move onto your assignment now."

"You look different." Walker couldn't help but get his two cents in.

"Well, people can look a little different on a computer screen than they would in person, that's true." I cleared my throat. "Now, if—"

"Do you want to come to my house? I could show you my Transformers collection."

Walker's offer brought a bright smile to my face. These kids had an innocence about them that most middle schoolers had outgrown. In fact, I would imagine the regular education kids wouldn't be caught dead inviting a teacher to their house. I was the lucky one who got to spend time with four amazing people who taught me the meaning of courage and kindness on a daily basis. "For now, Walker, I think it's best we all stay at our own homes. But thank you. I appreciate the offer."

"Yes, Mrs. Williams needs to go, so stop asking her questions," Walker's mom spoke up from nearby, although, I couldn't see her.

"Okay, good luck on your reading assignments. Take your time with it and read it more than once if you want to. There's no hurry. It's more important that you understand the story than how quickly you finish. Pay attention to the details. When you're ready, take the quiz. We will go over the answers later."

"Thank you, Mrs. Williams" came from three of the four, all of them sweeter than cotton candy. Trina waved her cat's paw at me.

* * *

I called Dr. Zeller at lunchtime, but she didn't answer (she was probably with a patient), so I left her a message, doing my best to describe the situation.

The rest of the day was uneventful.

I made chicken cordon bleu with mashed potatoes for dinner that night but kept walking across the kitchen, checking my cell phone for any texts or missed calls. At one point, Scott put his cell phone stand near the stove and placed my phone in it.

"You're going to wear a hole in my new floors if you don't stop pacing this kitchen." He kissed the top of my head and went back to work on his laptop.

He was right. My nerves were getting the better of me.

With the scent of melted Swiss cheese and baked ham infusing the air, I sat at our dining room table with Scott, enjoying our dinner. My phone remained perched on a stand nearby.

It wasn't until we were cleaning up the dishes and pans from dinner, when my phone finally rang. I just about jumped out of my skin. Standing by the dishwasher, I bolted for my phone, relieved to see the name *Dr. Zeller* appear on my screen.

"Hello?" I said, my voice eager.

"Hello, Sara. This is Dr. Zeller. I got your voicemail. I'm sorry I couldn't call you back sooner. It's been a busy day."

"No worries. I appreciate you calling me back."

Scott ushered me over to a bar stool to sit while he finished the dishes and wiped down the counters.

"Is this a good time? I have a few minutes if you'd like to tell me more about what's going on."

I took a breath. *Time to face the music.*

Chapter Six

Dr. Zeller had helped me break through some formidable barriers in my life that I had thought permanent. I met her during my freshman year of college, and I still sought her counsel six years later. I could have seen someone else locally, but I trusted her, and that wasn't something I did often. Especially when it came to deep-rooted issues as I was dealing with now. The mere sound of her voice calmed my fears. I placed the call on speakerphone so Scott could overhear. After he finished cleaning the kitchen, Scott sat right next to me at the breakfast bar working on his laptop.

I had just brought Dr. Zeller up to speed with my current situation, not that it was tied to me in any way. A threat posed in the community, which I also explained, trying to avoid stumbling over my words too much. The more I spoke about this stranger evading the police, the more bizarre I sounded—to myself. Was I arrogant enough to think that every mishap centered on my life? I was about to end the call, apologizing for being so paranoid, when she spoke up.

"What you are feeling is normal, Sara. When someone experiences a traumatic event, the remnants don't just go away. You learn how to manage those triggers and the anxiety. We've talked about this, remember?" She spoke with a reassuring tone; one meant to lower my guard and open my mind.

"I do. I'm sorry I keep falling apart every time something stressful comes up." I huffed at myself as Scott glanced over.

Brow furrowed, my husband shook his head as if to say, *Don't be so hard on yourself.* Bearing witness to my plight, he blinked compassionately with those beautiful blue eyes of his.

"Oh, no, no, no. That's not what I'm saying. And you're far from falling apart. This is very normal for you to feel right now, especially for someone with your past. I've told you many times, I admire your tenacity and ability to reinvent your life. That day in your classroom must've been terrifying. It would be for anyone. You got through it. You got your students through it. Give yourself some credit." Dr. Zeller had a way of embracing me with profound truths that lifted the burden from my shoulders.

"I know. You're right," I said, a shameful waver in my tone.

Once again, Scott glanced over, nodding with conviction.

I touched his arm. "Scott is here with me, and he's nodding with you."

"Oh, hi, Scott." Dr. Zeller's voice lifted. "I hope you are well. Sorry to hear about the news in your community."

"Hey, Dr. Zeller. Appreciate you taking the time to call Sara back. And I'm glad you're reminding her what a great job she's doing. I tell her that all the time, but she doesn't listen to her husband." He winked at me.

Dr. Zeller snickered over the phone. "Well, as you already know, Sara is a very unassuming person. And she can be way too hard on herself, but I'm glad to hear you keep reminding her."

"Yeah, he's been great, and I do listen to him." I took his hand, my gaze washing over my adorable husband in his gray pullover hoodie and black joggers. And then I welcomed a stabilizing breath into my lungs. "Okay, Dr. Zeller. I think I've got it from here."

A few minutes later, I ended the call, feeling much better. As Dr. Zeller had reminded me, I planned to resume my meditation right before bed. That seemed to help me in the past. I was good. This was just another bump in the road.

Scott paused working on his laptop. "I have an idea I want to run by you." He swiveled in his barstool to face me.

I swiveled mine, too, our knees lightly kissing. "Does this have anything to do with yoga poses?" I placed my hands on his thighs, thick and powerful, and then grinned.

Scott made a face as if considering this, his brow rising and falling. "Well, that will always trump anything *I've* got planned, but I was also thinking, what if we take a road trip to visit Amy and Luke in Richmond this weekend? You haven't seen Amy since September, and it would be nice to get out of town. The forecast for the weekend looks good for a road trip to Virginia."

Not only did I love his idea, but I was also touched he'd done his homework by checking the forecast. That was sweet of him.

"I guess I could call or text Amy and see if she's free." There were few people in my world that I would consider kindred spirits. People I couldn't live without. Scott was number one on my list, then Abigail—and, of course, my little sister, Mel—and then there was Amy. She was someone who had changed my life just by populating it. Bold, fearless, and refusing to follow the norms of pretty much anything, Amy put up with my insecurities and timid behavior from the start. We met as suitemates our freshman year. She saw right through me, but in a good way. And she stuck by me like glue when I really needed her. She'd fight a dragon for me, and I would do the same for her.

Scott's lips fidgeted as if holding back a grin. And his eyes shined with untold surprises. I loved that look on him. "I already texted Amy and Luke. They're both free. Luke told a friend of his that he'd watch him play at a club nearby on Saturday night, but he said we could join. He also said the place has a dance floor. They're both free on Friday night. We could have breakfast together on Sunday and then come home. Amy mentioned a Tacky Light Tour that's a big deal in her area. She said we could walk around downtown Richmond Friday night to stretch our legs after dinner. And Saturday night, we can check out the band." He watched me as if I had just opened a present, and he was waiting for that moment of joy to blossom upon my face.

And so I gave him the reaction he deserved. I beamed, both of my hands covering my mouth. "Yes, I would love that." The thought of seeing my best friend made my heart leap in my chest. "But don't you have work to do this weekend?" I knew Scott had a full plate, regardless of the time of year. His schedule was crazy.

Scott scratched his ear as he seemed to ponder this. "If I work late tonight, tomorrow night, and Thursday night, I bet Ben would let me quit early on Friday. And that should also help with my weekend workload. I'll catch up next week. What time do you finish up with your students on Friday? Will you still be working remotely?"

"Until they catch Randy, we've been told we're staying remote. We only have one more week before winter break, anyway."

If working remotely continued until break—which I assumed it would—that was fine by me. It was nice having this time at home. All I had to do was stroll down the hall toward my office. No rushing to get out the door. Plus, if I had a load of laundry to do, I could easily fit it in. I started my day at 8:00 a.m. (although, I was often signed on by 7:30) and my last online class with my students finished up by 2:30. I would normally work a couple of hours longer than that to grade assignments or quizzes and wrap up everything we had covered that day—and to prepare for the next day—but considering it was Friday, I was sure I could get most of that extra work done the night before or over my lunch break. Anything else could be taken care of on Sunday night.

"Hellooo." Leaning in, Scott waved a hand in front of my face. "Earth to Sara."

I combed a few strands of his caramel locks away from his forehead. He had the softest hair I'd ever felt. "Sorry, handsome. I was just running my schedule through my head. I'll check with Principal Robbins and our department chair to see if they mind if I leave a little early on Friday. I'll even see if I can have my afternoon class moved to one o'clock instead of two. That way, we can get on the road by two and be there by seven." I was practically bouncing in my seat, which I could tell Scott enjoyed watching. "Are you sure you don't mind doing all of that extra work this week? And what about holiday obligations?" The calendar in my head told me we were two-and-a-half weeks away from Christmas, with only one free weekend beforehand.

Scott exhaled. "After watching you start your Christmas shopping so early, I'm almost done with mine too. I've got to order a few more small things. And that's all."

He's right. Good thing I *had* started my Christmas shopping early—like August early. Running out at night with a town on high alert wasn't exactly at the top of my list these days. Plus, I kept finding things that reminded me of my loved ones, and I'd grab them while the selection was good. For Scott's mother and Abigail, I had found some beautiful handmade placemats with matching tablecloths, knowing how much they both liked to dress up their tables, along with a few other decorative items for their homes. I found a bath-bomb making kit for Mel (she liked to play scientist), and a nice fleece jacket for Scott's sister, Kelsey. For Theo and Joel, flannels shirts and fun food did the trick. I bought Scott an electric dartboard that he could use when he finished the basement or whenever he was mulling over a work issue in the barn. When we went out for drinks with his best friend, Jason, and his wife, Heather, Scott often gravitated to the bar's dartboard, so I knew he enjoyed them. Buying clothes for my man that would show off his muscles was always a pleasure. It was like dressing up Thor, and I knew what snacks he liked to munch on, or gadgets he was pondering a purchase of. Our biggest present to each other was, of course, the house, but I had a few surprises hidden away.

Scott leaned back in his chair and crossed his arms in a relaxed manner. "Let's see, we've already trimmed the tree at my parents' house and ours. Holiday Lights Run is canceled for the foreseeable future. Abigail is coming two days before Christmas. The only other plans we have are drinks at my boss's house on the twenty-first, and Jason and Heather coming over on the twentieth for game night. My parents will be here with Abigail and your family Christmas Eve and again on Christmas Day, along with Kelsey and maybe Stuart. We've got New Year's Eve planned with my parents, but that's later on." His gaze met mine. "I think we can handle one weekend away, don't you?"

"Oh, yes, Scott. I could really use some Amy time. Thank you. You are the best!"

Scott slid off his stool and nudged me up to do the same. He pulled me close for a hubby bear hug. "Anything for you, babe." He even swayed a little. "I'm hyped about it. It'll be fun."

* * *

Principal Robbins and the department chair didn't have a problem with me adjusting my Friday schedule as long as my students and their parents were okay with it. I emailed them right away, and everyone approved.

Not only did Ben accept Scott's altered Friday schedule, but he was also excited about the yoga studio project. If Scott got the job, Ben promised to loosen the reins, allowing Scott to supervise the project independently. Ben would sign off on the final designs. He felt it was important that he be there for the initial meet and greet, though. Scott had no problem with any of that. Now, he had to sell the job to Tanya and Andie.

He'd left a message at the yoga studio Wednesday morning, explaining who he was, why he was calling, and, by the way, he was married to one of their students, Sara Williams. A little common ground never hurt. Or so he told me.

Tanya called him back that afternoon. Once Scott told her he could do the job at a large discount—something he also worked out with Ben—she said they were interested. I had brought Scott's dinner out to him in the barn when he told me all about it.

"I'm so pumped about this, babe. Ben said I can use this job to build my portfolio. It will be my baby." He paced his office, his feet restless with energy. "Since I'm discounting my hours, Tanya agreed to write some testimonials and let me use images from the project for my website." He fanned a hand out. "That is, if she's happy with my work, of course." While chewing on the turkey-and-cheddar sandwich I had brought him, Scott circled around me. "Having a commercial job on my website will be fucking awesome." He took another generous bite of his dinner, his mind grinding like the gears of a clock. And then he stopped short. "This could be my first big job." He said the words as if to himself, the realization dawning on him.

I rubbed his back, his tan marled rib-knit sweater, soft against my palm, a plaid tartan shirt hidden underneath. Even through two layers of clothing, his body still felt as firm as a brick wall. "I'm so happy for you. Yay. We'll have to celebrate with Amy and Luke this weekend. When do you guys meet about the job?"

Having finished the sandwich, Scott set the plate on the counter in the kitchenette we had installed. He hadn't even touched the sliced apple or the small salad, which both remained on the plate, unattended.

Before I thought too much about it, though, the back of his Levi jeans distracted me, offering a perfect view of his round butt cheeks. No man could fill out jeans like Scott could. *Okay, focus.*

"I asked when they were free, and Tanya said they could come by tomorrow night after yoga class. If they sign on the dotted line, they want to get this job started as soon as possible. I've got a couple of trainees who can do some preliminary measurements on Friday afternoon. Are you going to yoga class tomorrow night?" He gazed over at me, catching my butt-wandering eye, not that he seemed to notice, his mind already working out this new job and what his next move would be. I could tell by the dazed look in his eyes.

I shook my head. "No. I won't have time. I've got too much to do to get ready for Friday. And my back feels much better now."

Scott nodded.

Thursday came, and soon Ben was driving up in his large double-cab pickup truck at 8:00 p.m. on the dot. Tanya and

Andie agreed to arrive at 8:15 p.m. The black onyx-colored paint paired well with the nighttime sky. He parked in a gravel area that Scott had graded just large enough for two vehicles. His headlights were so bright they left spots across my vision long after he had extinguished them. The gravel ran along the side of the barn, reaching a larger parking lot out back for delivery trucks or more customers that would eventually arrive. *Someday*.

Unfettered by clouds, the sky beamed with all its starry brilliance, the moon rising up to reflect upon the night. The temperature had dropped as the hours passed. The weather apps predicted no precipitation for the East Coast, but without clouds to provide a blanket for the warmer air below, gusts of Canadian chill drove south, right at us. We planned to take my Subaru SUV this weekend since it had four-wheel drive and comfy seats. Scott's big truck was great but a gas-guzzler.

I waited with Scott by his office's entrance. An LED barn light (with a new motion sensor) that I referred to as a second sun shone down, illuminating each breath in the form of fog, dancing around my face and Scott's. I zipped my winter coat up an inch higher, and with gloved hands, hugged my waist for warmth. "Hey, Ben." I waved as Ben hopped out of his tall truck and approached.

Pushing sixty years of age, Ben still had a full crop of mostly gray hair—a few strands of charcoal black weaved throughout—a pair of dark-rimmed glasses rested on his nose. "Well, hey, Sara." Wearing a three-quarter length, black wool coat, a casual seafoam-colored button-down shirt and a pair of khaki pants underneath, Ben shook his head and released a flabbergasted breath as he drew near. "What a strange week we're having. Most of my employees are working from home. I hope they catch that guy soon." Ben was of average height, maybe five feet ten and of medium size. He was handsome and had that x factor that attracted business ventures and set people at ease. Scott had that too. Ben carried confidence well on his shoulders, letting you know that if you entrusted your money or your project with him or his company, you were making the right decision. Scott's father had known Ben for years, which I suspected influenced Ben's decision to hire Scott.

"I hope so too. We've been watching the news and haven't seen anything new. Have you?" Whenever I had a free second, I checked my laptop or phone for updates on Randy. So far, the news outlets were only regurgitating the same information, other than an investigation was underway at the prison to determine how this had happened.

Still, every time I passed by a window in our house, I couldn't help but peer out at our property for any human movement. Even the walk from the house to the barn felt scary at night, which this time of year began before five o'clock. One hundred yards of the willies.

As he descended upon us, Ben leaned in for a hug from me and a handshake from Scott. "Not that I've seen." He released another flustered breath. "Not a good time of year for this. Judy's mother is supposed to be taking a train in from Connecticut next week and staying for the holidays. According to Judy, she doesn't want to come now." He quirked a brow. "Said too many crazy people down here." He made a face as he scratched his temple. "She's gettin' up in years. Cranky woman."

I thought about Abigail driving south from Vermont and started to stress over it. "I'm sorry to hear that. How is Judy doing? Scott said she was sick last week?"

Scott opened the door to his office and ushered us in, the air much warmer and welcoming to my cheeks and nose. "Oh, she's much better now. Just a cold. Probably caught it from our grandson, Logan. He's our little germ factory."

I nodded, knowing how true that statement was. "I bet you're right. It seems like there's always something going around at the middle school." Stomach bugs, flu, and every other virus known to man had me nagging my students to wash their hands on a regular basis. Another perk of working at home: less contact with pesky germs before the holidays.

A few minutes later, I watched a red Prius drive up and park next to Ben's robust truck through the office window. The size difference was quite remarkable. When the motion detector light blared on, Ben's onyx-colored truck looked like it could swallow Tanya's red Prius for dinner.

Sporting comfortable looking sweatshirts and leggings in shades of gray, heather, and black, Tanya and Andie headed for the office door. Tanya's short, dark curly hair bounced in the winter breeze next to Andie's short wisps of blond fluffing up like the feathers of a rooster. Both had tight expressions and hunched postures, a noticeable shiver jiggling their shoulders. "I should have worn my coat," Tanya said from outside our walls. "It's freezing out."

Andie offered her two cents. "Yeah, no shit, hon."

I giggled to myself at her response. Something about these two women reeked of cool, and I couldn't wait to get to know them better.

So far, I'd had more opportunities to chat with Tanya, especially since she was the one who taught my yoga class. I also liked Andie's style. It reminded me of Amy, who went from donning spiky black hair in college (complete with multiple facial piercings in her nose and lip) to more relaxed layers now, each one a different shade of the rainbow. Amy still wore piercings in her nose but, according to her, the lip stud had to go. Man, I missed my friend. *BFFs will be together again soon.*

Scott opened the door to his office and smiled. "Let's get you two out of the cold. Thank you for coming." He shook

Andie's and then Tanya's hands, who both shivered again with a *brrr*.

"It wasn't this cold earlier." Andie rubbed her hands together as if hoping to create a spark.

I nodded. "You're right. A cold front is moving in." I removed my coat and hung it on a hook by the door, my body relaxing into the warmth. "Ben, let me take your coat."

As Ben handed me his coat, Scott removed his own and hung it next to mine by the door. Poor Tanya and Andie didn't have any layers to shed.

"I always get so warmed up from yoga, I didn't think I needed a coat. Man, was I wrong," Tanya said in a bold voice.

Scott agreed. "Yeah, it's gotten a lot colder for sure. I meant to tell you when I was there taking pictures yesterday how much I enjoyed attending your yoga class last week with Sara. I was glad I came."

Yeah, right, I thought to myself. He still referred to it as *fart yoga,* not that I was willing to say so. I just stood back and watched everyone mingle with a smile on my face.

"That's cool." Standing in the center of the room, Tanya gave Scott a quick once-over. "I remember you. We don't usually get men of your ... physical build in our class, so it's nice to know you got something out of it." She glanced over at me, her thumb hooking in my direction. "Sara's getting really good at her poses."

From beside Tanya, Andie nodded. "I noticed that. Girl's got it goin' on."

"Thank you," I said with a bashful smile.

"Yeah, I noticed that too." Scott's gaze found me, his eyes revealing a secret too nasty for this crowd. Not only did he refer to the class as *fart yoga,* but he also called what we did the other night *sexy pose.*

Clearing his throat and hopefully his thoughts, Scott angled his body toward Ben. "This is my boss, Ben Miller."

Ben stepped forward and shook the clients' hands. "Nice to meet you both." He patted Scott on the shoulder. "I'll be overseeing the project from afar. But you're in good hands with Scott here. He's shown more talent than some of my finest architects who have been with me for years."

Ben's compliment pulled Scott's shoulders back a bit, the corners of his lips twitching upward.

"We're good with that. Did you remodel this barn, Scott? This space rocks." Tanya's eyes grew wide with wonder as she nudged Andie.

"Yeah, I agree," Andie said.

With a pitched ceiling, exposed wooden beams that promoted strength and stability, and tongue-and-groove walls made from fresh pine and other raw materials both old and new, the barn was able to reminisce about the past and revive for the future.

I understood Tanya and Andie's appreciation of it. You could practically feel the history of the farmers and the livestock from within the walls, the hard work and the spoils. Deviating from our museum of yesteryear was a concrete floor that promised to lay low and support the needs of the structure for many years to come.

"I love seeing old buildings revamped like this. You've designed the space well." Tanya inhaled through her nose as though enjoying the natural scent.

Adapting the room to a more office-like environment, Scott utilized two-drawer filing cabinets as legs to support a very large and very beautiful piece of wood he had sanded smooth to create an extra-long desk that ran along one wall of his office—the one adorned with his degrees, framed and hung proudly. A drafting table stood adjacent; its surface angled just enough to allow better viewing of blueprints.

Keeping the country theme alive, a pair of gooseneck barn lights hung from wooden beams providing plenty of illumination, and when the sun came out, two large windows, one peering out toward our house, the other, the parking lot, did their best to assist.

Promoting a more modern era, a small kitchenette anchored the left side of the room. A place where a full farmhouse sink harbored dirty dishes, coffee brewed on the marble countertop, and chilled beverages awaited in the full-size fridge for clients. A convection microwave substituted well for a stove in case Scott needed to warm up food for his lunch. And right next to it, a bathroom hid behind a closed door for whenever nature called.

But that only covered a fraction of the barn. Beyond an extra-large wooden slider, which we kept closed to conserve heat (although it did have heat when needed), Scott's warehouse awaited. Someday, he'd store supplies there as more jobs came in. For now, it was just a very large and very empty room.

What was my contribution? I scored a large, hand-knotted wool rug donning geometric patterns in shades of red, beige, and green at an antique mall in town, which added color to the room and softened everyone's footing, along with a pair of valances, in seafoam green that, somehow, matched the rug perfectly. I also took care of stocking the kitchen cabinets with plenty of mugs, glasses, plates, and silverware, not to mention all the paper and cleaning products Scott would need for the near future.

The scent of old wood and fresh possibilities ripened in the air, making the need for air fresheners unnecessary, with the exception of the bathroom, of course.

"Thank you. I enjoyed restoring it. There's nothing like

taking old buildings and finding the right materials to make them new again." He stared up at the ceiling and then around the room, his hand finding a post nearby to admire and touch. "My great-great-grandfather built this barn, and I was happy to bring it back."

Ben's eyes shined. "So that's why you work for me, is it? You like restoring old geezers like me?" He chuckled, inviting everyone else to do the same.

Scott grinned. "Not quite, Ben. You still gotta a lot of spring left in your step." He clasped his hands together. "I'd love to give you ladies a tour of the rest of the barn and the house if you'd like when we're finished."

Andie nodded, and Tanya said with a shrug, "Sure. We'd be down for that."

"Before we get started, could I offer you coffee, tea, or a bottled water?" Scott asked, being the great host that he was.

I was really enjoying watching him pour on the charm. He was definitely a *big guy* as my friend Amy had nicknamed him, but one with a gentle demeanor. Most of the time. *Just don't make him mad,* I thought to myself in jest.

"I'm good. Thank you, though." Andie gazed over at Tanya who said the same.

"Okay then"—Scott motioned toward some chairs sitting vacant by the elongated desk—"Let's get started."

* * *

The next day, we packed up my Subaru and headed for Richmond, Virginia. When I was pulling my suitcase out from the back of my closet earlier, I knocked the infamous dress I had obsessed over recently off the hook, the entire dress bag falling to the floor. When I picked it up, I couldn't help but unzip the cover and admire it. If I hadn't been short on time, I may have even tried it on, just for fun. Scott had offered to take me out for a special dinner, so I could wear it. And as I admired the delicate crab apple chiffon fabric with a flattering style meant to *wow* whoever was wearing it, I decided I'd do just that.

"What are you doing?" Standing at the doorway, Scott peered in at me.

I thrust the dress in front of me, my back doing its best to shield the surprise. "Don't look. I don't want you to see it until our dinner date."

"See what?" He paused. "Oooh. The dress." His voice teased. "The mysterious dress." I could hear the laughter in his voice. "That reminds me. I got us on a waiting list for Bon Appétit in Philly. Ben told me about it. He said he might be able to pull some strings for us. And from what I saw on the website, it's definitely nice enough for that dress. It even has a piano bar so we can slow dance, and I can get my hands on you and that dress." His naughty intentions brought a smile to my face.

"I'm glad to hear that. Now turn around, mister." I knew I was being silly, but he'd waited this long, what was a little while longer, right?

"Copy that, babe. I just came in to see how much more time you needed. I've got my stuff already loaded into the car."

With my shower bag packed and my clothes organized and folded on my bed, I calculated the timing in my head. "Maybe twenty minutes? Did you grab the wine bag? And my purse?" I was terrible about forgetting things and had on many occasions. Nothing worse than heading out on a long trip and realizing you'd forgotten your purse *with* your license. Happened once, and I was determined to not let it happen again.

"Yup, and the snack bag, small cooler, the fleece throw for your lap, and your neck pillow. Oh, and the presents." His hand patted the door casing. "It's already in the car. I'll be in the kitchen. See you in twenty."

And so, twenty-*five* minutes later, Scott drove, and I rode shotgun, my hand resting on his thigh. In my side mirror, our house grew smaller until trees and distance pulled it away from my view. While part of me (a big part) was thrilled to get out of town, I couldn't help but feel guilty about leaving our beautiful house behind. I'd checked the locks on the windows. Scott set the alarm. We still didn't have one in the barn yet or on the second floor. Regardless, our house was vacant. And if someone —more specifically, Randy—was determined or desperate enough to get inside, there wasn't much we could do about it from several hundred miles away. I just hoped and prayed Randy didn't wander in our direction.

This was our private sanctuary. Not his.

Chapter Seven

Scott stared down at my hand on his leg, which had ridden up a few inches unbeknownst to me. "You may want to pull that hand back down, babe. You're messing with a deprived man, and if you're not careful, I may have to pull this car over and make love to you in the backseat. It's been a while." With his body angled toward me, Scott rested one hand atop the steering wheel, the way he always did, the sound of soft rock emanating from the car's speakers. His eyes shined with amorous thoughts.

I removed my hand and scratched my head. "Been a while? Didn't we make love last Saturday? And didn't we have a quickie two mornings ago?" I barely remembered that one. He had woken me up before he crawled out of bed and left for the gym, his warm body rubbing up against the back of mine. *What a way to start the day.*

"Quickies don't count. Not when I have to sleep next to you every night. Do you know how hard it is, *hard* being the operative word here, to come to bed with you lying next to me?" Scott exhaled, his eyes caressing me from head to waist.

"Like I always remind you, it's your fault for being so damn hot, woman." And then he yawned, the intensity threatening to crack his jaw apart.

Poor guy was almost too tired to flirt. He'd been out in the barn all week long until late in the night. Business was good at Ben's firm, and it showed in the dark circles pulling Scott's bloodshot eyes inward. He also had that new job at the yoga studio.

"Why don't you let me drive?" I sat up and faced him.

"I like driving. It relaxes me." He yawned again.

"Any more relaxed and you'll be asleep." My hand found his shoulder. "Come on. You can take a nap, and then you'll be more rested when we get there."

With his free hand, Scott rubbed his eyes. "Okay, I give up. Next rest area I'll pull over. Just keep talking to me until then."

The winter sun beamed into our vehicle, forcing visors down and sunglasses on. A cloudy day would have been much more forgiving for tired eyes. But our sky wasn't having it, no clouds to speak of, just the blue abyss and a sun, trying its best to warm the chilly earth.

Okay, so what should we talk about?

"It was nice having Tanya and Andie over. I mean, I know it was all about the project, but while you and Andie were discussing expenditures in the kitchen right after you gave them a tour of our house, I visited with Tanya in the family room."

Tanya had made it perfectly clear that finances weren't her thing. "I teach the classes; she does the books." She kissed Andie after she said it. "The perfect match. Right, hon?"

Leaning her head closer to her wife, Andie had agreed. "You know it, T."

"I wondered where you two were. Hit it off, did you?"

I lifted my voice. "We did. I told her that I teach special-needs students, and she said she has a niece with Down's. Her name is Samantha. She's ten, and Tanya adores her." I tipped my head back and forth. "Anyway, we talked about other stuff. I asked her if she liked to watch movies, and she said she did. She likes suspense like I do. So I mentioned that maybe she and Andie could come over for a movie night sometime. She seemed down with that. And I also told her how much I enjoyed her yoga class." I elbowed Scott in the arm. "Way to pour on the charm about how much you liked her class, by the way." I cast him a disapproving glare.

"What?" From behind his sunglasses, Scott pretended to be outraged. "I never said I didn't like the class." He lifted his chin and pursed his lips. "Fart yoga is awesome."

I wagged a finger. "I knew it. Better not call it that in front of them." I filled my tone with as much sarcasm as it would hold. "You might just lose that new job you're so proud of."

A few more barbs pinged back and forth before I settled onto another topic. I kept my body angled in his direction, making sure his eyes stayed open. "Can I ask you a strange question?"

With the hand holding the steering wheel, Scott lifted a casual finger. "Rest area in five miles."

A large sign flew past on the side of the highway.

"Oh, good. You can stay awake that long."

And then Scott slid his sunglasses down, his eyes filled with curiosity. "What is your strange question? Should I be worried?"

I waved him off. "Worried? About what?"

"Never mind. What's your strange question?" He sat up straighter.

"What was it like to go to prom? I assume you went to your junior and your senior prom, right?" I mean, with his looks, he probably had girls waiting in line to go with him. I shook the thought from my head.

"Yeah, I went." His voice came out guarded.

"Did you ask JoJo to both proms?" With big brown eyes, long, silky black hair, and a body that did nothing but turn heads, JoJo was one of Kelsey's best friends and an old flame of Scott's. When I had first met JoJo, it was obvious to me that she still carried a torch for Scott, but she quickly learned that he and I were solid. Whatever bond they shared was in the past. We had a few awkward moments over the issue, but things quickly settled down. And then, JoJo met Kurt, a successful stockbroker who swept her off her feet. They were married six months later.

"I told you, after JoJo had graduated, we weren't exclusive. She dated whoever she wanted, and so did I." I could feel Scott's defenses rising. He removed his sunglasses, his eyes showing more clarity. Discussing any of Scott's old flames was never a fun experience.

I removed mine too. I didn't want him to misunderstand my intentions, making eye contact a must.

"Don't be so defensive. Geez. I like JoJo. And I enjoyed attending her wedding. I was just curious what it was like to go to prom. You don't have to tell me who you went with. I'm just trying to get an idea of what it was like. Did you make a grand gesture when you asked your date? I guess I've just been thinking about it since I had that conversation with Kelsey and your mom the other day."

Judging by the way his brow eased, Scott seemed to accept where I was going with my inquiry. "Oh, yeah. Now I remember why you've got proms on your mind."

"It's not just that. I'm also reading a romance right now that includes a prom." I fidgeted in my seat. "Well, prom happens within the story. The town was decimated by a twister, and it's about how all the townspeople coped with the aftermath, more specifically, these two seventeen-year-olds named Cala and Marcus. Marcus ends up dying in the storm, and Cala remembers the year before when he had asked her to prom." I paused, realizing I was veering off the subject. "Anyway, I didn't mean to go into all of that. Where were we?"

Scott ran a palm across the back of his neck, a definite sign of his discomfort. "Can we talk about something else? I don't want to discuss proms."

I leaned over and nudged him. "Come on. Indulge me. I'll never get to go to prom. I just want to know what it was like."

Scott snapped a little. "I don't want to talk to my wife about taking some other girl to prom. Why would you want to know that? It was a long time ago." His eyes hardened.

I faced forward, realizing our conversation was going nowhere. Scott had a promiscuous past. And I had accepted that fact years ago. But when he acted like this—all defensive and weird—it only fueled my insecurities. Like he was leaving me out of something, which, of course, only made me want to know more about it. "Fine. I wasn't asking for romantic details. I just wanted to know the gist. What people do, but never mind." I exhaled and crossed my arms.

Another sign flew past: two miles to the rest area. "We're almost there." Enthusiasm drained from my voice like water from a sink. "Maybe I shouldn't have asked." I stared out the window, my heart heavy with regret. If only I hadn't lost those six years after my parents had died—those six formative years— I would have known what prom was like. It was a rite of passage to me. Even if a boy hadn't asked me, I could have gone with a friend. The music, the dresses, and the dancing, it all sounded so cool. Not to mention, the photo booth.

Scott ran a hand down the back of my head and across my upper back, his fingers providing a light massage. "I'm sorry, babe. I know you didn't get to go to one. We can talk about it. We've got nothing better to do, right?" Scott turned the radio down. "Let's see. When I asked my date, I wasn't really into making a big production about it. I knew who I wanted to ask, and I knew she wanted me to ask her, so I put a note in her locker. It wasn't anything big. Some of my friends went all out, but I wasn't into that."

I turned back to face him, my spirit lighter. "What did the note say?" I wanted to imagine every detail. Well, not *every* detail.

"Will you go to the prom with me?" Scott's voice was as deadpan as mine was just a moment ago.

"Seriously? That's it? But you're such a romantic. How can that be true?"

"I'm a romantic with *you*. I wasn't really like that back then. I was a self-centered prick, to be honest." He took my hand and kissed my knuckles before releasing it. "And I suspect I'd still be a SOB if it wasn't for you. You changed me, babe. When I saw what you had been through and the courage you had to change your life, I was blown away. I'm still blown away." His eyes twinkled like the surface of a lake when the sun hit it just right. "Not to mention, you are the most gorgeous thing I've ever seen. Inside and out."

Of course, my heart melted. Scott always had a way of making me feel special.

"Aw. Thank you." I touched his cheek. "You don't give yourself enough credit, though. I know your family. You may have been that way when you were a high schooler, but you would have matured out of that phase. Otherwise, you wouldn't have even wanted to meet someone like me."

Scott scrunched his face. "I'm not so sure about that."

"Stop." I said in a tender voice. "*I'm* sure. Now let's get back to our fun chat. Tell me more about prom. Did you have pictures taken?" I stared off. "I would love to have a prom picture, even if it was with someone I didn't like anymore." All I could imagine was Scott (it had to be Scott, of course) standing next to me, decked out in a tux, me in my gown, a prepared photo stage ready and waiting to capture our special night. Punch bowls and snacks displayed atop long tables, streamers and balloons floating through the air, teachers reprimanding students to pull apart, even though all they wanted to do was mash their bodies together, hormones in full swing. Yup. I'd read too many books and watched too many movies. It was obvious. "You had punch, right? I mean, you had to have had punch. Was it spiked?"

Scott put his blinker on for the rest area. "Yes, we had punch, and our valedictorian spiked it. He almost lost his class ranking when one kid drank too much and threw up all over the table." He giggled.

* * *

Before long, my Subaru found Interstate 95 South and the clogged highways that came with it. One moment, traffic was sparse and then big trucks had sandwiched us in, the cars bumper to bumper. I thought we were never going to reach our destination. It seemed to get worse every time we took this route. Especially around Baltimore and Washington DC.

Scott reclined his seat back and fell asleep for most of the trip. My fleece blanket and neck pillow came in handy for him. I was glad he had a few good hours of shut-eye. He'd been working so late. I hadn't even heard him come to bed the past couple of nights. The man had energy beyond anything I could muster, but everyone had their limit. How he had stamina enough for sex the other morning was beyond me.

We passed by a sign that welcomed me and my sleeping

partner to Virginia. I was so excited to see my friend. After she had graduated from college, Amy had landed a great job as a graphic designer at a prominent multinational clothing company in Richmond, who interestingly enough, headquartered in Philly, although Amy's position didn't require her to travel there. *Bummer for me.* The pay was good, and the treatment of their employees was even better. Considering Luke was working hard to make his band famous, the steady paycheck from Amy's job came in handy.

They lived in a section of Richmond called the Fan District, known for the way an array of streets fanned out westward like the fingers of a hand. She and Luke were renting a house on Park Ave (very different from Park Avenue in NYC), which we'd stayed at before. It was a quaint section of town, populated by tall but narrow houses, with thin alleys in between, and small eclectic restaurants sprouting up like greenery in a bouquet around town. She even had a front porch, where we sat sipping coffee, tea, or wine back in September when Scott and I had visited for Amy's birthday.

Her banana-colored house with bright-green shutters was lucky enough to stand next to a slim driveway, just wide enough to fit her car and Luke's van. The streets were narrow, the parking spaces few, making parking a logistical nightmare. But Luke had sold his old van to a scrap yard when its transmission had died last month. He had his eye on another used van—he needed room for his band equipment—that would hopefully do the trick very soon. That meant we had parking, and we didn't have to walk like pack mules carrying our bags for God knew how far. I also liked having my car nearby where I could keep an eye on it.

The minute my wheels pulled off the highway, Scott's eyes sprang open as if his internal compass had alerted him to our location. The clock flashed 7:30 p.m.

"Where are we?"

"Richmond. Do you feel better? You were snoring pretty loud for a while." I smirked.

Scott only snored when he was way overtired, so I knew he needed the rest. And he got three-and-a-half hours of it.

"Sorry, babe. I wasn't much company, was I?" He rubbed his face and then blinked a few times and stretched, his hand caressing my shoulder. "How are you holding up? I bet you're tired." He spoke through a yawn.

"Oh, no. I'm good. Just a little stiff. I'm ready to get out of this car, that's for sure." I took a sip of water from my stainless-steel water bottle, my throat welcoming the hydration. Not wanting to wake Scott, I had refrained from drinking much of anything to avoid the need for another rest area stop, not that we had utilized the last one. We had simply switched drivers. The needle on my gas gauge inched below a quarter of a tank, telling me I would need to fill up soon, probably on Sunday before we drove home. A problem for another day.

A turn onto Arthur Ashe Blvd led to another eventual turn onto Hermitage Road, which brought us to Park Ave. My best friend was only half a block away, her banana-colored house, a sight for sore eyes. And backs, and hips ...

Visiting this time of year, Christmas in Richmond, Virginia, brought the city to life in various forms: nearly every tree trunk wrapped in lights, along with skyscrapers dressed up for the occasion. No snow on the ground, but it didn't matter. The city sparkled. I was excited to walk around and check out the tacky lights that Amy had mentioned, a few I could already see from a distance.

I crept my SUV down the drive, parking behind Amy's used hybrid, careful not to ding my side mirrors on anything. Light shone through the side windows of Amy's house, shadows moving around, until a storm door at the back flung open, and Amy emerged. Luke stood behind her, wearing a big smile.

Scott and I climbed out and stretched our backs and legs, Amy making a fast approach.

"How was the drive?" she asked.

"Long. The traffic was insane." I edged my way around my car to fold into Amy's welcoming arms. "I missed you."

When I had met Amy six years ago, she wasn't much of a hugger, or a person who showed outward affection of any kind, but that wasn't the case anymore. We were like two soldiers who had been through some stuff and had come out stronger as a result. We saw each other's weakest moments and celebrated each other's strongest triumphs. We were sisters, not by blood but by our love and commitment to each other.

"Yeah, missed you, too, Al."

Amy had nicknames for everyone. She referred to Luke as Sky after Luke Skywalker of *Star Wars*, due to his sandy-colored hair and lanky body. The movie series was something she and her older brother Griffin used to watch a lot. She'd labeled Scott, Big Guy almost immediately for his obvious physical attributes. And I was called Al, short for Alice as in *Alice in Wonderland*, which was how I felt when I had first arrived at college. More specifically, like I had traveled down a rabbit hole that I wasn't sure I could handle at the time. But Amy knew I could. And even though I wasn't the same naïve and timid girl I was back then, the name stuck, a tribute to the struggles and accomplishments of my life. No one called me Al but Amy. It was our thing.

My husband drew near, straightening his sweater from being crumpled in sleep-mode. "Poor Sara had to drive. I slept the entire way." Scott's eyes still carried a level of fatigue that hopefully a strong cup of coffee would remedy.

"She seems okay to me." Amy gave me a smirk.

I offered a nonchalant gesture. "Yeah, it was no big deal." The only thing I regretted was not calling Abigail during the drive. Once again, I didn't want to wake Scott. I planned to send her a text, assuring her I'd be calling on the ride home.

"Glad you guys made it. Let's get your things inside and then have something to eat. I made chicken parmesan, and the smell is driving me *craaazy*. You're lucky I didn't eat it before you got here." Amy pointed a thumb over her shoulder at her hubby jogging down the steps. "Or Luke, for that matter. I had to kick him out of the kitchen more than once. Takeout is our normal routine around here."

Luke met Scott at the back of my car. "Good to see you, man."

They bro hugged, a slap on the back for good measure.

"Got some bags I can help with?" Luke stood ready and waiting to help.

Just like Amy and me, Scott and Luke had a history, one that bonded them for life. Considering their wives were best friends, it was a good thing they got along so well. When they met, Scott was a frat boy and a star soccer player at Commonwealth. Luke had long hair and played in a band, the scent of weed wafting off his clothes like cologne, not that anything had changed in that area. We still loved the guy to death. Luke had proven his devotion to Amy, and in my book, that put him at the top of my very short list of good humans. Scott's too.

"Thanks, man. Sure. I've got a few things you can take." Scott reached into our car to divvy out the cargo.

"Want some help?" I called out.

Amy waved me off. "Nah, they got it." She laced her arm inside of mine. "Let's get inside. It's cold out." She *brrred* through her lips.

* * *

After a delicious dinner of chicken parmesan, garlic bread, and a winter salad, plus two bottles of red wine, Scott ran off to take a quick shower before we ventured out on our Tacky Light Tour. He'd taken a shower that morning, but he said he needed another one to finish waking up.

Amy and Luke's upper floor provided just enough space for three bedrooms, one of them a makeshift office for when Amy worked remotely, and one bathroom, which we all shared. A half bath resided downstairs. With neighbors living on both sides of the house, only a few feet away, Amy used sheer curtains to cover the large windows, offering privacy while also inviting some semblance of light into each room. The house was old, the wood floors warped and weathered, and the rooms relatively small. But Amy's personal touch shined in the antique lace curtains hanging from the windows downstairs, the local artwork embellishing the walls, and the retro furniture that brought with it a cozy yet reflective style from an earlier time. She'd even sponge painted a few walls, giving them a textured feel. Wool rugs provided traction for our footing while sandalwood—Amy's signature scent—wafted from the essential oil burners running on both ends of the house. "Either that or the house would get musty," she'd professed.

One other scent lingered in the air. A small Charlie-Brown-style Christmas tree stood modestly in the corner of her living room. A real one decorated with a few old-fashioned ornaments, its tender branches offering the air a light burst of balsam, but only if you were standing close to notice. A few presents sat underneath, keeping the little tree content.

Amy had hung string lights over the insides of her first-floor windows, but she kept those up year-round. I remembered them from my last visit here.

For the most part, vintage was Amy's thing, and for that reason, I suspected she'd like our barn, which she hadn't been able to see yet, not since the remodel. Her family lived in Farmington, Connecticut, and I hoped to convince her to stop by on her way home sometime, maybe even stay for a night or two. We were practically on the way.

While Luke researched the best spots within walking distance for our Tacky Light Tour—and Scott took a shower—I stood in the galley kitchen, wiping dishes Amy had washed (she didn't have a dishwasher) while listening to a grumbling quartet, otherwise known as Amy's old furnace, hot water heater, and aged washer and dryer—which was now doing a load of wash—living between two parallel walls just off the kitchen.

"How's your job going?" I took an antique dinner plate decorated with a garland of flowers around the rim from Amy's soaking wet hands. She'd bought a whole set of vintage mugs, bowls, various-sized plates, and serving dishes, all stacked together in the open cabinets above.

"Good. I just got a raise. My boss is pretty chill. She's not one of those types that feels like she needs to micromanage everyone." Amy handed me another plate, which I dried and stacked in the cupboard to my upper right. "In fact"—Amy's face brightened—"she may see a promotion for me in the future."

I put my last plate away and bumped my shoulder against hers. "That's awesome, Amy. You deserve it."

Not only was Amy a hard worker, but she was also gifted artistically. It wasn't just local artists gracing her walls. She had a few pieces of her own work displayed as well. Maybe someday she'd have enough to warrant her own art show.

Keeping her enthusiasm under control—another Amy-ism —she simply shrugged. "Yeah, I'd be pretty hyped about it. But nothing's happened yet." She gave me a side look. "How's your job going? I bet those kids are fun." Amy loved the special-needs students I used to tutor in college for extra credit. I tutored one girl named Gwen for two years. I still kept in touch with her through email, and Gwen still sent me notes and cards from time to time.

"Great, other than what happened last week."

At that moment, the furnace groaned to life. It reminded me of an old man trying to get up from his not-so-easy chair. "I bet you don't have noises like that in your *brand-new* house." Amy loved to mock, and mock she did, every chance she got. "I'm sure everything is just perfect, just like Ken and Barbie who live there." Her smirk told me she was having fun amusing herself.

I decided to add a little mocking of my own. "Well, you'd know that if you ever came to visit." I took a saucepan from her hands, dried it, and placed it in a lower cupboard. "Next time you go to Connecticut, you should stop by on your way. We aren't even that far off the interstate. It could break up the drive. And if you left early enough, you could stay for a night or two."

Amy pulled the drain and rinsed the sink clean. "Yeah, yeah. Luke's schedule is hard to predict these days." Sponge in hand, she stopped and faced me, a shadow passing over her face. "He's been driving all over the fucking place trying to get gigs. That's why his van shit the bed. He had like two-hundred-and-fifty-thousand miles on the old clunker." She blew out a breath. "I'm not even sure we can go to Farmington for Christmas this year."

I placed a hand on her arm. "I'm sorry, Amy. That sounds rough. Poor Luke."

She scratched her chin. "Yeah, well, he really wants to get some steady gigs. But there are too many other bands out there doing the same thing. He just scored some DJ equipment, hoping to branch out. It wasn't cheap, either." She peered into the dining room where Luke sat at Amy's laptop, and then, she lowered her voice. "I'll give him another year, maybe two, and then his ass is finding a steady job. I love the guy, but love doesn't pay the rent, and I'm getting tired of pulling this gravy train on my own." After she placed her sponge at the head of the sink, she grabbed her satchel off the counter and fished through it, pulling out some deep-red lipstick that matched well with her winged eyeliner and colorful hair. Wearing a tan-and-black striped crewneck sweater, the material fluffy enough you wanted to touch it, Amy had rolled up her bell sleeves to wash the dishes. It matched perfectly with her black, high-waisted pencil pants. Amy always looked stylish wherever she went.

"I meant to tell you. I love your outfit, Amy."

She looked down at herself. "Thanks, Al. I found it a—"

"Let me guess, a vintage shop?" I grinned with catlike fervor.

Our gazes landed on my thick, gray-and-black plaid fleece button-down, black leggings for pants, a white tank playing camisole. *Plain Jane.* "I brought a better outfit to wear to the club you're taking us to tomorrow night." I flattened out my fleece shirt. "I will never have your sense of style, Amy, but at least I'm warm. And I figured this would be perfect for walking around outside tonight."

Amy approached, her head shaking slightly in a I-don't-understand-you sort of way. "Al, when are you ever gonna get it? You're hot! I'm getting a little tired of reminding you about your big blue eyes"—she took a few strands of my hair between her fingers—"long blond hair, with just the perfect wave to it, big boobs, long legs, and a body that says you work out constantly, even though I know you don't. *And* you eat like a horse, which makes me hate you even more." She placed both of her hands on my shoulders. "I have to slap on layers of makeup and dress up to look good, but you don't. You could wear a garbage bag and still have men chasing after you down the street." She quirked an eyebrow. "In fact, that would probably make them chase you even more." She settled her gaze on mine. "And you have a husband who looks like he should be starring in the next action film." She pinched her face a smidge and rattled her head for effect, sarcasm rolling off her tongue. "I think you're good."

She was wrong, of course, and certainly about her own natural beauty. In fact, Amy had the most beautiful green eyes I'd ever seen, but I wasn't in the mood to argue. As I always did in these situations, I took the compliment in stride.

A combination of fresh soap and musky cologne entered the room a second before Scott emerged wearing his own thick flannel shirt, only he'd paired his with jeans not leggings like mine. "Luke said he's got the route all figured out. You ladies ready to check out those tacky lights?"

When Amy had talked about the Tacky Light Tour, she didn't do it justice. The only thing I could compare it to was the Holiday Lights Run back home. Some of the houses on our Richmond tour gave way to a New Orleans theme, donning layers of lights hanging over the home's portico or front door like beads in a Margi Gras parade. The effect was quite spectacular. One house displayed lights cascading down from a two-story window to the street in the shape and flow of a small waterfall. Lit up in large, block-style letters, RVA beamed from another roof, with more lights exploding from the exterior and the front lawn, every square inch devoted to illumination. I imagined the power company loved these people. We even found an old vintage Cadillac convertible, flooded with colorful lights inside and out. The back seat burst with bright inflatables, bows, and lit-up candy canes, all pretending to be Santa's treasures, ready to dazzle a precious child on Christmas morning in this story. A team of reindeer stood guard tethered to the old car with strings of more Christmas lights.

I walked along holding Scott's hand, taking it all in, Amy and Luke guiding us like Rudolf, their noses almost as red from the cold. Luke kept his arm draped over Amy's shoulders, the two of them as casual and relaxed as anyone could appear.

We ended our walking tour near an iconic office complex called the James Center, known for its Christmas flair. The expansive lawn housed a large herd of lighted reindeer, all of them posing or grazing on the frozen ground. Illumination shined from every tree, some with glowing spheres that dangled like low-hanging fruit. A procession of lights ran along the edges of the skyscrapers, a large Christmas tree taking root in front of the state house, not far away. Like us, people walked around in droves, admiring the pageantry.

By then, my tired feet hurt, so we decided to head home.

"You'll have to come next year, and I'll take you on the driving Tacky Light Tour. You won't believe how decked out some of *those* houses get."

Amy looked cute, her colorful hair spilling out from under her red knit hat and a matching red wool coat that she found at, you guessed it, a vintage shop.

We finished another couple of bottles of red wine back at Amy's place, the alcohol doing an adequate job of warming my muscles. For the first hour, I sat on Amy's camelback vintage sofa with Scott, ranting about the lights and how nice the area was. I ran my hands along the couch's silky fabric, appreciating how its floral pattern harmonized well with Amy's sage velvet accent chair and Luke's wingback, matching the shade of a yellow zucchini. The furniture didn't match, but somehow, it blended nicely. Even the ceramic lamps, the color of robins' eggs and formed in the shape of an hourglass, along with the mismatched end and coffee table, played a role. Anchoring the street side of the room, an antique red cabinet stood in the corner watching over it all. I imagined Amy stored blankets or extra pillows there. How she knew they would all mingle so well was beyond me. Amy was truly an artist.

With my legs tucked under my butt, I continued to boast. "I know we're in the city, but this area has a real neighborly feel about it." I followed another train of thought, sparked by Randy back home. "How bad is the crime here?"

Snuggled into the velvet of her accent chair—an afghan draped over her lap—Amy sat forward and placed her empty glass of wine down on the coffee table.

"Of course, we get our share of crime. Mostly cars get broken into." She made a face. "We don't currently have an escaped convict running around town if that's what you're wondering."

During our walk, we had told Amy and Luke about what was happening back home, which they had already known about since the story had gone viral several days ago.

Scott placed his wine glass, also empty, on the same coffee table. "I'm beat." He rubbed his eyes. "I think I'm going up." He yawned, his cell phone flashing 12:30 a.m. from the arm rest beside him.

We'd been listening to Luke play his guitar, which included a new song he was experimenting with. He considered his band alternative rock or post-grunge, grouping him in with bands like Foo Fighters, one of Scott's favorites. It was nice to lay back against Scott on their couch and let the music mellow my mind.

"You coming up?" Scott sat forward, gazing over at me.

I yawned as well and stretched. "Yeah, I think so."

"What? I thought you'd want to stay up and chat, Al." My BFF stared me down, but not with intensity, just hopeful longing.

I stood. "I promise to stay up with you tomorrow night after we get home from the club." I arched my back feeling fatigue settle into my bones. "After working most of the day and driving here, plus our fun walk around town, I'm so tired, Amy. I'm afraid I'll just fall asleep on you." I blinked, my eyes reaching out to her generous side.

Amy got to her feet. She moved to collect the empty wine glasses while Luke opened his guitar case and stored his precious instrument away.

"Let me help you." I stepped forward.

"Nah. I got it." Using both of her hands like claws at an arcade, Amy hooked all four stemless glasses together, two at a time, and lifted them. "Go rest. Cause I'm making you stay up with me tomorrow night." She made her way toward the kitchen. "Hand towels, washcloths, and bath towels are in the cabinet under the sink to the left."

She had two sinks up there, which made it nice for four people. "Scott knows." She stopped briefly. "The reason you have a drying rack in your bedroom is because I don't have enough hooks in the bathroom. Just put your wet towels in your room and then you can reuse them tomorrow and Sunday." Her voice drifted away and out of sight. "Night" was the last thing I heard.

Our teeth clean, Scott snuggled up behind me, our bodies warming the chilly sheets. "You said something to me on the way here that stuck with me." The scent of mint from his luscious lips infused the air around my face.

"Oh, yeah. What was that?" I closed my eyes and molded into my human-sized spoon behind me.

"I can't remember exactly how you put it, but you said something about how if I hadn't matured when we met, I would have never even wanted to be with someone like you." He let that thought settle into my ears.

Not sure what to say, I simply said, "Yeah?" hoping he'd continue.

Diffused light from neighboring houses and streetlights brought definition to Amy's antique dresser standing against the wall in front of me, along with everything else inhabiting the room.

Scott moved even closer, his face cresting over my shoulder, his breath warming my cheek. "Just so you know. I was still a self-centered prick when I met you. But I took one look at you." He paused. "What those blue eyes of yours did to me had rendered me helpless, not to mention your other attributes." His gaze slid down my body for a brief moment. "I had no choice. I had to have you. And when I realized what kind of person you were." He brought his hand around to lightly touch my cheek. "How genuine your heart was." He pulled his hand back. "I said to myself, you can either grow the fuck up and do everything in your power to win this gorgeous creature's heart, or you can spend the rest of your shallow life regretting having let her go." His voice shook a little, making my eyes water.

I didn't dare move for fear of interrupting him.

He eased my shoulders back, so I was lying below his handsome face. "What you did to me was unfair, you know. I never stood a chance." With his elbows pressed into the mattress, he brushed my tousled hair away from my face. "I had never met anyone like you. You're funny. You're kinder than anyone I know. You're honest, and you're more beautiful than anything I've ever seen."

"Don't forget, I'm a klutz." With moist eyes, I smiled up at him.

The softest giggle floated from his lips. He shook his head as if my criticism had only reinforced his point. "Yeah, that sealed it for me. I was a goner. You own my heart, Sara Williams, and you always will." His lips landed on mine, his tongue exploring my mouth, sensual and hungry. "I know you're probably too tired for this right now, but I have to make love to you. I promise I'll be quick, and I'll be quiet."

I leveled my eyes with his, cupping his face in my hands. "I don't want you to be either of those things." My body longed for his touch. "I prefer you slow and loud."

Chapter Eight

The morning sun delivered a fresh new day to our little guest room. I awoke with Scott still spooning me in our queen-sized bed with brass frame. His deep breaths fanned the back of my shoulder; his body pressed against mine as though we were still one.

What a night. Scott made love to me last night like it was our first time. Slowly and methodically, he touched me, he kissed me, and he showed me with his body and his words just how much love he had stored in his heart. No dirty talk this time. Instead, he spoke with a tender voice. "You're all I ever want . . . . I'd be lost without you . . . . You changed my life forever."

He kept his movements gentle, his intention to connect and to savor. With his eyes watching and appreciating, he brought his hands between my legs, his fingers gliding inside a body that was already moist and ready for him. In and out, his fingers teased. Then, up and down along the folds of my female flesh, provoking my inner cravings.

As my lungs expanded and my eyes glazed over—my back

threatening to arch—he watched me groan and writhe, a smile spreading across his face. At one point, I caught my breath, realizing how one-sided this show had become. "What are you doing? I want you inside of me." And I did, my core was screaming for him. I started to move, putting myself in a more favorable position to satisfy him back, but he stopped me.

"Soon," he said. "I want to watch for a moment." After he kissed and suckled my nipples, his fingers slid inside me once again, massaging everywhere that he knew would drive me wild. I felt like a stick of dynamite, and he was the lit fuse, crawling toward certain detonation.

I cried out.

Just thinking about it now made me tingle all over.

A pan clanking from the lower floor stirred Scott, whose breath grew deeper, filling his lungs with new air.

"What time is it?" he whispered, hugging me tight and then rolling over onto his back.

I peered over at the clock on my nightstand. "Ten o'clock. I guess we were tired." I flipped over to face him, my bladder letting me know it required my attention and soon.

"Wow. It's ten?" Scott lifted his head and squinted until his eyes relaxed into the light.

Whether it was a weekday or a weekend, Scott was an early riser. Much more so than I was. I could sleep until ten without much trouble, but not him. So, this was rare.

I caressed his blond stubble growing steadily down the side of his strong jawline with my palm. "Thank you for last night. It was amazing."

His eyes drank me in. "For me, too, babe." He ran a hand down my hair and steadied his gaze. "I meant every word."

For a moment, we remained on our sides facing each other, our eyes sending out love notes, our hands interlocked.

I moved to get up. "I really need to pee before my bladder bursts."

Scott had just laced his arm around my waist as I rose but released it when he realized why. And then he swung his feet over the other side of the bed. "I need to get up too."

* * *

Bladder empty, I brushed my teeth, Scott doing the same right beside me. I had brought in my clothes, which sat stacked on the lid of a wicker hamper in the corner, so I could shower. When the shower warmed to my desired temperature, I stepped inside. And then, Scott came right in behind me.

"What are you doing?" I don't know why I continued to ask these questions. It was obvious what he was doing, although he answered me anyway.

"Saving water," he whispered back. "Scoot over."

By the scent of hazelnut infusing the air, I determined Luke had just finished brewing a pot of coffee when Scott and I entered the kitchen holding hands. I felt like a newlywed again. Busy schedules, job obligations, and a dangerous escapee from prison had taken a toll on my mental health. I knew this because of how much better I felt in this moment. Right now, all of those things were miles away. I could relax, even if it only lasted a day or two. A reprieve was a reprieve.

Standing by the stove, Amy picked up a mug of hot tea. "I heard the shower. I heard a few other things last night too." Wearing a black rib-knit cardigan and matching wide-leg pants, Amy brought me my tea, the scent of cinnamon promising a pleasant morning. She placed an indignant hand on her hip. "You're too tired to stay up and chat, but you obviously had enough energy for what I heard through the walls? Sounded like a porn flick over there."

I thought Scott was going to choke on his own oxygen, his eyes avoiding Amy at all costs.

I cringed outwardly. "Sorry, did we wake you? And thank you for the tea. I really appreciate it." My voice grew all sheepish.

Amy raised her chin, her eyes filled with satisfied vigor. The girl sure liked to make people squirm. "I gotcha covered. And there's stevia and oat milk creamer in the fridge. You know where the spoons are. No worries about last night. I told Sky he better up his game if he wants *me* to moan like that." She shot him a look.

Now it was Luke's turn to choke, this time on his coffee.

I lifted a finger in the air, hoping to stop Amy from making everyone in the room feel like we wanted to run for cover. "I am *not* going to touch that one. And I do remember where the spoons are, thanks." I made my way around the narrow kitchen flavoring my tea to my liking, the quartet playing their mechanical songs in the room next door. Amy's dryer sounded like she had sneakers inside of it, even though I was pretty sure she didn't.

"Nice sweater." My best friend's gaze explored my winter red cashmere tunic that paired well with my black leggings (I had a lot of those). "Looks soft." She reached out and touched the material, confirming her suspicions.

"Thanks, Amy. You look nice too. Then again, you always do."

A goofy grin washed over her face. "Well, thank you," she said in a funny voice, never quite taking my compliments seriously.

Luke's faded blue jeans hung from his narrow hips, his dark-gray fleece shirt a perfect little jacket for the striped T-shirt hidden underneath. "Coffee's ready, Scott." He handed

Scott a large mug. "Help yourself, dude. You take yours black, right?"

"Yeah. Thanks, man." Wearing a tan long sleeve quarter-zip pullover on top of his white T-shirt that peeked through at the neckline, Scott's light-gray joggers not only complemented his outfit, they made me want to grab hold of his perfect-sized butt and squeeze.

Especially after last night (and a very satisfying shower), I was smitten with this man. If I could crawl on top of him and mold my body to his, I would.

He caught my lovey-dovey gaze and smiled as though he could read my thoughts. His eyes softened, sending me a message back. *Love you, too, babe.*

With our mugs full, the four of us ventured into the living room and found the same seats that had served us so well the night before. Luke located an alternative rock station on his iPhone, using a small wireless speaker to fill the room with music. I was glad he kept the volume nice and low. I also remembered how much Luke liked to listen to music at any hour. *What musician didn't?* I thought to myself.

"I've got pancakes planned for tomorrow. Luke scored us some local sausage." Amy's gaze found me on the couch with Scott. She wagged a finger. "I knew you were going to bring me more maple syrup, so that's why the pancakes. I also have eggs that I picked up at the farmers' market." Coffee in hand, she settled into her sage velvet chair. "Tomorrow's covered, but I thought I'd take you to Grove Street Café right up the road on the corner of Park Ave and Grove. It's small, but given the time, we've hopefully missed the morning rush, and they make great breakfasts." She took a sip of coffee. The hazelnut competed with the sandalwood in the air. "So, drink up, and we can head out whenever you're ready. They serve breakfast on the weekends until three."

* * *

Two things occurred to me as we ventured out for breakfast. One, I was surprised how close the restaurant was in proximity to Amy and Luke's place. Good thing, since it was freezing out. We were there within minutes. And two, when she said the place was small, she was being generous. If Scott and I stood side by side with our arms spread wide, we would probably touch each of the opposing walls, all of them covered in framed artwork, quotes, and photographs, some antique-looking. There were only two tables large enough for four people. The rest were two-seaters, and then a modest-sized counter with half a dozen stools bolted to the floor, all but two occupied. On the counter, a few glass-domed cake stands displayed delectable-looking desserts that I guessed were homemade. The scent of fresh bacon, onions, and something sweet made me hopeful we had picked the right place.

From what I could see, one woman worked the counter, one woman waited the tables, and one large man cooked behind a half wall at the back of the room, the fruits of his labor sending succulent scents around the room. My hungry mouth began watering immediately.

Given the size of the place and the fact that it was Saturday, we had to wait for a few minutes for one group of four to finish their meal and leave. And there wasn't much room for standing around, either. I felt like a vulture looming over everyone's table. My empty stomach didn't help matters, making me feel like one too.

At one point, I bent closer to Amy's ear. "Should we wait at your house and come back?" It was too cold to loiter outside.

Amy shook her head subtly. "We'll lose our place. Just chill, Al. They're almost done." Just as Amy said those words, a petite waitress wearing a tight sweater, its zig-zag pattern covered in colors of burnt orange and brown, along with a pair of bell bottom jeans, approached. Her hair was the color of charcoal (too dark to look natural), her bangs cut short, and the rest of her hair just reached her shoulders. The style reminded me of the one Bettie Page was famous for in the 1950s. My mom told me once that, back in the day, her father used to have a pinup of the famous model in his garage. "It was the only one he had," she'd said, adding that since it wasn't a nude, her mother had allowed it.

The waitress handed a woman at the table in question their check, and soon, they were all putting on their coats and heading out the door.

"Hey, Amy. Hey, Luke," that same waitress said as she closed in on us.

Of course, she knew Amy. They had probably met at a vintage shop judging by how they both dressed.

"Hey, Harper. Working again, huh?" Amy offered her a friendly smile, and Luke gave a short wave from behind his wife.

"Oh, yeah. I'm off tomorrow, though. Give me a minute to clean this up, and then you guys can have a seat."

"Thanks. Appreciate it. This is my friend, Sara. She's here from Pennsylvania. And her husband, Scott."

Scott and I both raised our palms to greet Harper. "Nice to meet you," I said.

As Harper cleaned our table, Amy stood nearby catching up with her friend. From what I could overhear, Harper lived nearby too. I couldn't help feeling a tad jealous of Amy's talent for making new friends. I wished I was better at it. I thought about Tanya and Andie again. I'd have to make a point to invite them over for a movie sometime soon. I also thought about Giselle, my paraprofessional. We were close to the same age, and I really liked her. I'd even asked her out for a drink once after work, but she was busy. Which was fine; I was happy to keep trying.

Harper cleared the dishes from the table. "Okay, have a seat, and I'll bring over your menus." Holding a wet rag in her hands, she darted off as we descended upon the table.

Another party of four carried a cold blast in with them as they entered the diminutive room. Per usual, Amy was right. If we had left, we would have lost our place.

* * *

While I savored my eggs Benedict with hollandaise sauce and hash browns, Scott enjoyed a large plate of chicken and waffles. Amy and Luke each chowed on a breakfast burrito as we discussed our day.

"I can take you to Lewis Ginter Botanical Gardens today if you want. Or we could do some Christmas shopping. There are some great shops in Carytown."

"What's Carytown?" Taking a break from my food, I sipped on my second cup of tea for the day.

"It's a part of Richmond that's full of privately owned shops and good restaurants. Very trendy, but nice. We could grab an appetizer there later and a drink. If you don't want to go there, we have a lot of breweries nearby, too, that we could hit or even a winery if you'd like." Having finished her burrito, Amy nibbled on her blueberry muffin as she spoke.

I took my last bite of eggs and, using my napkin, wiped the excess hollandaise sauce from my lips. "That reminds me. I brought some gifts for you guys. And I also brought you some wine to thank you for having us. We need to schedule a short window so you can open them later. But everything else you said sounds good to me. I'm not fussy. We're just glad to be here."

Scott nodded as he chewed on his food.

Amy grinned. "Yeah, I got gifts for you guys as well. Sounds good, Al."

Scott's gaze lifted, his brow tensing. He swallowed his last bite. "Looks like something is happening back home." He pointed toward a small TV mounted behind the food counter, perpendicular to our table. "I wish they'd turn up the volume."

Both Luke and Amy peered behind them to see what he was referring to.

I also followed his gaze to what appeared to be a breaking news story about Randy, according to the headline scrolling across the bottom of the screen. It was hard to read from my angle, but I distinctly saw "Breaking News" and "Randy Meyers."

Scott got to his feet and approached the counter. "Hey, would you mind turning that up?" he asked a woman wearing a black knit top and leggings, along with an extra-wide floral-patterned bandanna, doing its best to secure her wildly curly hair.

"I don't know where the remote is," the woman said sympathetically as she took an order from a man and a woman who had just arrived at the counter.

Scott stood there for a few minutes, watching the screen before returning to our table. "They don't have the closed captioning on, but the ticker said something about Randy carjacking some woman in Phoenixville." He pulled his cell phone from the front pocket of his joggers and started tapping and swiping.

"Can I get you all anything else?" Harper had returned.

Since Scott was busy on his phone, Amy zeroed in on me. "Do you want any dessert, Al? I saw you eyeing them."

I extended my back and neck so I could see over the heads of the patrons sitting between me and the food counter, more importantly, those domed cake stands. "What do you have for desserts?"

Harper surveyed the inventory from afar. "Let's see, we have buttermilk pie, strawberry cream cake, and wild berry crumble."

"Yup. It looks like Randy carjacked a woman last night off Main Street."

"Here?" Harper's voice rose with alarm. "That's like two streets over."

"No. Sorry. It happened in Pennsylvania." Scott glanced sheepishly up at Harper and then returned his attention to his phone.

"Oh." Our waitress relaxed her shoulders.

"Says here he left her on the curb and stole her minivan. I think she had stopped at a four-way intersection. It must be the end of Main, which is on the way out of town. It's a lot less populated there."

"Did he hurt her?" My stomach tightened at the thought. "Does it say anything more?"

Keeping his focus on his tiny screen, Scott said, "I'm checking, babe."

At that point, Harper cleared her throat. "So, did you decide on a dessert?" She stood there with a slightly impatient look in her eye. Since she was covering all the tables on her own (not that there were many), I understood her need to move on. She used the eraser side of her pencil to scratch behind her ear while she waited.

"Bring us two of each dessert to go," Amy said. "And thanks, Harper. We'll take the check whenever you're ready."

"We can turn on the news when we get back if you want." Luke watched Scott, his eyes curious.

I pulled my wallet from my bag. "First of all"—I pointed

with a stern finger—"*we're* paying for breakfast. You're kind enough to put us up, so no arguing!"

Amy crossed her arms and smiled. "Fine. Thank you. And I wasn't going to argue. Is there a second of all?"

I fished my credit card out. "Yes, you have a TV? I don't remember seeing one."

"You know that red cabinet in the living room?"

I nodded. "Yeah, I thought it was for blankets or something."

"Nope. It's got a TV in there. We don't watch it much, but when the weather sucks, we may stream a movie. And Luke likes to watch concerts."

"Oh." I don't know why that surprised me so much. I realized we never watched any TV when I came in the fall. The weather was too nice for hanging inside. "I do remember you had one at your last apartment."

Harper approached, and before she could give me the check, I handed her my credit card while Scott remained fixated on his phone, Luke now checking his own.

* * *

Amy carried the takeout bag as we all hustled back to their house, where the red cabinet awaited. Once inside, Luke flipped through streaming channels while Scott continued to research on his phone. Every now and then, my husband's face would tighten, but he wasn't saying much.

I was surprised Randy was being so brazen, and on Main Street in Phoenixville, no less. Didn't he know the cops were out looking for him? Was he that desperate? And how come the police hadn't caught him?

Sitting next to Scott on the couch, I finally asked, "Do you know anything more yet?"

With a somber face, he nodded, scaring me more than he realized. "A little more. It just says Randy carjacked a woman at an intersection on the western end of Main Street. When she stopped at a stop sign, he ran over to her car and pointed the gun at her through the window. According to this report, he told her to get out or he was going to blow her head off."

I couldn't imagine the terror that woman went through. Well, actually I could.

"Did he hurt her?" This was the second time I had asked this question. I kept hoping for better news.

Sitting on the edge of his seat, Scott shook his head. "I don't think so. The police interviewed her, so she was healthy enough to tell them what happened."

"Phew." I exhaled. "At least she's okay, right? A car can be replaced."

But Scott wasn't exhaling or acting like this was good news. *Why wasn't he?*

I almost didn't dare to ask. "Is there something else?"

His eyes flared for a moment, his brow tensing up even more. "The woman's toddler was in a car seat in the back of the minivan at the time."

Oh, my God.

Chapter Nine

So that was what Scott was laboring to tell us. There was a toddler in the car? My heart sunk, the eggs Benedict forming a rock in my stomach. "Did he let her take her child with her?" The pitch of my voice was only one symptom of the anxiety storm brewing inside of my body. How awful. And how much worse could this get? "Does it say if she got her child out?"

Amy shrugged. "Don't look at me. I have no idea. I hope so. Luke, hurry up and find us a station."

"We don't stream news stations, but I'm sure I can still find one." He patted the air. "Just give me a minute." I was sure finding anything outside of movies and concerts provided a challenge for him. Back home, we had local stations that would tell us everything we needed to know.

Amy hopped up and darted out of the room. "I'll check my laptop."

I gazed over at Scott who had been checking his phone the entire time. Surely, he'd found out more. "Scott?"

He just shook his head dumbfounded. "I don't know, babe. It's not saying anything more than I've already told you. Hopefully, we can find out something on the news."

"Found one." Luke returned to his chair, Amy rushing into the room.

"Good. My laptop is taking forever to load. It's doing an update."

We all stared at the TV expectantly, and then came ... more commercials. Too many to tolerate—most of them about prescription drugs—before the TV finally began to answer our questions. A man and woman appeared: the man had short brown hair and wore a light-gray suit, and the woman had long blond hair and wore a navy-colored dress. Both had flawless complexions and perfect smiles, a news desk providing arm rests and a place for notes in front of them. A blue banner ran along the bottom of the screen with the names Philip Thompson below the man and Samantha Cleary below the woman, the letters CBN and Channel 13 in the lower right-hand corner.

Samantha spoke first. "Thank you so much for joining us here on CBN, I am Samantha Cleary."

"And I am Philip Thompson," the man said in a robust voice.

Samantha continued. "We are covering a breaking news story out of Phoenixville, Pennsylvania, where convicted criminal Randy Meyers escaped from Faulkner State Correctional Facility just over a week ago."

A different picture of Randy appeared in the upper right-hand corner of the screen than the one I had seen when the story had first aired. This one looked more like a mug shot, Randy in civilian clothes, not the orange jumpsuit like before. What hadn't changed were those intense, angry brown eyes of his, the ones meant to do nothing but provoke nightmares, the

Gothic cross on his temple. He was actually glaring, and I couldn't help but wonder if the person taking the mug shot had gulped at the time. *I* would have.

"Since then, Pennsylvania State Police and other law enforcement have joined forces to apprehend Randy. What we know at this time is that Randy has stolen a hunting rifle from a Phoenixville citizen's truck, making Randy not only dangerous but armed. Last night, another Phoenixville citizen, a woman this time, fell victim when Randy carjacked her at an intersection just outside of town. Police have reported the incident occurred at approximately 10:30 p.m." The beautiful blond with big blue eyes glanced over at Philip, who carried on.

"That's right, Samantha. The female victim's name has not been released yet. And I'm afraid that isn't the worst of it." He paused. "It is with a heavy heart that I report there was also a toddler in the back seat of the woman's minivan, secured in a car seat, when the incident occurred. Our sources tell us that Randy drove off with the child inside of the vehicle. So far, there has been no indication of any other witnesses on scene." The man blinked, sadness shadowing his eyes.

I was sad too. My heart broke for that family.

"Sources from within the police department have stated that the toddler is most likely a boy, although, we cannot confirm that to be true. The toddler's name has also not been released to the public at this time."

As the camera panned out a smidge, both anchors shook their heads as if in disbelief. "I can't imagine the grief that mother must be going through," Samantha said with a heartfelt sigh.

I had said something similar two minutes earlier.

Philip agreed. "Let's hope this story finishes with a happy ending."

Samantha stared into the camera. "Stay tuned to CBN. We

will continue to provide updates throughout the day as details emerge."

So, nothing new.

Luke muted the TV when another commercial governed the airwaves.

I placed a hand over my heart, my stomach in knots. "He couldn't have known the child was in the car. Do you think he'll release him? That poor family."

Amy shook her head while Luke stared at the floor. What was Scott doing? Keeping a watchful eye on me.

I placed my hand on his thigh. "I'm fine. It's not about me."

"I know, babe. But remember what Dr. Zeller said. It's normal for stuff like this to trigger you."

My gaze wandered over to Amy next who didn't look much better than I felt. "You okay, Amy?" Although she always presented herself with bull-like strength, I knew my friend better than anyone. She'd had her own set of demons to work out.

As I expected from her, Amy squared her shoulders, her eyes filled with resolve. "Oh, yeah. I'm fine, Al. Stop worrying." She waved me off.

Still, the somber vibe never left the room. This was terrible news. *And* in the place where we lived.

"Wait. This happened on the western part of Main, right?" After two years, I was still trying to orient myself with the streets in Phoenixville.

Scott nodded. "Yeah?"

"That's not too far from our house, is it?"

The crease forged across Scott's forehead told me he'd already thought of that. When we were watching the news report, he had placed his cell phone on the coffee table in front of us.

"Do you think it's anyone we know?" I racked my brain

thinking of anyone who lived near us and who had a toddler but came up short. I hadn't lived in Phoenixville for all that long, though, unlike Scott who grew up there. My inner circle included my students, a few workmates, and Scott's family and friends.

Growing up in the small town of Middlebury, Vermont, it seemed everyone knew who you were. When my parents died, there was no loss of sympathetic stares and "I'm sorry for your loss" rumblings at school, at the grocery store, and even at the gas station. I couldn't escape it, until I did just that—escape it— by leaving town.

Phoenixville was three times the size of Middlebury, but that didn't mean it was large by any stretch of the imagination. Could this woman be someone Scott or his family knew?

"I have no idea whether or not it's anyone we know. I hope not. But I'll text Jason and my parents to see if either of them know anything. I'll also ask Jason if he can check on things at the house. He can bring his brothers." Scott grabbed his cell. "I don't want anyone going out there alone." He seemed to ponder something. "I can also call my buddy Alan who works on the local police force. I'm sure they're all stretched pretty thin right now, but I'll mention that we are out of town." He got to his feet and walked out of the room, the words, "I could call our neighbor, Bart too," trailing behind him. He was worried, I could tell, his mind processing how to handle things.

Amy joined me on the couch. "You guys are welcome to stay with us until they catch that lunatic, you know."

From across the room, Luke nodded. "Absolutely."

I wrapped my arm around my best friend's shoulders. "Thanks, Amy. I wish we could, but I didn't bring my laptop with me, and I'm teaching remotely for another week. I haven't given the school any notice to find me a replacement. Plus,

Scott has a ton of work right now, and a new project that he just sold."

"Got it." She thought for a moment. "Well, do you want to get out of here for a bit and get your mind off things?"

Removing my arm from Amy's shoulders, I leaned forward searching for Scott in the other room. "Let's wait and see what Scott finds out." And then I thought about that mother and the anguish she must be going through. I was sick about it. I knew what loss felt like. And how a person's world could come crashing down in an instant.

My cell phone vibrated from my purse. I took it out as the name Abigail Saunders flashed onto the screen. "I better take this." I accepted the call. "Hi, Mom." I rose and wandered out of the room.

"Oh, my God, Sara. We just saw on the news what happened in Phoenixville last night. That's horrible. Did it happen anywhere near where you and Scott live?"

"It's kind of close, but Randy's been spotted in different areas, and we have an alarm system. I'm so sorry I didn't call you sooner. I've been so busy with work and everything, but I should have called anyway. And we are in Richmond right now visiting Amy and Luke, so you don't need to worry about us. I was going to call you on our way home tomorrow."

What an afternoon. I spent the better part of an hour on the phone with my mother, trying to ease her mind. I also tried to talk her out of coming for the holidays to no avail. She said she would feel better if we were all together. She even asked if we could come to her in Vermont, which I ran by Scott after I had gotten off the phone.

"First of all, I don't know the woman who was carjacked.

Jason's mom seems to think it may be Mrs. Pruitt, who *she* knows, but Jason said she's not sure. If it's the person Jason described, I think I have an idea about where she lives. And second, I can't go to Vermont over the holidays. I'm too busy with work. If I'm home, I can take time off and make it up during off hours. Plus, I want to keep an eye on the place. I'm sorry, babe. But you can go." His eyes blinked with sadness.

I made a *pfft* through my lips. "I'm not gonna spend Christmas away from you." The thought left me empty inside, and Scott, too, who had perked up by my response.

I texted Abigail about what Scott had said, hoping she would be okay with it. She replied immediately: *Tell Scott we understand. We will come to you. No arguments.*

I hoped her driving to our location was a good idea. Randy was brazen enough to carjack innocent women and kidnap toddlers. Would he dare break into a house with people inside?

And then I thought about Scott's gun, hiding in our nightstand. If Randy broke in, he'd certainly find it. And then my inner voice took over, assuring me Scott had not only put on the alarm before we had left the house, but he'd also put on the motion sensor. That meant any movement on the first floor would alert us. And so far, we'd had no alerts. *Not yet.*

Scott's best friend, Jason, and his two brothers surveyed the area around our house. He reported back a couple of hours later that everything looked fine. Unfortunately, Scott wasn't able to reach his buddy on the local force or our neighbor.

Instead of running around town, and since we were planning on going out for the night, Amy ordered pizza and salads to enjoy from another of their favorite restaurants, which we enjoyed as we played a couple of used board games that she had scored at a thrift shop, one of them from the '80s called Win, Lose or Draw. It was fun. You had to draw old-time phrases like "Roll with the punches," "Pull the wool over one's eyes," or "Two peas in a pod" that your partner had to guess before the hourglass timer ran out. The TV stayed on, but no new reports had aired, just the same information.

As the afternoon sun made a beeline for the horizon, Scott and Luke enjoyed a few beers, Amy and me, a couple glasses of red wine. We opened presents, which was also fun. Amy seemed to like the cashmere tunic I had bought for her and the fuzzy socks to match. The sweater was the same style as the one I had been wearing all day. "When you complimented mine, I was hoping you'd like the one I got for you too. It's really comfortable on a cold day."

Amy held it up, admiring the winter-white fabric. "It's nice. Thanks, Al. And thanks for the wine and the chocolates." She put on the socks next and wiggled her toes.

"Cool shirt." Luke held up the flannel shirt I had bought him from L.L.Bean. Its plaid pattern and the hat with braided tassels down the sides from the same store reminded me of him.

"I hope it fits."

Luke appraised it with welcoming eyes. "It will definitely fit. Awesome, thanks."

I gazed over at the dining room table, where my new essential oil burner and a pack of oils for me to experiment with sat. A faded periwinkle scarf made with cozy material matched perfectly with a pom beanie completing the set. All from Amy and Luke. Next to my pile of treasures, two bottles of red wine from a local winery, which my friend knew I loved, stood ready for consumption. It was funny that we had both bought each other wine. I didn't drink that much, but a glass or two was nice when the occasion warranted. *Like maybe with Tanya and Andie?* I had told Amy about them and how nice they were. Knowing I was an introvert, she was happy I was making friends.

For Scott, Amy chose various samplers of microbrews from

area breweries, two pilsners etched with Scott's initials, and some trail mix, all of which he loved.

Scott thanked her with a hug, Luke with a friendly pat on the shoulder.

We warmed up the leftover chicken parmesan and garlic bread from the night before to enjoy for dinner before we all trudged off to get ready for our night out. I made sure to hydrate from the wine earlier and used that time to also check my phone for any updates. Still nothing new about Randy or the toddler. My heart broke every time I thought of the mother and what she must be going through. And the father. For some unknown reason, I kept forgetting about him. And what about siblings? A tragedy of this magnitude sent torment throughout the entire family and beyond.

While Scott took yet another shower (the man couldn't seem to get clean enough), I dressed in my black top that cut just above my black jeans, allowing a few inches of my abdomen to peek through, and my black cropped denim jacket, which blended nicely. Aside from the jacket, the outfit had a skin-like fit. And to finish it off, a pair of suede black ankle boots with a four-inch heel added just the right accent to bring the outfit together. Tonight, I was the woman in black.

Standing in front of an antique mirror overlooking the dresser in Amy's guest room, I added a little extra makeup to my eyes, giving them a smoky effect, and a little extra mousse and hairspray to my hair, hoping to fluff my natural curls to another level. I rarely went out dancing and wanted to feel sexy while I was doing so. This wasn't my typical attire. Somehow being around Amy always made me feel a bit more daring and uninhibited.

When Scott entered the room smelling fresh and looking hot in a pair of faded blue jeans and a dark-gray button-down shirt that molded perfectly to his luscious body, his mouth practically hit the floor.

"Holy shit, babe. You look sexy as hell." He came around behind me, his hands wrapping around my waist, then down my hips and thighs. "I may need to sample some of this before we go out." His lips found my neck as he inhaled my scent.

I gazed at him through the mirror, a smile spreading across my face. "You don't think it's too much?"

Scott's eyes found my reflection. "I think you should dress like this more often." He ran his fingers along my exposed abdomen. And then, he reached out and kicked the door closed with his foot. "I want to make love to this hot, sexy woman right now." With his body mashed up against the back of mine, another part of his anatomy prodded me.

His hands roamed from my stomach to between my legs where he stroked the area over my pants, sending moisture to all the right regions.

It wasn't easy, but I had to squash this moment before it went too far. I didn't spend an entire hour getting ready, only to throw my efforts to the wind. "How about we try that later, handsome. It took me too long to get my makeup and hair right. I don't want to mess it up."

Of course, Scott wasn't giving up that easily. "How about I pull your pants and your panties off—if you're wearing any—and I'll put those sexy boots back on for you. And then you can wrap your long legs around my waist and let me take care of the rest." From what I could feel pushing up against the back of me, he was already rock hard. "I promise you. I won't mess up your makeup or your hair."

My knees weakened. My heart ramped. "Okay." I mean I wasn't made of stone.

* * *

We took an Uber to Carytown, where a pub called Party Animal had already gathered a small crowd, all of which stood hovering by its door. Once Luke told the bouncer he was helping the band, we made our way inside without even being carded, the bouncer's eyes giving me a full once-over as I walked past.

I had thought we came to strictly watch the band and dance, until Luke informed us on the way over he'd also promised his friend, Mike, who played bass in the band that he'd help him set up. Scott piped right up, offering his able hands as well.

The pub was dark, several black lights casting a purple hue around the room, the kind that made white shirts even whiter, the air musky and thick. Strings upon strings of white Christmas lights ran along the walls and across the ceilings, some cascading downward, resembling a small meteor shower. A patchwork of oriental rugs led the way toward a dance floor layered in wood. And one step up from there, a modest-sized stage, also wood, awaited the talent. Round tables and booths surrounded the dance floor, each one scattered with fairy lights at their center. A large bar stood off to the side, its back wall displaying every kind of liquor known to man, string lights intermixed to promote the liquor's natural tinge.

People milled about the area, some hanging at the bar, others clustered in conversations, a few taking selfies.

As we made our way through the semi-crowded pub, a few more men stared at me and my outfit. It made me a tad uncomfortable but flattered at the same time. I did dress for the occasion. One guy's eyes almost bugged out until my husband shot him a glare, which seemed to shut him down as he quickly found something else to focus on.

Scott took my hand. "I'm starting to rethink that outfit of yours." He kissed me and then grinned.

When we approached the stage, a skinny guy with messy, dirty blond hair that fell just above his shoulders, barreled out from the back. "Thanks for coming, man. Appreciate it. Hey, Amy." He gave Luke a bro handshake as Amy raised a palm to greet him. "We go on in an hour, at nine. First time playing here." He pulled his skinny jeans up a tad as he spoke, the scent of fresh cigarette wafting off his distressed Led Zeppelin T-shirt.

"Need any help?" Luke turned to Scott, placing a hand on Scott's shoulder. "This is my man, Scott, and his wife, Sara. They're here staying with us over the weekend. Scott offered to help too."

Luke turned back toward Mike and fanned one hand out. "This is Mike, the dude I was telling you all about."

Mike's eyes widened a little at Scott. "Wow. You look like you could lift a few pounds." He gave Scott the same bro hand-shake he had given to Luke. "Nice meeting you, dude."

"Yeah, you too."

And then he glanced over at me. "Wow. Your friends certainly are attractive. Does Sara happen to sing?" He ran a hand over his lower jaw. "She'd be a great backup singer. Crowd would go crazy over her."

With tense eyes and a slight flush to his cheeks, Scott rubbed the back of his neck the way he always did when dealing with something uncomfortable. Most of the time, it involved him having to tell me something that he knew I didn't want to hear. Today, however, the neck rub reflected a different sort of discomfort: all the attention his wife seemed to be getting. Every now and then when we had joined Jason and Heather for a drink, I'd hear a catcall or two or some guy's gaze would find me and stick around for a few extra seconds, but those were isolated incidents that never amounted to anything.

Being Scott's wife, I was used to the gawking *he* received.

He was handsome. I didn't fight it. And I'd always thought, of the two of us, he was far more attractive than I was. Not that it mattered either way. But then there were times, such as tonight, when things didn't follow that same equation. Before Scott, I'd never dated, so part of me loved the attention, even if Scott didn't.

I stepped forward to greet Mike when he took my extended hand and kissed the back of it. I blushed and giggled a little. "Oh, wow. Uh, no, I can't sing. Not well enough to be on stage."

Mike's eyes shined. "Bummer, you'd be perfect. But nice to meet you anyway." He turned to Luke. "And, yeah, I could use some help dragging the last of my equipment in from the van. One of my amps isn't working, so I'm hauling ass here. Rico and Jeff are out back getting their own shit ready."

Luke glanced over at Amy. "You ladies okay for a bit?" He focused on something behind her and then pointed. "Grab that table, Amy. And I'll get you both some drinks."

Following Luke's suggestion, Amy and I sat at a round table loaded with fairy lights and cushioned chairs to keep us comfortable. Amy requested margaritas from her husband, which he was happy to retrieve. When he returned with drinks for the women and beers for the men, my husband bent down to kiss me. "If anyone hassles you, text me." Something dark brewed in his eyes, something I didn't quite understand before he left with Luke. Was he that bothered by the attention I was receiving? For me, it wasn't a big deal. It was all in fun.

"Maybe I shouldn't have worn this." I tugged on my shirt, hoping to narrow the gap where my abdomen remained exposed.

Sitting right next to me, Amy waved me off. "Look around, Al."

I let my eyes wander over many women wearing outfits like mine, some way more revealing. One girl wore a skirt so short, I feared she'd flash people if she were to ever bend over. And her top was close to a bikini.

"You look hot, but you're mild compared to a lot of the women here. You're just a lot more attractive. Cheers." She clanked her glass against mine, and then we both took a sip, the taste of lime and tequila landing strong on my tongue.

When the clock struck eight-thirty, according to my cell phone, recorded music flew from the speakers, pumping the air with enthusiasm, enough that I wiggled in my seat ready to dance.

"You're staying up with me tonight, right? We can polish off one of those bottles of wine you brought." Amy took another sip of her drink, encouraging me to do the same. "We haven't had any time for girl talk yet." She bent closer to my ear. "I'm sure the shit going on in your hometown must be freaking you the fuck out."

"Yeah, I actually called Dr. Zeller and spoke to her about it." Enjoying the sweet and sour way too much, I took my third sip. "You remember her, right?"

Amy nodded. "Yup. Did she help?"

I told her more about it as we finished our drinks, my mind relaxed, yet my body full of dancing energy.

"Wow. That night you thought Randy was in the upstairs of your house would freak anyone out." She surveyed our empty glasses. "I'll go get us another one. Stay here and hold our table." Grabbing her clutch, Amy pushed her chair back and darted off to the bar, which from my perspective wasn't that crowded yet, although, people were now spilling in rather quickly.

One guy bumped another guy on the chest with the back of his hand to get his attention, both of them staring right at me, their lips moving. I hoped they wouldn't come over. I was never good at this kind of thing. And I wasn't a flirt, either. Too many stumbles and bad experiences from my past told me it was never a good idea.

The scent of fresh lime flew past my nose as my next drink landed on the table in front of me, Amy falling into the chair on my right. "Drink up."

Another "cheers" and we were off and running.

Every now and then, Scott and Luke would appear on stage, placing this piece of equipment or that in its rightful place. A few women started whistling at them, one yelling, "Take it all off, stud!"

I couldn't help but laugh, even though neither Scott nor Luke acknowledged them before they were gone backstage again. *Scott can sure excite the women.*

The drinks had us cracking jokes about a few people in the room whom Amy thought were worth mentioning in a comical sort of way. "What the fuck is she wearing?" She was referring to a blond woman wearing jeans so torn they were in shreds, especially around her butt, where her cheeks were literally falling through the fabric. "Why doesn't she just write 'Fuck me' across her forehead?"

With a slightly drunk hand, I slapped her arm. "Amy, you're awful."

"Oh, look," I said with excitement in my tone. I pointed to a group of women who had just entered, one of them wearing a bride's veil. "Aw. Must be her bachelorette party." I burped. "Oops. Excuse me."

Amy cracked up.

"Did I tell you, Scott said I fart in my sleep?"

Now she was practically doubled over. "I lived next door to you freshman year and slept next to you enough times to know, he speaks the truth."

I slapped her arm again. "No way. You two are full of it."

Speaking of the devil himself, Scott came out a few minutes

later, prompting more hoots and hollers from the female crowd, especially the bachelorette party, who had just noticed him. "I'd pay *him* for a strip tease for sure."

He came over. "How's it going? You ladies doing okay?" He reeked of weed, his eyes red and glazed over. I knew Scott smoked from time to time (mostly with Jason), but it wasn't something he did often. Then again, we were on vacation, and that was exactly how it felt. We had made love as many times in twenty-four hours as we had in two weeks. And I was enjoying every minute of it. Randy and the missing toddler tugged at my heart, but before I could obsess over it, Scott answered my thoughts as though he could read my mind.

"Hey, by the way. I came to tell you that they found the toddler. It was a boy as they said on the news."

I fidgeted in my seat, antsy. "Is he okay?"

Scott crouched lower as Amy leaned in. "He's fine. Apparently, Randy abandoned the minivan at a gas station near Parker Ford. It's west of Phoenixville. I hope that means he's heading away from town. According to the report on my phone, the boy was pretty upset, but unharmed. Maybe a little dehydrated, but he'll be okay. I knew you'd want to know."

I kissed him with gusto, the air instantly lighter. "Yes, thank you for letting us know." What a relief.

"Yeah, thanks, Big Guy. Good to know that asshole didn't hurt anyone else."

Scott straightened up. "I'm grabbing another beer for me and Luke. You two want another margarita?"

"Does a bear shit in the woods?" Amy said with conviction.

I shook my head at my friend. Cursing wasn't something I did often, but that wasn't the case with my BFF who swore just about every time she spoke. Not quite, but she definitely didn't have an issue with it. For me, it was only part of what made Amy ... well, Amy.

Scott rattled his head as he wandered off to the bar, a broad smile stretching across his yummy face. "Copy that," he called out.

I tipped my head back and watched him walk, right along with all the other women in the vicinity. "Man, my husband has a nice butt."

"Yeah, yeah. Rub it in." Amy finished her last drink and set the glass down, smacking her lips. "Luke doesn't have much of an ass, but he's got a good-sized dick." She bumped her shoulder into mine. "And he knows how to use it." She wiggled her eyebrows at me.

There it was. The sex talk. Amy loved having it. In fact, it was during my freshman year that Amy had dragged all sorts of sex talk out of me. She was the first person I told when Scott and I had made love.

Taking another sip of my drink, I sat forward. "Oh, yeah? Well, we've been having a great time since we've been here." I wiggled my eyebrows back at her. "If you know what I mean."

"Yeah, we established that this morning. I heard so much moaning, I thought a ghost had taken up residence in my guest room." Amy chuckled and shook her head in a what-am-I-going-to-do-with-you sort of way. "You better slow down, Al. I don't want you stumbling out on the dance floor."

"Slow down? You can't be serious." Scott placed two new drinks in front of us, pretending to be outraged. "I say, drink up and have a good time, ladies."

Scott bent over for another kiss.

"You smell like weed." I touched his chin with the tips of my fingers. "You taste like it too."

He cast me a bashful glance. "Is that okay? Mike had some and wanted to repay us for helping him."

I lightly shoved him. "Of course. Go have fun. We'll be here when you get back."

The minute Scott was out of view, I leaned into Amy's ear. "So, do you want to hear about our fun?"

"Wow, those drinks are definitely going to your head, Al. You *never* volunteer sex talk, but let's have it." She fluttered her fingers in a come-hither sort of way. "Do I need to burn the sheets after you leave? Is that what you're telling me?" Amy's breath reeked of lime, her green eyes shining with a slight margarita haze.

I giggled, a hiccup popping up in my throat. "Excuse me." She was right. I never opened up like this. But I was having too much fun to care. "You don't need to burn the sheets because we only did it once *in the bed.*"

If Amy leaned any closer, she'd be in my lap. "I want details. What did you two do in my house?"

"Well, I have to say, I have never in all my years of coming to these dumps, ever seen a woman as beautiful as you here."

Amy and I both looked up at four men standing before us. Judging by their tailored hair and expensive-looking suits, they were successful somethings. A collage of colognes swirled around them, the scents complex and robust. *Who wears a suit to a bar?* I gathered they worked in town. Lawyers, maybe? Or financial advisers?

The nicest looking of the four, with short brown hair and decisive blue eyes, had a body that filled his suit well. Someone who exercised for sure. He bent slightly forward. "My name is Trevor. I'm an entertainment lawyer. Could I buy you ladies another round?"

Amy didn't hesitate. "Sorry, dudes, this is a private conversation. And we are both here with our husbands." She flashed her wedding ring and then lifted my hand to do the same.

Trevor gazed around in an exaggerated manner as though checking to see if anyone would object to his presence at our table. "I think I'm safe for the moment. I wasn't planning on extending any marriage proposals tonight, anyway."

His friends smiled at his joke.

Trevor stared down at me. "Do you mind me asking your name? Are you from around here?" He pulled himself back a moment as if flustered, raising a palm. "I apologize. I don't mean to come on so strong. I've just never seen you here before. And I come here often."

I palmed my drink. "I'm not from around here. My name is Sara. This is Amy."

Amy whacked my arm. "What are you doing? Don't tell him our names."

Trevor took a step closer. "I can assure you, Amy. I am not a threat. I was just stopping by to say hello." He smiled, his face brightening. "Even married women are allowed to say hello, aren't they?"

Amy didn't respond, so Trevor kept going. He faced his friends. "I'll meet you guys at the bar. I just want to chat with these ladies for a moment."

Chat with these ladies? Why? We'd already established we were off limits.

"Sure, man." A short, stocky man with hair so short it looked shaved, placed a hand on Trevor's shoulder. "See you in a minute." He turned to his friends. "Come, lads, we need bourbon." He pointed his finger over their heads as though he was a colonel sending his troops into battle. "Onward."

They all wandered off mumbling something about what sounded like a case that was causing them stress. Since none of them had a drink in their hands, I gathered they had just arrived. If that were true, lawyers worked long hours.

Trevor took the seat across from me. He wore a smile designed to dazzle, his aura brimming over with self-assurance. Add in his good looks, and I imagined this guy didn't go home alone often. "I don't mean to sound like I'm hitting on you, Sara, because that is the last thing I'm trying to do. Not that you aren't worthy of such advances." Clasping his hands together, he placed his elbows on the table, his chin resting on his hands. "I was just curious, are you a model?" He sat back and pulled a business card out from the inside of his suit coat, which I took but didn't really look over. What I caught was Trevor's first and last name in large type, the scales of justice at the top. "If you're not, I would be happy to set up some photo shoots. I know several successful photographers who do excellent work."

Amy balked. "Seriously, dude? You're gonna play that card?"

An attractive waitress appeared carrying a large tray loaded down with drinks. "Here you go, Mr. Austin." As she bent over to place a glass containing dark amber liquid on the table in front of Trevor, the meteor shower of lights dangling above her head shimmered off of her long brown hair.

How in the world did he order this ... and so quickly?

Wearing a tight black skirt and an equally tight knit top in Christmas red—the outfit promoting her skinny frame—the waitress kept her voice light and airy. "And these are for you." She placed a pair of margaritas in front of our already filled drinks, followed by two waters. All I could think was, they have waitresses here? And how am I going to drink all of this alcohol? I had two drinks in front of me now. And I was a lightweight, my head already starting to swim. I took a large sip of the water.

"Thank you, Emily. Hey, tell Stevie to put on some smooth jazz until the band starts. Been a rough week."

"As you wish, Mr. Austin."

Trevor smiled up at her. "Trevor, please."

Does he own the bar?

The waitress walked off without even collecting payment.

A few short minutes later, the music changed to a more relaxing tempo. *Wow, who is this guy?*

Our uninvited companion took a sip of his drink and then closed his eyes momentarily as though savoring the flavor. "So, where were we?"

My eyes searched for Scott but didn't find him anywhere. Not that Trevor was being forceful. It was just that I didn't really communicate with men like this. Scott was always with me.

"You were finding ways to convince my friend here that you can turn her into a star." Amy giggled and took a long sip of her drink. "Thanks for the drink, dude, and the waters."

"My pleasure." Trevor straightened his posture, confidence rolling off him like soundwaves. "I can assure you, Amy, this is not a ploy, and I admire your loyalty to your friend. Let me also say that I don't offer things to people that I can't deliver." His blue eyes slid over to me next. "I will admit, I came on a little strong. Been a rough week with a very difficult client." He fanned his hands out, his tone softening. "But then I saw you. And you brightened my day." He took another sip of his drink. "So, tell me Sara *and Amy*, what do you two do?"

Amy hesitated to answer as she continued to study the man with her critical eye.

I guessed it was up to me to answer him. The man did just buy us drinks. *He knows we're married. Where's the harm?* Needing some liquid confidence, I took a large sip of my margarita. It wasn't every day that I met people like Trevor, a man so confident and well connected. "I teach special-needs students." I was proud of my profession. It was a dream come true for me. I didn't offer what Amy did. I figured that was up to her.

Trevor tipped his head, a smile washing over his face. "You teach special-needs students." He didn't say it as a question.

Was he making fun of me? Again, I searched for Scott.

"So, you're not only stunning, but you also have a good heart." Again, he didn't say it as a question. More matter of fact. He scratched his temple. "Well, Sara-who-teaches-special-needs-students, I would like nothing more than to help you start a modeling career. May I ask, how old you are?" His eyes seem to take me in, much like Scott's always did, and I found myself flustered by the attention.

Of course, it felt good to hear these things, and Trevor didn't strike me as someone who needed to work all that hard to get a date. Not that he was going to get one here. The diamond on my finger wasn't exactly small. And Amy had already established the rules.

Requiring more liquid vigor, I took yet another sip, knowing deep down that I was pushing my stamina. It wasn't the number of drinks I was having; it was the pace. And whenever I drank quickly, I regretted it. But I was enjoying myself. Again, where was the harm in feeling a little rusty the next day? It was the holidays. "I'm twenty-three."

"Okay, well, not as young as most agencies would prefer. But if you'd like to sit for a photo shoot, I'm sure we can create a portfolio that will draw interest." He pulled another card out. "Here is the card for a photographer I know very well. His name is Howard Baker." He pointed to the card. "You can see his work on his website, Google, or IMDb. If you decide you want to give it a go, I'll set up a meet and greet." He brushed his fingers down the side of his face in a delicate manner. "You have great facial structure and expressive eyes." He sat back in his chair, his gaze discerning, his finger running across his upper lip like some people do who were mulling over an issue. "There's something else that I can never describe but tends to be a factor with successful people. And I suspect you have that too." Trevor's phone rang, diverting his focus. Bowing his head and covering one ear, he took the call.

"Nice one, Al." Amy nudged me and then leaned in to whisper something into my ear. "It took me a minute, but I think I've seen Trevor in our office building before. In fact, he may have done some legal work for the owner. If I'm right, he's big time."

Being discreet, we both looked him up on our phones. It didn't take either of us long to discover that Trevor was, in fact, a lawyer who dabbled in the entertainment industry. The photo on his website confirmed this guy was legit.

Okay, so he wasn't hitting on me. He was merely proposing something pretty grand. How often do women get offers such as this one? Amy was taking him seriously too. The excitement of it all lifted my spirits even higher. This weekend was fast becoming one for the books.

Call finished, Trevor rose and sipped the last of his drink, placing the glass down on the table. Then he exhaled and straightened his suit. "I pride myself on finding talent in various forms: music, modeling, art. I think we could do something with you, but I don't want to push it. Think it over. It was nice meeting you, Sara." He bowed his head. "And Amy." If he'd worn a cowboy hat, I suspected he would have tipped it at us.

I stood and reached my hand out to thank Trevor for coming over. No harm in that, right? Only the alcohol in my bloodstream had other plans, the effects sloshing around in my brain like water in a leaky boat. I stumbled forward, and right into Trevor's arms.

"Wow. I see you've had a few already. You okay?" He chuckled and straightened me up, his eyes searching my face for an answer. "Let me guess. You're not much of a drinker?" His demeanor told me he was being kind, his voice reassuring.

"I'm so sorry." I was mortified.

"Nah, no harm done." Trevor stayed close, probably to make sure I didn't flop on the floor in front of him. "Drink some of that water, and if you need food, I can get you whatever you'd like."

"I'm good on food but thank you." My cheeks were on fire.

The only comfort I took was knowing that Scott hadn't seen the whole thing. Until I heard.

"Get your fucking hands off my wife!"

Chapter Ten

Now that my legs were stable, Trevor removed his hands from my arm and my waist. He stepped away.

Even though it may have looked otherwise from a distance, the man wasn't behaving inappropriately. Falling into his arms was my fault. And I *was* literally in his arms when Scott came out.

Feeling like a complete idiot and flushed from head to toe, my gaze located Scott glaring at me, something I hadn't seen in a very long time. "Scott. It's not what you—"

"I saw what was going on. Did he put something in your drink?" He closed in on me, his eyes watching, observing. "Are you okay?" He spoke with a firm voice, telling me he wasn't messing around.

"Scott, he wasn't—"

"Save it, Amy." He glared at my friend.

Amy had already risen from her chair. She stepped forward, her palms raised. "Listen, Big Guy, I know it looks bad, but it wasn't like that. I was right here. Trevor was just offering her—"

"What? A nice fuck in his penthouse suite?" Scott widened his stance, the cords in his neck ready to burst, two fists dangling by his sides like wrecking balls. He turned his head. "*You* still here, dipshit?" He practically growled the words at Trevor, whose friends were returning, all of them focused on Scott.

"Jesus Christ, come on, dude. Calm the fuck down." Amy kept her tone even, not the confrontational tone I was accustomed to hearing when she found herself butting heads with a foe. And I'd seen *that* side of her often, especially back in college when preppy, immature men had disrespected her often.

Scott wasn't a foe. Not to her. He was more like a brother; one she trusted through and through. Years of turmoil and triumph had paved the way for that relationship to fuse, their bond as solid as stone.

Before Scott could respond, Luke came bounding over from the stage. "What's going on?"

Trevor cleared his throat. "Why don't you ask *Big Guy*, who can't seem to handle his wife speaking to someone besides himself." He crossed his arms. "I can see why Sara doesn't model now. Her Neanderthal of a husband wouldn't allow it."

Scott lunged forward, Luke trying to stop him but with little success. He shoved Trevor back a few feet. "I know a slime ball when I see one. What did you put in her drink? Tell me now before I rip your fucking head off." Scott was unhinged, rage burning his eyes and cheeks.

Had my husband lost his mind? "What? No. He didn't put—"

"Are you nuts? I didn't put anything in her drink, asshole." Trevor fanned a hand in my direction. "Look at her, she's fine. We were just talking." Trevor stared Scott down. "But that's the real problem, isn't it? You can't stand her talking to another man, can you?"

Trevor's friends were behind him now with wide stances and arms crossed. It seemed everyone in the bar was watching us, even the bartender.

I was humiliated.

"You had your hands all over her. Don't act like you didn't."

Trevor rubbed his jaw thoughtfully, and then let his hand drop. "Would you have preferred I let your wife fall to the floor? Did you not see her stumble? If you care so much, maybe you should have paid more attention to how much she was drinking."

"Please, both of you stop." I thought I was going to be sick. My head was pounding as though I had been thrust from buzzed to sober, a hangover shoving the good vibe away in an instant. I put a hand over my mouth to stabilize my stomach and my lungs.

Scott took another purposeful step toward Trevor and pointed. "How about I ram my fist—"

"You lay another hand on me, *Big Guy*, and I'll sue you for everything you own. I will fucking bankrupt you. And that's *after* I have you thrown in jail." Trevor's jaw set, his eyes filled with disdain.

Oh great. Scott couldn't afford this fight. The stakes were too high. And it wasn't even worth it. Nobody was doing anything wrong. Except for my husband, that was. How I was going to explain that to Scott was beyond me.

"And he's not bluffing, either, dickhead. You know who you're dealing with?" the stocky guy said, the one who had suggested bourbon to his friends earlier. "Best attorney in Richmond, that's who."

"Oh, I see. You and your lapdogs are all bigwig attorneys?

You think that scares me?" Scott blew out his lips, his breath loaded with disgust. "How about we solve this argument like real men?"

I stepped between the two human bulls ready to lock horns. "No, that is not necessary. Trevor didn't do anything wrong. I had too many drinks and felt lightheaded." I peered over my shoulder. "Trevor, I think it would be best if you left. I am so sorry about all of this. Thank you for your offer. If my bullheaded husband hasn't ruined it for me, I'll definitely consider it."

Scott shook his head, another huff sounding from his lips. "Nice job, Sara. Way to stick up for your husband who was trying to rescue you."

I snapped my head in his direction, a hand braced over each hip. "Did it ever occur to you that I didn't need rescuing?" I flung one arm back toward Trevor. "That maybe what you saw wasn't what you *thought* you saw? No, you'd rather punch your way through a problem, fist first. I didn't need your help! And Amy was right here."

Trevor straightened his jacket and adjusted his tie as though he were going into a board meeting. "My offer still stands, Sara. You know how to reach me." He locked eyes with Scott once more. "Dude, you've got issues. And if you're this insecure about your wife speaking to other people, maybe you oughta think about why that is. I've seen men like you who think they own their spouse. You call all the shots, right? From what *I* can see, you don't deserve someone like her."

I closed my eyes, wishing Trevor hadn't said that. And it wasn't true. Scott had never acted like he owned me, but I could see why Trevor thought otherwise. I also knew Scott would react and could very well find himself behind bars tonight if he did so. I had to do something to stop him.

Not two seconds passed before Scott advanced again, but

this time, I cut him off. Before Scott could make any moves, I slapped him hard across the face, leaving a red welt on his cheek and a stinging sensation on my palm. It was that or let him make one of the biggest mistakes of his adult life. "Enough!" I stared into my husband's crestfallen eyes, feeling horrible and yet angry for him making me feel horrible. Scott needed a shockwave, and I had just given him one. "Don't you dare take another step in his direction! If you do, so help me God!"

Needless to say, the night was ruined. I didn't even stay for the band's first set. I apologized profusely to Luke and Amy and took an Uber back to their place, Amy coming with me. I guessed we were going to get our girl talk after all. Scott wanted to come, too, but I refused to let him. And then he stormed off without saying another word, Luke promising to keep an eye on him. From what I could tell, Trevor had left, along with his friends. That was a relief.

There were so many things wrong with what Scott had done. If he had been truly watching my interaction with Trevor, as he had said he was, Scott would have seen that Trevor wasn't leering over me or making me feel uncomfortable in any way. I didn't ask for him to help me. Because I never felt unsafe. And I *knew* what feeling unsafe felt like. I could write a book on the subject. When he asked me if I was okay, why couldn't he have listened and accepted my response?

Either Scott didn't trust me or my instincts, or he felt possessive, as though I was his property, as Trevor had so eloquently pointed out. When did *that* become a thing? Neither scenario sat right with me. Yes, I was his, but because I chose to be his. Not because I was falling in line with his rules. This was the first time I had ever spoken to a man in a bar, other than a few fleeting words.

Bad things had happened in our past, no doubt. *Very* bad

things. And if we were still back there, Scott's reaction would have made more sense. This was six years later. We were past those horrible times. I'd worked my tail off to get where I was now. And I couldn't let Scott drag me back there again, even if he wasn't meaning to do so.

I also had to consider that if I had been willing, I was sure Trevor would have taken me up on a night of sexual exploits, but he knew I wasn't. And Amy knew I wasn't. Scott coming into the situation hostile did nothing but make Scott *and* me look like fools. Like our relationship couldn't withstand something as harmless as me having a conversation with a man in a bar. We weren't kids anymore. *Did he think Amy would sit right there and let someone drug me?* And once he saw I was okay, why couldn't he have just backed off? *Argh!*

* * *

The next day, I drove home while Scott slept again, nothing but silence weighing heavily in the air. I wasn't sure if he was really sleeping or just avoiding talking to me.

At least the subdued atmosphere limited itself to the inside of my car. Outside, white puffy clouds skidded across the sky, revealing a bright winter sun and patches of deep blue whenever they saw fit. I was glad it wasn't raining or snowing.

Last night, Amy and I had chatted until midnight, and the guys still hadn't come home yet. We talked about the escapee and how it was affecting me, Scott's behavior earlier, and Amy's concerns about Luke's career, or lack thereof. She hoped his DJ business could help supplement his income during the slow periods. She even thought about suggesting he teach music at a school.

"I wonder if Trevor can help." I had mentioned. "Maybe

we can call him and see if he'd be willing to watch Luke's band play."

My friend seemed to ponder that.

I rolled my eyes. "That is, if Scott hasn't ruined Luke's chances."

Amy waved me off. "No big. If Trevor is turned off by Scott, then so be it. We'll find another way."

It was nice talking to Amy about Scott. She knew him, so I didn't have to stress that she thought he was a psychopath or anything. She seemed to understand the situation a bit more than I did.

"The big guy came out at the worst possible moment. You were basically in Trevor's arms. I'm sure he was wondering what the fuck was going on."

"Yeah, but I tried to tell him, and he wouldn't listen." It was Scott's stubborn streak that drove me crazy sometimes. But I also had to accept that when put to good use, his stubbornness was the reason he had a master's degree in architecture and IT and why he would most likely have a successful business someday. And it was also that perseverance that had probably played a strong hand in winning my heart. Back then, I wasn't exactly looking for romance.

"Don't forget he'd had a few beers already and was pretty stoned. Trevor wasn't really all that nice, either, but I guess I could see why. It was just one of those fucked up situations that didn't go well for anyone." Amy stared off.

I tried to listen. And I knew I'd forgive him. Of course, I would. But I wasn't there yet. I wanted Scott to understand who we were now. As adults. Not college kids trying to figure ourselves out. We'd grown past that phase. Plus, what if I did want to pursue a modeling career? The thought felt alien to me. How would that work? Did the photographer live in Richmond too? That would be a very long commute. Too many questions tangled my thoughts into a ball.

As the night wore on, Amy kept tabs on our men through Luke. Scott watched the band play, had a couple of shots, but didn't really say much. I guess those women, who I had spotted out for their bride-to-be's bachelorette party, harassed Scott with selfies, all of them fawning over him. One woman was persistent, according to Luke. No surprise. Again, *that* type of behavior, I was used to.

Luke also said that Scott never really went along, even refusing to dance or take a shot that the persistent woman had tried to push on him. He had made himself politely off-limits. They arrived home at 1:30 a.m. when I was already asleep in bed. Amy texted me the time, which I saw this morning.

I had to wonder, what if I had confronted that situation and tried to pick a fight with those women? I wouldn't, of course, but what if I had? Would I have been justified by acting like a crazy jealous person when all that *most* of them had probably wanted was a fun moment with a gorgeous man on a special night? From what I'd heard, at least one of those women would have been more than happy to take Scott home with her and ravage him. But I wasn't threatened by them. Why? I trusted my husband. That's commitment. That's marriage. I glared over at my sleeping companion.

"I thought he was doing something to you, and you were trying to get away from him." Scott sat up and rubbed his face. "I'm not sorry I stuck up for you."

I let his comment settle into the air between us, crowding the cabin with his judgment. I wanted him to rethink his words before I had to correct him.

"Okay, okay. I *am* sorry. But that guy was a dick."

I turned my head, my expression deadpan. I wasn't letting him off the hook, not without some serious self-reflection first.

Scott fidgeted in his seat. "What? You're not going to talk to me now?" His eyes were red, dark rings implying he hadn't slept much. "I know you're mad at me. And if you want to pursue a modeling career, you know I support you. Just not with that asshole." He pursed his lips and stared out the window for a few seconds while I kept silent.

Scott had shoved the man and threatened bodily harm. What did he expect Trevor to do, blow him a kiss? He'd known Trevor for all of five minutes. How ridiculous. But I refused to say so, not yet.

He was working something out, and I wanted to give him plenty of time to do so. We had two more hours on the road.

Another hour passed, and he tried again. "All right. Maybe I misunderstood the situation. And you were right that I didn't need to be thrown in jail over it. I can be a bullheaded asshole sometimes. Is that why you're so angry, or is it because of those girls at the bar? I'm sure Luke told Amy about it. I didn't give any of them the wrong idea."

I turned my head again. "No, I'm not upset about that. I trust you, Scott. They were just having fun. I get it. I also know that if you had wanted to, you could have easily taken at least one of them home for the night."

Scott's defenses rose, right along with his voice. "I would never do that!"

"I never said you would. I said, 'I. Trust. You.'"

I let that comment stab at his resolve or, at least, chip away at it.

He rubbed his eyes and exhaled, the tone of his voice wavering. "Fuck, I don't know what to say here, Sara. I was a dick. I'm sorry. But I was looking out for you. Doesn't that account for something?" He let his hand fall to his lap.

I swallowed a sip of water from my travel bottle, placing it back in the cup holder. "That isn't the point. I thought we were past all of our petty insecurities. Last night, you showed me that we aren't. I understand why you initially thought something was wrong. I was basically in Trevor's arms when you came out. But I had just drank several margaritas in a very short time, and you know I'm a lightweight. When I stood up to thank him for offering me some pretty incredible things, I had a sudden head rush and got a little dizzy. That's all. Thank God Trevor caught me. If you had come out five minutes earlier, you would have seen Trevor sitting at our table behaving like a perfect gentleman."

Scott watched me, his eyes taking everything in. "That may be true, but he wanted you. Don't deny that he didn't."

"So what? Just like those girls wanted you?"

That shut him up.

"It doesn't matter anyway. He knew I was married."

Scott made a face and hissed. "Like that would have stopped him."

"Just like that would have stopped those girls?" I stared him down as much as I could without driving off the road. "It doesn't matter what he or those girls wanted. I trust you. And I thought you trusted me."

Scott placed his hand on my arm. "I do trust you, babe." His voice softened, his eyes reaching out for forgiveness.

"No, if you had trusted me, then you would have known that I had the situation under control. And Amy was right there. She even recognized Trevor. She said he was the real deal. He saw something in me and reached out." I flung one hand up and then let it fall. "When does that ever happen?"

Turning his body my way, Scott touched my cheek. "I've always told you how beautiful you are, babe. Just the other day, I said how you could put any supermodel to shame." He stared forward for a minute. "Do you want to try modeling?" Something in his voice sounded different, unhappy. Was he hoping I'd say no?

Just thinking about the possibility left me flustered. "I don't know. I've never thought about it before."

A truck hauling two trailers behind it flew past me, a few stones kicking up from its tires. Thankfully, none chipped my windshield, something I always paid attention to when I found myself behind large vehicles. Since we'd left the Baltimore area, the traffic was easing a bit. I was able to loosen my grip on the steering wheel, my palms and neck stiff.

We didn't discuss the situation beyond what we had already covered, but Scott did stay awake for the remainder of the trip. He even offered to drive, but I told him I was okay.

When we reached Phoenixville, we stopped at the local grocery store to stock up on things we were low on. We also decided to tick away at our list of items for the holidays. Christmas Eve, I planned to make crab cakes, roasted Brussel sprouts, and home-made mac and cheese for my little sis. Prime rib, garlic mashed potatoes, green-bean casserole, tossed salad, and cinnamon rolls would feed us Christmas Day. I'd already made chocolate walnut crumb bars and an assortment of Christmas cookies, which I'd stored in my freezer. Together, Abigail, Mel, and I planned to make chocolate fudge and strawberry trifle on Christmas Eve as well. And that didn't include the goodies that Abigail, Beth, or Kelsey planned to bring. We'd eat like kings and queens.

We discussed the menu while Scott made a detailed list as we drove into town.

* * *

The doors to the grocery store whooshed open, and I was soon confronted with a populous of stressed townspeople. No one was gathered or anything. But as we wandered the aisles, I couldn't help but feel the tension hunching a few sets of shoulders. I remember my parents telling me that after 9/11, everyone walked around with somber expressions, others downright stressed. That was what I was witnessing today. Two older women in the cereal aisle mentioned Randy's name a few times in hushed tones, telling me the reason. I just couldn't hear the specifics.

"Did you hear that?" I asked Scott as he grabbed a box of cereal that he knew Mel liked from the shelf.

He placed the box into our cart. "Yeah, I did. Sounds like something else may have happened."

Scott and I headed for the deli next, where a high school friend of his worked. "Hey, Carl, how you doin'?" Scott smiled at his friend.

Wearing a soiled apron over a long-sleeved gray T-shirt, Carl looked up. "Oh, hey, Scott. Hey, Sara." He snapped on some food-service gloves. "What can I getcha? Also, we'll have that prime rib ready for you on the twenty-second as planned." Carl was one of those people who wore many hats. Not only was he the manager of the deli, but he also dabbled in handyman work and was starting his own plumbing business. The solidly built Latino man with short, dark hair slicked back had a lot of energy, much like Scott. He was also extremely nice.

"Thanks, I'm looking forward to it. And I'll take a couple pounds of honey-roasted turkey and uncured maple ham, both sliced thin, thanks. Oh, and a half pound of Swiss, also sliced thin."

I lifted up on my tiptoes to peer over the counter and the baskets of food on display, sitting on top. "Can you put each pound in its own separate bag, Carl?"

"You got it, Sara." Carl reached into the glass case in front of us, which displayed large sides of various meats, and pulled out the requested order. Starting with the ham first, he unwrapped one end of it and placed it on a slicer, adjusting the thickness dial. "So, how are things coming along out at that new house of yours?" He proceeded to slice the meat as he spoke, his arm going back and forth in a rhythmic pattern as if he were sawing wood.

"Good. You still doing plumbing jobs on the side?"

"Yeah, man. Why, you need some plumbing work done out at your place?"

With his hand gripping the handle of the grocery cart, Scott nodded. "Yeah, I just might. I'll give you a call."

Carl placed the deli meat on a scale, punched a series of numbers into the display, and then inserted the sliced meat into a plastic bag and sealed it. A price tag printed out, which he slapped onto the front. After he sliced the second pound, he rewrapped the ham and put it away, then grabbed for the turkey next.

"Hey, any news about Randy, the guy who escaped from prison? We were out of town, but we heard about the carjacking." Scott looked at me, his eyes telling me he was fishing for information.

An elderly man and woman walked past with their cart nearly full, the man discussing a sale on canned soup. As more people strolled by us, I took notice of a few more tense eyes and even dark rings. Either it was my imagination or the residents in this town were missing out on sleep.

When he was finished slicing the turkey, Carl put the next two bags on the only vacant spot at the top of the glass case for Scott to take. "You said, Swiss, right? Which kind?"

Scott looked over at me for an answer as a woman and her two young children descended upon the deli for Carl to wait on next, one of the kids talking a mile a minute. He reminded me of my student Daryl, the speed demon.

I turned to Carl. "Anything imported is fine, Carl, thanks."

He nodded and reached into the cheese case. "What did you ask me again, Scott?" Then he caught himself. "Oh, yeah. I remember. Did you hear the latest? It looks like Randy may have killed someone?"

Scott and I exchanged a look. My pulse ramped up, a sick feeling festering in my gut.

Suddenly, I wished we were back in Richmond.

Chapter Eleven

Scott tried not to interrogate poor Carl too much at the deli. We figured we could find out the full story when we got home a few minutes later. Plus, more people were lining up for Carl's services. So much so, he had to call on someone from the back room to assist.

As we entered our lovely home—and Scott punched in the alarm code—I was met with another feeling of uneasiness. Like our safe haven may not be so safe anymore. I figured most of the residents in town had to feel that way. Randy could spring up anywhere, destruction in his sights. He was like a human tornado.

The house still carried that new wood smell, despite the candles I burned and air fresheners pumping from the outlets. Though, I actually preferred the natural aroma.

Together, we hauled in our travel bags and groceries, plus the gifts Amy and Luke had given us. With everything indoors, Scott turned on the TV in our breakfast nook, finding a local station for updates. We unloaded the groceries as we listened.

It wasn't long before we heard the whole breaking news

story on TV. Local police had discovered a body behind a hunting cabin in the woods near Parker Ford, close to where Randy had carjacked the woman and kidnapped her son a couple of days ago. The victim was a man in his mid-seventies, cause of death, a gunshot wound to his chest. According to the reporters, the investigators believed the man had been there for a few days, but they were waiting for autopsy reports and forensic pathologists to confirm their findings, along with a definitive cause of death. There was also evidence that Randy had been holed up in that same cabin. That meant he had access to food, water, and shelter. It seemed as though Randy was still going strong. And now that they had found his hideout, he was back on the move. No wonder everyone was on edge in town. What I couldn't understand was why Randy hadn't left the area. Leave to places like Mexico or even Canada. Then I realized it wasn't so easy to cross borders these days. I also wondered if he knew someone local.

I looked at Scott, trying to contain my fears.

He blinked, his eyes surveying me, I could tell. "If you're okay finishing up here, I'll put our suitcases back in our bedroom. Then I'll check through the upstairs and basement before I pull your car into the garage."

I lifted a bag of golden potatoes out of my canvas shopping bag and nodded. "Good luck." Other than a few last-minute essentials—prime rib being one of them—we'd stocked our cupboards, our fridge and freezer prepared to serve our guests for days. I took comfort in that, knowing we didn't have to venture out too much.

I had just finished unloading and then folding my shopping bags when Scott returned. "House looks fine." He continued toward the door, not slowing his pace. "I'm gonna check the barn after I put your car away."

Carrying my empty shopping bags with me, I followed him

to the foyer closet to store the bags, noticing a thick protrusion coming from the back waist of my husband's pants: the gun. Even with his coat still on, I could see it.

That was how dire things had gotten. Scott didn't feel comfortable checking his own office without a weapon. I cringed at the thought of him confronting Randy. Scott was a big man, no doubt, but Randy was a murderer. And Scott had never killed anyone, *thank God.*

It was hard to relax and enjoy the holidays with all of this going on. When I was at Amy's place, I was able to let down my guard and enjoy life again. That was, until Scott had decided to squash that too. We still hadn't resolved the issue with Trevor, and I wondered if we ever would. I had too much on my mind to deal with it now.

As the nighttime sky darkened the little corner of our world, I made sandwiches for dinner, got myself organized for my Monday morning class, and then I curled up on the sofa next to Scott. He said he still had a lot of work left to do, but I begged him for a few minutes of rest first. It had been a long day. What I really wanted was some cuddle time (real cuddles) with my hubby.

I had already turned on every Christmas light in the house, hoping to cast a comforting glow within the confines of our new home. Somehow that helped, reminding me that it was still the holidays, and my family was still coming to visit.

The wind gained new strength, rattling the outside of the house and bending the trees with its force, at least the ones I could see from our back window. The motion-detector light hanging above our back patio clicked on and off like the flash of a camera as the wind played tricks with its sensor. Every creek of a branch and thump had my body primed to spring off the couch and run for safety. Only I wasn't quite sure where safety was anymore. While the cartoon movie *Shrek the Halls* played on the TV, I ran a different movie through my mind titled "What to do if Randy brakes in?" I played out several scenarios such as where to run and where to hide. How to contact the authorities. I had plugged my cell phone into the SUV the entire way home while using the GPS, so it was fully charged. Our bathroom had a secure lock, and a small window for escaping.

"Are you even listening to me?" Scott's voice snapped me back to the moment.

On the TV, Shrek struggled with how to make the perfect Christmas for his family. I could relate to his monumental task.

"No, I'm sorry. What did you say?"

"I said, did you keep that dude's business card? I saw you take something from the table when you grabbed your purse to leave the bar last night. It looked like a business card to me."

Not the question I was expecting. "Uh, yeah, I think so. He gave me two, why?" I sat up and turned my body in his direction. The lights from our imitation balsam fir may have softened the features of our living room, but it did little to amend the hard expression washing over my husband's face.

Scott's jaw clenched in a way I didn't like much. "Because I'm not comfortable with you having some guy's contact information, especially someone you just met at a bar. What was the second card for?" His brow lowered.

"A photographer he knows."

"He's already setting up photo shoots? What the fuck, Sara?" He blew out his lips. "It could all be complete bullshit, for all you know. You don't even know this guy. He seemed shady to me. Him and his cronies."

I almost wanted to laugh. He had to be kidding, right? Only the intensity of his stare told me that he wasn't. "Are you being serious? He's not some lowlife trying to hit on me. He's the real thing, Scott."

My husband's cheeks flushed red, his eyes unforgiving. "Oh, really. How do you know he wasn't just a con man? Christ, he could've been a sex trafficker." He flung up a defiant hand in the air. "You are way too trusting."

"Because I looked him up. He's an entertainment lawyer. He was telling the truth."

Scott flew to his feet. "That doesn't mean a goddamn thing. Watch the news lately? Some of these guys come off one way, but that's not who they really are. There are shady lawyers all over the place. They know the law, and they know how to hide behind it." His nostrils flared, his hands flying this way and that. "Do you think I was dumb enough to think that those women at the bar all had good intentions? A couple of them grabbed my ass more than once. No, I knew what some of them were up to. And if I had given them any leeway, I would have had my hands full. And so would you if I hadn't come along."

"That's not true. I was handling it just fine on my own. And if those women were acting so badly, why didn't you leave?" I got to my feet, unwilling to lose this ridiculous argument.

Scott leaned into his anger. "Because you left me there, remember? I tried to go with you."

I had hoped since our conversation in the car, he'd had second thoughts. Apparently not. "Doesn't matter. How those women acted and how Trevor behaved were not the same thing, and you know it. Those women were obviously flirting with you. Trevor approached me as a professional."

Scott's temper continued to tighten the muscles in his jaw and neck. "Stop saying his name like he's a friend of yours. You. Don't. Even. Know. Him!" He raised his chin indignantly as his tone jeered and insulted me at the same time.

I was flabbergasted, my mouth hanging open. "Do you hear yourself? He said he saw potential in me." My own temper had my eyes starting to water. "And no one has ever approached me like that. He was nothing but polite. He paid me a few compliments. He offered me a chance to model. He bought us a drink. That was all." I paused to gather my thoughts. "I thought you'd be excited for me."

Excited for me? Scott was outraged, judging by his stiff posture and glaring eyes.

"Is it so hard to believe that someone could possibly think I could be a model?"

Scott crossed his arms as though he needed a place to restrain his flailing hands. "Don't put this on me. I've always told you that. But you're not going to find a talent agent in a bar, *Sara*." He looked away, his head shaking as though it pained him to have to point out the obvious to his idiot wife. "I can't believe you'd fall for that."

"I'm not stupid, Scott." I could feel my teeth baring. Why was he acting this way? "And Amy—"

"You already told me Amy was there. Amy doesn't know him any better than you do. Wake up, Sara." He flung one hand out in my direction. "You're gorgeous. And this guy wanted to fuck you. He doesn't go out to bars to find models or start business ventures." Again, the demeaning tone.

"So, you obviously don't believe I have what it takes." I pointed with an irked finger. "Because if you did, you wouldn't be acting this way. Do you even realize how much you have insulted me? You act as though I don't have a brain in my head, and that there is no *possible* way Trevor could see potential in me. It *has* to be something seedy in your eyes. That I couldn't distinguish a con artist from the real thing. I'm surprised you even let me go out at all. Maybe you oughta buy a leash, so you can keep an eye on me at all times."

Scott hissed at me. "Now who's being ridiculous?" He let his hands fall to his side.

I stormed out of the room, found my purse in our bedroom, fished out what I needed, and then stomped back into the living room—Trevor's business card and that of his photographer, clutched in my palm. I slapped both cards into Scott's hand.

"Here! You can tear them up, or you can throw them away. You can do whatever you want with them. I'm finished with this conversation. I won't pursue a modeling career. I'll continue to teach, and that will be fine." I turned around. "I'm tired, and I'm going to bed."

* * *

Snow fell from the sky the following morning, carpeting the ground with the potential of eight inches of white powder, according to the forecast. As I dressed for work, I glanced over at my husband's side of our bed, untouched and lonely. If I hadn't been so dog tired, I might have tossed and turned all night, but I didn't. The only comfort I took from Scott's outrageous behavior was the hope that he'd come to his senses and beg me for forgiveness. *I was just tired, babe. I realize what an ass I was being. I don't know where that was coming from. Blah, blah, blah.*

Nothing yet, and as more time passed, my inner critic edged closer to a very disturbing conclusion: he wasn't sorry at all. We'd been married for well over a year now and together for nearly six. Not only that, but we'd also been through hell and back. What was this really about? I had to believe it wasn't just jealousy or possessiveness, even though that was exactly what it appeared to be. Was he really that shallow?

I passed by our family room where a spare comforter sat folded beneath a guest pillow, both resting on the end of our couch. The arrangement told me where Scott had slept last night. When I entered the kitchen, I gazed out our breakfast nook window, loving the sight of thick flakes tumbling to the ground with their comforting silence. For a little while, Mother Nature had granted dead vegetation and dormant trees permission to hide their winter blemishes behind a duvet of frozen fluff. In this moment, I wanted to hide there with them.

That wasn't the only thing going on outside my window. I watched as my husband shoveled the area between our house and the barn—a walking path, anyway—as more snow scoffed at his efforts, accumulating on his hair, coat-laden shoulders, and the ground around him. At least he was wearing gloves. I was tempted to run out there and help. I loved playing in the snow, but my resentful side forbade it.

Since the county had already switched over to remote learning, we continued with our school day. In other words, no school cancellations. I was sure that left more than a few students disappointed. When I was a kid, there was nothing like a snow day. Since my mom was a teacher, it felt as if we had both been given permission to play hooky back then. And if the weather was bad enough, Daddy could even join us in building our snowman, having snowball fights, sliding, and then enjoying hot chocolate afterward. Those were precious memories for me.

At least, everyone was home, where they could dash outside and make the most of those breaks in between classes. Remote learning didn't require the strict calendar that in-person learning did.

During my lunch break, I was eager to get out. I shoveled the back patio, letting chunky flakes grace my skin with wet kisses. In the distance, the woods stood quiet, everything taking a pause to enjoy the storm, except for a lone woodpecker, who echoed from inside the thicket. When I was finished, I sipped a cup of hot tea and let the winter wonderland in front of me lift my spirits, my mind primed for reflection. I recalled how Scott and I had made love back when this land was untouched, and summer was in full bloom. My gaze found the cluster of pines on the far right side of our property—our place—away from neighbors or prying eyes. Those were beautiful memories.

For the life of me, I couldn't understand where Scott was coming from. And I tried. I really did. I even put myself in his shoes, imagining an attractive female lawyer approaching him in the same manner. Scott was often the center of attention. And I knew I'd be okay with it. Other than my stumble into Trevor's arms, I never came close to flirting with him. So, once again, what was really going on here? What was Scott battling with? Did he think that if I became a successful model, I'd leave him? If that were true, then he didn't know me at all. And how selfish. I'd supported his career at every turn. I lived in his hometown, for goodness' sake.

Christmas was next week and normally I'd be excited by this, but I wasn't. Not with Randy out there and Scott in a perpetual bad mood. It was hard to be excited about much of anything these days. If it weren't for Abigail, Joel, and Mel's impending visit, I'd be just as happy to skip Christmas this year. And that was saying a lot, considering it was my second favorite holiday (Halloween being my first).

I made spaghetti and meatballs for dinner, both homemade, along with a fresh salad. Scott came shuffling through the front door as I was finishing up, carrying a cold breeze through the foyer with him. I listened as he pulled his boots off by the door and hung his coat in the foyer closet.

It was still snowing, but as the sun fell and the temperature dropped, those vibrant snowflakes from earlier grew thin, robbed of their budding moisture until they diminished into tiny white particles of their former selves.

"Hungry?" I said as Scott entered the room, his eyes sunken and a new layer of blond scruff growing thick along his jawline. His hair was wet from melted snow, and he was wearing new clothes from the night before, telling me he must've snuck into our bedroom at some point to change. Since I hadn't seen any evidence of a shower in our master bath, I also suspected he'd used the shower in the barn, something we decided to install since we were already putting in a bathroom. We had a washer and dryer in there as well. One never knew what messes a business could commit.

Scott turned on the TV in the breakfast nook. "I could eat." He didn't approach me. No kiss hello. No, how was your day? Was he ashamed or still angry? It was anyone's guess.

"How much snow do you think we got?" I placed two dinner plates on the breakfast bar side of our island. I wasn't in the mood for anything more than informal dining or discussion.

"Not sure, maybe nine inches by now. It's tapering off. I'll shovel out front again after dinner."

Keeping with my informal presentation, I moved the pot of sauce to the edge of the stove, along with the pot of pasta, leaving the salad at the breakfast bar within arm's reach. "Want some help shoveling after dinner? I cleared the back patio earlier, but I'm sure it also needs to be done again."

Scott filled his plate and then sat at the breakfast bar, his head bowed over his food. "No, I got it."

"Want to make a snowman?" I sat next to him and smiled, hoping to thaw the icy mood he was so determined to embrace.

He chewed on his food with his attention diverted elsewhere. "It's too cold for that. Snow is too dry." His voice held no emotion or enthusiasm.

I twirled my fork through my pasta, letting it fatten before I tucked a generous bite into my mouth, the tangy, garlic sauce exciting my taste buds. As we continued to eat our dinner, the

TV performed the role of a third person in the room, filling the awkward silence with news about Randy, the weather, and a few less critical issues around town, a broken water main being one of the more serious stories. And I let it. I wasn't sure what I could say to make Scott come around. I gave him Trevor's business cards. I told him I'd also forget any notion of a modeling career. What else could I do? Bow before him and render my soul entirely? That wasn't going to happen. In fact, I was disappointed in my husband. On a level far too serious to comprehend fully.

I had always felt like we were equals in every way. But his recent behavior threatened the delicate balance of our marital scale. Was this the beginning of a long line of disappointments that would later lead to resentment and eventually a fractured marriage? I shook the thought from my mind. I didn't want to believe that was possible. This was Scott, my soulmate.

Having wolfed his entire portion down, Scott rose. "Thank you for dinner." His voice remained monotone.

Normally, he'd go for seconds, or even thirds.

Instead, he rinsed his empty plate in the sink and then placed it in the dishwasher, his water glass going on the upper rack. "I'll clear the patio again and then shovel the path between the house and the barn. My dad's employee, Leonard, will be here to plow the entire driveway first thing in the morning. I've got a few deliveries arriving for that yoga studio job. So, you may see some trucks coming and going." He took a breath and rubbed his tired eyes. "I've actually got a lot of work to do this week before your family comes, so you won't see much of me I'm afraid. I can sleep on the couch, so I don't wake you." He lowered his chin, his eyes staring up at me from under his brow.

Did he want me to object? *No, please, Scott, stay with me in our bed.*

I just couldn't force those words from my lips.

"I've gotta run. Thanks again for dinner." And then he was gone, back into the night, leaving his wife disappointed and confused. At least he set the alarm on his way out.

The next day, I worked. I ate. I watched Christmas movies. I meditated. I went to bed. The day after, I worked. I ate. I watched Christmas movies. I meditated. I went to bed. Rinse and repeat. I didn't even have presents to wrap. I had already taken care of that. Other than a few conversations with Abigail about her visit and my class interactions with my students, I became a loner.

Scott appeared every now and then to eat, wash, or change out his clothes. He barely spoke. He barely even acknowledged me. A hot tea sat on the stovetop waiting for me every morning, Scott's bedding folded neatly on the couch.

The tea was a nice gesture. His cold shoulder was not.

A few times, I awoke with a feeling of dread lodged in my chest. In those moments, I wanted so badly to nestle next to my husband on the couch, but I didn't. He was probably working late in the barn, anyway. If I gave in on this—even though I *had* in a lot of ways—there was no telling where we'd go from here. I didn't need to become a model. It wasn't that important to me. But I did need my husband to trust me and the decisions that I made. And it was *my* decision, not his. I had faith in him. And I *thought* he had faith in me.

By Thursday evening, I was climbing the walls. I couldn't watch another round of movies all by myself. Friday was a half day, so I planned to spend the afternoon organizing myself for the following week and prep meals for our weekend activities. Friday night, Jason and Heather were supposed to arrive for game night, but I didn't see how that was possible, considering Scott and I weren't even speaking. Either he'd have to cancel, or I would. And then his boss, Ben, was hosting a holiday gathering at his house the following night. That was on the twenty-first. I'd either fake illness and force Scott to go it alone, or I'd find a way to throw on a plastic smile and make it through the evening. And then, two days later, on the twenty-third, my family would arrive. For that, I couldn't wait, talking husband or no talking husband.

Once Leonard had plowed our driveway, trucks and vehicles of various sizes traveled to and from the barn, the light shining from the windows well into the night. Given the time of year, it reminded me of Santa in his workshop. A grumpy and very immature Santa.

In need of human contact, I dressed for yoga and ventured out to class. The exercise and the company would be just the pill my spirits needed right now.

I could have stopped and told Scott where I was going, but I sent him a text instead. I figured that if he couldn't even face me, why should I bother? This thing, whatever it was between us, was growing like a tumor on the DNA of our relationship. How would this end?

* * *

"Oh, hi, Sara," Tanya said as I approached the yoga studio, the sun already hiding behind the horizon, the parking lot lights burning bright. A large canvas grocery bag hung from her hands. In the other hand, a key ready to unlock the door. Diffused lighting shined from within the building, the yoga room on the outer edge, cast in darkness.

And then I spotted a large note stuck to the glass door. "Closed until December 27th. Happy holidays. Stay loose."

If Tanya hadn't been standing there, I would have turned on my heel and left.

"Are you here for class?" She tapped the sign with her key.

"We're closed until the Thursday after Christmas. I sent out an email blast, didn't you get it?"

I shook my head in a subtle manner. "I'm sure it's in my inbox. I haven't been very good about checking my personal account this week." I waved my hand causally in the air. "It's no problem." I fished my keys back out of my bag. "Have a nice holiday and give my best to Andie." I turned to walk away, feeling lower than I did when I had arrived.

"Hey, if you're not busy, why don't you come in for a bit? Andie's experimenting with some new smoothie recipes." She lifted the canvas bag higher to imply she had brought supplies for the occasion. "You can be our human guinea pig." She smiled. "I'll even sneak some rum in if you'd like. We were going to do this at home, but all of our blenders are here, and we didn't feel like carting them back and forth. They're heavy as shit."

"Sure. I'd be down for that." My spirits lifted.

* * *

"Okay, try this one." Andie handed me a small plastic cup filled with thick, reddish-colored liquid.

"This one has strawberry, coconut butter, almond milk, orange juice, and organic protein powder." She poured herself and Tanya a cup as well.

It was the third drink I'd tried. "Okay, give me a minute to finish this last one." I held up my half-empty cup containing a mixture of kale, mango, banana, coconut water, and blueberries. Plus, a splash of rum. "To celebrate the holidays," Andie had said as she poured it. It was yummy. Although, I only allowed her to spike one drink since I was driving.

Holiday garland decked the tops of what few cupboards this tiny kitchen, located at the back of the yoga studio, allowed.

An abundance of holiday cards and photos wished Andie and Tanya greetings from the front of their full-size fridge, everything either taped in place or secured by magnets. A collage of good cheer. It reminded me of one of those cars I'd seen on the highway plastered with bumper stickers from one location or another.

Keeping with the gleeful theme, these two energetic women whirled around the room wearing Santa hats, creating concoctions while I sat at their miniature breakfast bar enjoying their company and positive vibes. Christmas music floated through Tanya's wireless speaker nearby. The song "Christmas Wrapping" by The Waitresses came on. Both Tanya and Andie stopped working and woo-hooed. Tanya grabbed my hand, dragging me off my stool to join them in a dance. Our audience was a cluster of fruits, vegetables, and various containers of plant-based protein powders and milks cluttering the counters. They kissed, they sent love notes with their eyes, and they made me jealous every time I thought about Scott.

Once that song ended, another marched its way through, titled "Santa Clause is Comin' to Town," by Bruce Springsteen. We danced some more.

"Okay, okay, I have to sit." I raised a palm, feeling extremely full from the drinks.

Both women stopped dancing as well and stood next to their two high-powered blenders, admiring their work. "I think we've got some good recipes, don't you all?" Tanya asked with a nod. "Minus the rum." She giggled, raising a finger.

"Yeah, that oughta go over well. We offer customers rum drinks, and we'll make a killing." Andie placed her hand on the full pitcher, pressing a button for a quick boost, the noise loud and then silent.

Tanya laughed outwardly. "Could you imagine my yoga class, Sara? Everyone would be falling all over each other."

I chuckled. "Oh, my God, you're right. It's hard enough to keep those poses."

"Right?" Andie said with a raised brow. "She gets it." She wagged a finger.

Tanya leaned over the counter in my direction, her elbows propped to support her chin, which she rested in her hands. "Your husband has been an absolute gem to work with. He's had people out here measuring and asking all kinds of questions. He's been keeping tabs on us all week, making sure we're happy with our plans." She pursed her lips and nodded in an approving sort of way. "When I first saw your hottie of a husband show up for class, I was like, what the fuck?" She glanced over at Andie, who agreed with a smirk.

She straightened up. "I know, he's the size of a linebacker," she said as she topped off her smoothie. "But he's actually a really nice guy." She picked up her drink. "You did good, Miss Sara. Landed yourself one of the few fine-looking men who isn't an asshole."

Andie came up beside her, lifting her own cup, her other arm sliding across her wife's lower back. "And that's worth a toast. Grab your drink, missy."

I grabbed my drink and raised it. My smile implied that I agreed with their assessment. I mean, I did agree. My thoughts kept tripping over themselves between the Scott I knew and loved, and the Scott who was acting like a childish brat right now.

"Hey, is that shit about Randy Meyers freaking you out as much as it is us?" Andie used her finger to wipe a drop of smoothie from the corner of her mouth. "I hope they catch that lunatic soon. I'm getting tired of stressing out every time I walk anywhere at night. I was at a stoplight the other night and couldn't help thinking, what if Randy comes running out from the bushes with a frigging gun?"

"I know, Jesus." Tanya furrowed her brow. "And poor Mr. Wilkins."

I lowered my drink from my lips, the strawberry flavor coating my tongue. "Who's Mr. Wilkins?"

Andie picked up a container of strawberries and brought them over to the sink to wash. "Arthur? He's the unlucky dude who was shot behind his hunting cabin. I take it you didn't know him?"

I shook my head. "No, I didn't even know who it was until now." The news hadn't released the name, last I heard.

"Oh, well, he used to own a small hardware store in town. Went out of business when his wife, Esther, got sick with cancer. She died about five years ago. They had three sons. The oldest died in Afghanistan. His name was Barry, and the other two moved away. Kind of a lonely man. My dad went to school with Barry, the one who died. Arthur used to use that hunting cabin with his boys when they were younger." Pausing her work, Andie placed a hand to her mouth to suppress a burp. "My dad and my brother went there once." She placed her washed strawberries in a strainer and let them dry in the neighboring sink. "Tragic. From what I heard, shot right through the heart." She wiped her palms with a hand towel and tossed it onto the counter.

Tanya took a sip of her drink. "Sure is. A case of being in the wrong place at the wrong time. Sucks." All at once, her face froze, her brow inching downward. "Hey, did you guys just hear that?" She used her cell phone to lower the volume of the wireless speaker. Then she listened again. We all did.

Only I didn't hear anything.

"What did you hear?" I asked.

With her head tilted and her eyebrows slanted from concentration, she listened again then relaxed her face. "I thought I heard someone knocking out front. I'll go check." She dashed out of the room, returning a few seconds later. "I don't see anyone out there. We're good. Maybe it was another person for yoga, although I didn't see anyone returning to their car." She made a face. "See, I wouldn't normally think twice about someone knocking out front, but with this Randy shit going on, I get all wigged out."

I slid off my stool and went around the counter to place my hand on her shoulder. "I totally get it. I get freaked—"

Bang, bang, bang.

We all jumped, my heart skipping a beat, adrenaline rushing through my body so fast it was painful. Even my toes felt the jolt. Andie dropped the bananas she had just picked up from the counter onto the floor, both her and Tanya placing a calming hand over their chests.

Andie was the first to speak, which came out in a whisper. "Who the hell is at our back door?"

We all turned toward the menacing metal gray door, the only barrier between the kitchen and the back alley. And then it sounded off again. *Bang, bang, bang.*

Chapter Twelve

s though we'd been turned to stone, we all just stood there, frozen. I could tell neither Tanya nor Andie knew quite what to do. Neither did I.

"You weren't expecting anyone?" I asked in a low voice.

They both shook their heads no. Andie motioned with her hands as she grabbed a thick cutting board made of wood, holding it up like a weapon. Taking her wife's lead, Tanya grabbed a large knife from the counter.

From my bag, I fished out my heavy stainless-steel water bottle, holding it high like a club.

We all tiptoed closer to the door. It reminded me of when Scott and I had checked our second floor, not too long ago. This was crazy.

"Who is it?" Tanya yelled, her hand gripping the knife so tight, her knuckles turned white.

A voice floated through the door. "It's Scott Williams. Is Sara there?"

As though we were all puppets and our master had just let

go of the strings, our postures slumped, our lungs releasing one big exhale.

Tanya grabbed hold of the knob, when I raised a palm. "Wait. How do we know its Scott?" I moved my ear closer to the door, Tanya standing back. "Who did you say it is again?" I listened with intent.

"Sara, it's me. Open up. No one's out here. You're safe."

I exhaled again. There was no mistaking that voice. I opened the heavy door. "Sorry, but you scared the heck out of us."

Carrying a cold blast of air with him, Scott came into the room, closing the door with a thud, a long roll of paper clasped in one of his hands. He smelled like the outdoors, fresh and chilly. "Sorry about that. I saw Sara's car in the parking lot and didn't want her to ride home alone. I knocked out front, but no one answered." His gaze found me next. "I sent you a couple of texts. Didn't you get them?" His eyes remained fixed.

I hurried to the counter and grabbed my bag. "No, sorry. I had turned my ringer off, thinking I'd be in class. I did send you a text where I was going, though."

"I know. I was in the back room of the barn, going over my new inventory, when you sent it. I didn't notice it until about half an hour ago. I didn't want you to drive home by yourself. Not with Randy carjacking people. I'll follow you back." He turned toward Tanya who was placing her knife back on the counter and Andie who had just put her cutting board down and was now retrieving the bananas from the floor. "I'm sorry. I didn't mean to scare everyone." Scott's eyes grew sheepish. "While I'm here, I wanted to give you some preliminary floor plans. It's still pretty rough, but take a look when you get a chance, and we can go over it together when you're ready." He handed the roll of paper over to Tanya.

"Thanks," she said. "We'll take a look in the morning."

"It doesn't have any details yet. It mainly includes the outer walls and where we had discussed cutting through from the yoga studio to the space next door. I wanted you to have a visual of what it would look like."

"Wow, you work fast." Tanya held up the roll, and then she waved him off. "And no worries about scaring us. It's all good. We were just startled, really." She grinned. "We had it under control." Her eyes shined with amusement as though seeing the comical side of the situation.

Scott chuckled and rubbed his chin. "I can see that." He put on his flirty face. "I'm sure Randy would be no match for either of you. If you'd like, I can follow you and Andie home as well."

* * *

We drove past our barn and up our gravel driveway, the one that transformed into a small pad of blacktop just outside of our garage. Eventually, Scott hoped to pave the entire road. But like with everything else he wanted to do, it wouldn't come cheap.

I admired the garland and lights wrapped around the pillars holding up our front porch, a large lighted wreath hanging from our front door. Timers, installed by Scott, ensured the lights didn't stay on all night, so I enjoyed these moments when I could actually appreciate this perspective. Lately, I hadn't been out much.

What a beautiful house we lived in was all I could think.

Scott continued into the garage, my car rolling into the bay next door. We climbed out of our vehicles. When he spoke, the smile Scott had been wearing at the studio was long gone. "You forgot to put the alarm on when you left." He headed for the door. "It's on now, but I'll turn it off and check the house to be safe." Apathy controlled his volume.

I rode his heels into our mudroom where hooks hung along one wall to handle our coats, and a long bench with a cushion provided a place to put shoes and boots on or off, along with a space to store them underneath. "Thank you for following me back." Tanya and Andie had declined his offer to follow them home. They had each other was their argument.

I took off my coat and boots and then placed my hand on his lower back. It was the first time I had touched my husband since we'd returned from Richmond.

Scott bent down to remove his boots but didn't place them under the bench. Instead, he held them in his hands. He also kept his coat on. When he straightened up, his cheeks flushed to the color of a watermelon. "I can't believe you would be so careless." He set his boots on the floor then pointed at my face in a demeaning way. "You take off without turning on the alarm. You send me a text and don't even tell me *in person* where you are going, so I can prepare." Scott liked to talk with his hands, and when he was angry, they went wild. He reminded me of a composer guiding his orchestra, only a lot less pleasant. "Randy just shot a man and could have killed that woman and her son. And you go jaunting off to yoga class?" Wiping a hand over his mouth as though to collect himself, he stood back and stared at me, his eyes fuming.

Nice job, Sara. I felt like a complete imbecile. And then something occurred to me. "I'm sorry, but you left our window open upstairs and all the others unlocked so you have no room to talk."

And I never yelled at you like this.

"Randy had just escaped when that happened, and I've had everything locked up like a drum ever since. What you did tonight was risky." He started ticking off tasks. "I put locks on the barn, I added a motion sensor above the front door to the barn, and I've checked and rechecked all the doors every night." He was practically spitting at me, a wall of frustration standing between us, one he created. "You said you wanted to feel safe? Well, I've done everything I can to make you feel secure." A storm cloud passed over his eyes, his shoulders standing tall like two formidable boulders. "And what do you do? You take off across town without even telling me."

It was hard to side with him on this. He was so angry and cold. But deep down I knew he was right. What *was* I thinking? I stuttered, trying to redeem myself on some level. "I'm sorry. You're right. I wasn't think—"

"Damn right you weren't thinking. You want me to take you seriously? Trust your instincts?" He paused, as if letting the first blow in his speech knock me down. "Maybe don't act so goddamn impulsive, and think"—he tapped his temple with an aggressive finger—"before you do things."

This time he pointed toward the door. "Randy is out there fucking killing people. Have you lost your mind? Do you have any idea how much you scared me tonight?"

I felt like a ten-year-old being scolded by her father. My eyes watered as I stood there taking my poison. "I *said* I was sorry. I won't do it again. What more do you want from me?" That was the real question. Given all the mistakes Scott had made in the past, one more recent than the others, how could he act like this?

Without saying another word, Scott huffed, then picked up his boots, allowing his irritated feet to carry him throughout the house. *Stomp, stomp, stomp.*

I stood in the kitchen waiting for his return while, at the same time, wishing he'd take off for the night. I knew it was irrational given the Randy situation. I loved the man, but I didn't *like* him right now. I was tired and defensive, which made it very difficult for my brain to also be sorry.

When he emerged through the doorway from the basement, he never even looked at me. He went straight through the kitchen and into the foyer. "House is clear. I'm going back to work." He threw on his boots and then stood by the alarm near our front door, calling out to me like I was an employee in need of reprimanding. "Hey!"

I inched my way into the doorway between the kitchen and the foyer. I felt like a dog who was about to be swatted with a newspaper, my eyes doing their best not to spill tears, fists dangling by my sides. Inside I was a volcano, about to erupt and, from what I could ascertain, so was Scott.

He'd made his point. I felt horrible about it. Where was the forgiveness and understanding? I had never been this unrelenting with him. That night with Trevor, he almost got himself thrown in jail if it hadn't been for me. *Jerk.*

Not that he was willing to admit to any of that. No, I was the stupid wife. *You want me to take you seriously?* The unsaid message within that insult told me that he clearly didn't take me seriously now. I had to earn his trust and his confidence in me. I never knew this. After everything we'd been through, I assumed he felt all of those things already. The chords in my neck clenched so tight, I could barely turn my head. And the smoothies from earlier only exacerbated my nauseous stomach.

"From now on, I want this alarm on at *all* times." And that was the last thing he said before he flung the door open and then slammed it shut behind him.

At midnight, I couldn't take it anymore. I'd tossed and turned all evening. Nothing helped. Not watching Christmas movies, not reading my latest novel, nothing. I had to speak to Scott. I put on my flannel pants, a sweatshirt under a thick coat, my boots, and then I stood by the alarm, trying to decide whether this was a good idea or a bad one. Tomorrow—now today, given the hour—was the beginning of our winter break (mine started at noon). We had gatherings planned, parties to attend, and even game night with Jason and Heather. This was *supposed* to be that one time of year when everything felt special and joyous. We even had snow on the ground to fit the occasion. I'd extend an olive branch, nothing more, and we could go from there. The rest we could work out later. I wasn't giving in. I was calling a truce.

With new resolve, I punched in the alarm code to exit and then reset it as I dashed out the door, my arms hugging my upper body for warmth, my house keys securely in my pocket. Outside, the moon shone bright encouraging the white landscape around me to glow. My eyes had no trouble seeing where I was going, even without the aid of Christmas lights, which had already timed out. With no clouds to obscure them, stars poked through the abyss, providing the earth with a glittery canvas to appreciate for the next several hours. Only *my* eyes were too focused on the woods in the distance and the sounds of the night. My cell phone weighed down one pocket of my coat, ready to dial 911 if needed.

Snow crunched under my boots as I approached the barn where lights shined through the windows, and the second sun flashed from above the door upon my arrival. But when I reached the door it was locked, so I knocked loudly, hoping Scott would hear me. Given all the illumination around me, he'd see who it was without any trouble. I tried not to focus on the fact that someone else could possibly see me as well—if Randy happened to be nearby. The darkness behind me loomed a few feet away, keeping me nervous and paranoid. I pounded again, this time with more fervor.

Scott appeared a few seconds later, thank God, taking my anxiety down a notch. He opened the door but stood in my path. "What are you doing out here?" His brow bared down like the Burgermeister himself.

"I came to talk." I bowed my head and then gazed up at him

with hopeful eyes. "Can I come in?" I really needed my Scott back, the man who always made me feel special and safe. Not the one who seemed to have deserted me for the time being, leaving this iceberg of a person in his body.

Scott looked around behind him as if someone were there, and he was hiding them, which I knew wasn't possible.

"It's cold out here. Move over so I can come in, and we can talk."

Instead of doing as I asked, he nudged me back and stood in the cold with me, closing the door behind him. "It's not a good time. I've got a lot of work to do."

What?

I used to love Scott's eyes, the ones that always carried a flicker of adventure in them, and those lips that curved up just enough to hint that a joke might be hiding there. His eyes were still beautiful, but they were far from adventurous or warm, and those lips did nothing but frown at me.

I stood back. "Let me get this straight? You're not going to let me in?" Even though tears stung my eyes once again, they weren't hurt tears; they were mad ones. "You're that bullheaded?" Shock and cold trembled my lips.

He exhaled, his frozen breath creating its own vapor cloud. Then he placed his hands on his hips. "Look. If you want me to be able to take time off when your family comes, I've gotta get caught up. I've already told you this. And running off to the yoga studio earlier only put me further behind." And then, he mumbled, "That and our trip to Richmond, which I am starting to regret as well." He gazed into the darkness behind me. "You shouldn't be out here."

With my arms hugging my body tight for support and warmth, I struggled to absorb everything he was saying to me. "You regret going to Richmond, now?" I thought of all the times we'd made love. And that special night when he'd confessed his true feelings about me when we'd first met. All of it meant nothing now? Why? And then I realized the reason. How stupid of me. He didn't regret the trip. He regretted who I met on the trip. Trevor. Was all of his anger coming from that one encounter?

He rubbed his eyes. "I'm tired, Sara. I've gotta get back to work." He turned toward the door. "Let me grab my keys, and I'll walk you home." When he came back out, I was still standing there stunned. "Next time you want to come down here, call me first." His voice was nasty and unfeeling.

I let him walk me home. Mainly because I was scared. When we reached the door, I punched in the alarm and stepped inside where warm air soothed my frigid skin. The scent of my citrus pine candle that I had burned earlier lingered in the air.

Scott came in behind me, his eyes boring a hole through the back of my head. Maybe they weren't, but I wouldn't be surprised if they were. "All right, I'm going back to work. You good?"

I made my way to the foyer closet to store my coat and boots. "I'm far from good, Scott. But you can go now." I didn't bother to face him this time; I just kept walking toward our bedroom.

* * *

Scott hovered over the breakfast bar the next morning eating a bowl of cereal when I entered the kitchen. "I made you a cup of tea on the stovetop," he said with a hoarse voice.

Ignoring him, I went to the cupboard, pulled out a fresh mug, and filled my electric kettle before plugging it in and turning it on.

Scott watched me. "I said, I made you—"

"I don't want it!" I slammed my mug down, hoping it wouldn't crack against the marble countertop.

With a spoonful of cereal halfway to his mouth, Scott let it drop, creating a small splash of milk from the plunk. "Great. Now you're mad again." He stood, the legs of his barstool scraping against the wood floor as he pushed it back with his body.

I laughed without any humor in my heart. "You know what? It doesn't really matter. I've had enough of your nastiness, Scott. I can barely even look at you anymore." I'd never been a mean person, but I was tired and raw, and I needed an outlet. "If you want to spend Christmas at your parents' house that would be fine by me."

Eyes beyond red, Scott's dark circles were making him look more like the undead. He ran a hand down his face. "I can't deal with this right now."

"Then, don't." I grabbed a tea bag from the canister on the counter, making sure I chose one with plenty of caffeine. Thankfully, I only had one class this morning.

Before Randy, I had planned to spend the remaining time watching a fun holiday movie with my students in my classroom. *Since* Randy, I found a way we could watch a movie together through one of my streaming services. I'd already coordinated it with the parents. We'd chew on popcorn, watch the movie, and even comment on it, using the chat feature. It was all supposed to be fun. Now, I worried I wouldn't be able to stay awake.

"Stop acting like a child. I was trying to keep you safe." Scott brought his bowl of half-eaten cereal to the sink and said under his breath, "Doesn't matter."

The water in my kettle roared as steam strengthened within the confines of its stainless-steel walls. I imagined the frustration in my veins doing the same. "It *does* matter!" I faced him, my heart drained of forgiveness. "You're treating me like a complete idiot, and I won't have it. I'm tired of your insults. I am *not* an imbecile!"

His face sagging with fatigue, Scott faced me. "I never said—"

"I'm speaking!" I thrust my palm up. "I see where this is all coming from now. And I don't like it much. I stumbled in a bar, and you acted like I was having sex with the man who, thank God, caught me. You embarrassed me in front of the entire place and in front of our friends. I told you I wouldn't pursue a modeling career. And, even so, you've done nothing but belittle me ever since. I'm sorry I went to yoga, but I went because I've been alone in this house every night, and because my husband won't even come to bed and lay next to me. I have a hard time believing that you are *that* busy with work. You were sending a message, and I received it, loud and clear. Never once did you act excited for me or allow me to share with you how I felt about Trevor's offer. You wouldn't even let me speak his name." My head shook with disgust. "You were too busy pouting and acting like a jealous jerk. It's all about *you*, Scott, isn't it? I moved here to support you and your career. I never even hesitated. That's what partners do. Trevor called you a Neanderthal, and that's exactly what you are acting like."

Scott's face tightened, a look I'd seen a lot of lately. He even clenched his fists, dangling by his sides.

I didn't care. I marched up to him and pointed my finger right into his chest. I almost wanted to punch him. "How dare you treat me like that! After everything we've been through." I stomped my foot; my anger unleashed. "I am telling you right now. I will *not* put up with this from you. I would rather divorce you than let you treat me this way."

The tea kettle whistled, the bond between us on the verge of detonation.

"Go back to work. Go stay with your parents. And you can forget game night. I'm not interested. I may just go to Vermont after all." My lips quivered. My tone wavered. I knew I was ranting, but I was too upset to hold back. I couldn't seem to control my words. I had to get away from this man. And so, I ran out of the room, slammed the door to our bedroom shut, fell onto our bed, and cried my heart out.

By the time I was online with my students for our first class of our last day before winter break, my eyes were so puffy, they commented. "Are you sick, Mrs. Williams?"

I lied and said that I was.

Chapter Thirteen

"Okay, you all have a wonderful Christmas. And don't forget to read over break. We'll have our holiday gift exchange when we return to the classroom."

"Bye, Mrs. Williams" came from four excited faces, all ready for two weeks off, fun in the snow, and Christmas surprises from Santa (for the ones who still believed, anyway). Annabelle's mom appeared on the screen, saying, "I hope you feel better," before all four boxes disappeared, taking my students with them.

I got up from my desk and went to my bedroom, collapsing onto my bed and falling asleep immediately.

What seemed like minutes, turned out to be a couple of hours as two o'clock flashed from my nightstand clock, my tired eyes struggling to flutter open. I crawled out of bed, took a quick shower to revive myself, and got dressed in comfy clothes for an afternoon of meal prep for our weekend plans and the following week. I had told Scott I'd make lasagna, one of my favorite dishes, for Heather and Jason, who were supposed to be coming later for game night. Even though I suspected Scott had canceled the night's plan, I was hungry and in need of some comfort food. Plus, I had all that spaghetti sauce from the other night, and it needed a home. That would be my first task. The taco dip and brownies, for Ben's holiday party the following night, were still up for debate. I didn't mind making them. I only minded accompanying my husband to the party. For that, Scott would have to go it alone. And even though I had threatened to go home to Abigail to spend the holidays in Vermont, it was an empty threat. Not only did I lack the energy for such an excursion, but I also wanted to be in my new home, though I still wasn't sure I wanted my husband in here with me. Once again, Scott didn't come to bed last night, and this time, I was glad for it.

It was hard to argue with someone who refused to see your point of view. And I was tired of trying, the task like climbing a mountain as its peak continued to rise higher. What added immense amounts of salt to this marital wound of ours was the time of year. Would I always look back on this Christmas with unfavorable memories? What stressed me the most was the question: *could we survive this?* Before our trip to Richmond, I would have scoffed at this crazy notion.

I brewed myself a cup of hot tea and stood in our kitchen assessing. *Okay, get your head in the game.* My gaze drifted to the fireplace furnishing our formal dining room next door, which beckoned for my attention. The lights weaved throughout the garland draped across its mantel, ready to twinkle with delight. I plugged in the lights, then flipped the switch for the fireplace, inviting warmth and the sight of colorful flames to overflow into my kitchen as I pulled out this pan and that to prepare. Needing more Christmas cheer, I put on some music next, using the touch panel in the wall. And then I turned on the rest of the Christmas lights in the house, flooding the square footage with holiday ambiance. For a moment, I stopped at our tree to admire the ornaments from my youth, something Abigail had held safe for me as I was maturing and going to college. One was a hand-painted frame with my baby picture staring out at its center. Scott loved that one. "You were so cute, babe," he'd often say, holding it in his hands for a few extra seconds before hanging on the tree.

I sighed. *Moving on.*

Inspired by my festive burst of energy, I filled my diffuser that Amy had given me, sending scents of rosemary and mint into the air. I even considered mixing myself a cocktail, but realized I needed to stay awake if I had any hope of making this lasagna in time. I added a touch of Baileys to my tea instead.

Inside my pantry, I located my red apron, which I draped over my head, the belt tied tight around my waist. Enough stalling. *Get to work.* And so, I did.

An hour later, an impressive pan of lasagna sat on the counter, prepared for baking. It felt good to complete a task, and it helped get my mind onto other things. Feeling motivated and fully awake now, I also pulled out some garlic bread to thaw and gathered the ingredients for the brownies.

At four thirty, Scott came wandering in the door, looking as grim as he had the night before. *Was he trying to kill himself with work?* I almost felt like asking.

But I didn't. In fact, I didn't address him in any manner. I just kept working as if he weren't there. As I read through my cookbook, a strong hand came down, covering one of mine, the words, "Can we talk?" floating past my ear, his voice soft and tender.

I turned, not liking the bloodshot eyes or the pasty complexion camouflaging my husband's handsome face. "I postponed our game night for another time." His voice was kind, the way it used to be.

Good. I wanted to rest my weary head on his chest and stay there, but I couldn't. Not yet. Not after the way he'd been treating me.

"Can we talk?" he asked again, his eyes two pools of despair, imploring me to pardon him.

"I don't know, Scott. *Can we?*" I huffed. "I mean, I tried to talk to you last night and you weren't interested, so why should I—" I stopped abruptly. Mainly because my focus became the tear that ran down my husband's cheek.

Scott rarely cried.

I took a step closer. "What's going on with you?"

The dam broke, and my statue of a husband crumbled before me. As his body bent from the strain, I caught him and his sorrow in my arms and let him release whatever was torturing his poor soul. I backed up to the counter to support his weight, which was massive. He blubbered, drawing tears from my own eyes. Soon, we were both crying with abandon.

Finally, he caught his breath and pulled back, his hands smoothing down the sides of my hair, his cheeks drenched. He sniffled. "I'm so sorry, babe. I've been a fucking mess. I can't sleep. I can't eat. I don't know what to do." He was floundering, and that was also something Scott never did. He was always the man in charge.

I took his hand and guided him onto the couch in the family room. We both sat, Scott looking like he'd just lost his best friend, his shoulders bent as though he were carrying cinderblocks.

"What have you been so upset about? This thing with Trevor? Because that makes no sense to me."

Scott wiped his eyes and shook his head vehemently, mucus running from his nose and mouth. "It's not about Trevor. But I can see why you think it is. And I have to admit, Trevor did remind me of ..." He cast his gaze downward.

It took me a second, but it clicked. The *who* he was referring to clicked.

"That's not the point. I was wrong."

Okay, that was a bit of a revelation. I could meet him halfway. I was open to that. "Hang on." I ran to grab him some tissues which he used to wipe up his emotional mess. As I watched him, another epiphany hit me. This wasn't work exhaustion Scott was dealing with. It was mental exhaustion.

I used a few tissues myself, then blew my nose clean.

"I want you to know that I do trust you and your judgment. Christ, Sara, you saved my life. Remember when you told me how worried you were that something bad was always going to happen to us?" He sniffled some more. "The night we thought Randy had broken into our second floor?"

I nodded, caressing his forearm, staying close.

"Well, I didn't dare tell you that I felt that way too. In fact, that night we heard the noise upstairs, I was pretty freaked out by it. I couldn't sleep all night."

I leaned closer. "Why didn't you say something?"

His distressed eyes softened. "I didn't want to freak you out any more than you already were. I know how these things can trigger you."

I let my brow rise and fall. "Yeah, but you don't need to protect me from your feelings, Scott. In fact, telling me how you really feel will only make me feel better." I took his hand in a tight grip. "We're in this together. So, tell me everything. I promise you won't make me feel worse." I scooted back a few inches on the sofa to give him some room.

Scott looked down at the sodden tissue in his palm. "Well, after that night, I found myself waking up a lot, having bad dreams, all of them involving me trying to find you or the both of us trying to escape something bad. I woke up in a cold sweat one time." He took a stabilizing breath. "I was afraid I was going to wake you. That's why I've been sleeping on the couch. When we went to Richmond, the burden lifted, and I felt like myself again." He moved his head back and forth in a subtle manner. "I may have indulged a little too much on the weed as a result. When I came out and saw you in Trevor's arms, I couldn't figure out what had happened. Those triggers went off like cannons inside of my head. I saw red and overreacted. I heard you tell me everything was okay, but I was too wired and upset to believe it." He wiped his nose with the weathered tissue and then tossed it onto the seat next to him. "When we talked about it in the car on the way home, I felt like we'd started to move past it, but then I began obsessing about you leaving. What would I do if you were working on photo shoots all over the world? I was terrified of losing you, but I was even more terrified of something bad happening to you. If you are right in front of me, I can keep you safe." He cleared his throat, his lips pursed. "I do think there are people out there like Trevor who could prey on innocent women, but I also know you would never fall for that, neither would Amy. And I'd be there with you. I had to remind myself about all of these things."

I could tell he was trying to hold back another round of sobbing.

"I was so messed up by it, I called Dr. Zeller earlier today."

My eyes grew wide, my cheeks finally starting to dry. "You did?" All this time, I had thought he was being selfish, and he was, sort of, but there was something else going on. He was dealing with some very profound feelings. I could relate to that. Fear could make a person do strange things, masking itself as jealousy or outrage, which I had seen a lot in him lately.

Scott nodded, his gaze resting on me again. "Yeah, she helped me. She reminded me that I had also been through a lot, and that I may need some counseling to help me deal with these situations moving forward. She said that if left untreated, these types of fears can turn into phobias that can control a person's life. But all my fears manage to do is turn into anger, which just pushes you away. I was awful to you. I am so sorry, Sara. You didn't deserve it." He reached out and ran his fingers down the side of my face. "And I'm not worried about Trevor. In fact"—he reached into the back pocket of his jeans and pulled out two business cards—"I called Trevor earlier today." He handed me back the cards. "I apologized for my behavior, explaining that we'd been through some scary shit here, and that I had overreacted. I also told him that I had no problem with you setting up a photo shoot. I said that I agreed with him, you are the most beautiful woman *I'd* ever seen."

It was a good thing I was sitting because if I were standing, my knees would have given out by now. I was moved beyond words. I wished I had known what was going on inside of my husband's worried head. And I was so relieved to discover that his motivation, although intense and destructive, didn't come from selfish behavior. He wasn't shallow. He was anything but.

My heart opened to him. My love even stronger than I had ever thought possible.

"And that's why you were so angry last night. My taking off like that, only triggered you more." I didn't say it as a question, more of an understanding on my part.

He nodded. "I'm sorry, babe. I realized that I'd pushed you too far, and that I had to do something, or I was going to lose you." He cupped my chin. "You see, most people think the worst thing that could happen to them is death." The love from his eyes showered over me, and I basked in its rays. "For me, the worst thing that could happen to me is divorce. I'd *rather* die than lose you. I will seek counseling and get my shit together. Dr. Zeller gave me some names. I want to be there for you. And I'd be proud to have my wife gracing the covers of magazines."

A smirk played across his face, his eyes appearing less misty and more hopeful. His voice shook. "You'd fucking blow this world away with your beauty."

I fell into his arms, and we hugged, our grips strong, our hearts unbarred. "You will never lose me." I pulled back. "I hate that you've been carrying this burden all alone. You've been there for me. And I want to be there for you too." I shook his shoulders, hoping to punctuate my message. "But I can't be there for you when you push me away and act like you have been acting. I was worried you were turning into someone I didn't recognize anymore. Promise me, you will *always* be honest with me." For a moment, I didn't blink.

"I promise." He brought my hand up to his face, then kissed my palm, holding it against his cheek. "I don't ever want to go through the past several days again. And I never want to sleep away from you again, either. I love you, Sara Williams, with my whole heart. I told you when I proposed that I knew you were a better person than me, and that I didn't deserve you. Trevor was right about that one. Even after all these years, I still keep expecting you to come to your senses and leave my sorry ass."

"Trevor was not right, and I would never leave you." Yes, I was angry at Scott, and I also had my moments of doubt (my triggers), but deep down, I knew we'd move past this.

He kissed my hand again, his lips soft and supple. "You definitely didn't deserve what I've been dishing out this past week. I'm sorry I put you through that."

I cradled his face in both of my hands now, the bristles from his jaw prickling my skin. "I'm sorry that *you* went through that. And that you didn't feel you could tell me. I'm yours, Scott Williams. And I always will be."

"Thank God for that." He grabbed my head and kissed me with so much passion that I almost forgot where we were. He took my hand and guided me to our bedroom.

We were going to make love, my insides quivering at the thought of it. As we passed my walk-in, I thought of something I had purchased during my months of early Christmas shopping, somehow knowing I'd find an occasion for it.

When we reached our bed, I stopped. "I bought a surprise I want to wear for you." I put up a finger. "Give me just one minute." I went into my walk-in where a spicy negligée hung seductively on a hanger. The shimmery satin was Christmas red, the neckline so low, it reached my belly, and the slit so high, it left nothing to chance. Outfitted for fun, I sauntered into our bedroom, ready to dazzle, but what I found was a man sprawled out on our bed, snoring like a bull.

I smiled and admired his beauty and strength.

I covered my relaxed husband's body in our microsuede light-and-dark-gray striped comforter, draping him in softness and warmth. My lips placed a tender kiss against his forehead. Once I had changed back into my comfy clothes, I even cuddled up next to him for a few minutes, enjoying the warmth of his body next to mine, the sound of his lungs singing a healing melody.

For the next several hours, Scott slept while I baked the lasagna, toasted the garlic bread, and refreshed the salad from the other day. With that accomplished, I went to work on those brownies for Ben's party, the taco dip to follow, since I planned to attend after all.

The smell of garlic and tangy tomato sauce must've roused Scott from his slumber. Wearing a fleecy, long-sleeved T-shirt in black and a pair of gray sweatpants, he entered the kitchen with wet hair and a fresh, musky scent tagging along for the ride.

"Smells good in here, babe." As his lungs expanded, he glanced at the clock on the wall, its hands pointed at 8:30 p.m. "I hope you didn't wait to eat." He was practically salivating.

What had *he* eaten over the past few days? I wondered. Given the state of him, probably not much. In fact, I guessed he'd lost about five pounds.

"I had a few snacks to tide me over." I took his hand and led him into the dining room, where the fireplace blazed. The table welcomed him with elegant dishes, placemats, and a woodland centerpiece, two cranberry-colored candles positioned stylishly at each end. "I made us a special dinner." As Vince Guaraldi emanated from the hidden speakers, I retrieved a lighter from a drawer in the china cabinet and lit the candles. "Do you like it?" I put the lighter away.

"It's awesome." Scott took in the fancy decor and the bottle of wine, ready to fill the Christmas goblets standing at the head of each setting. Slightly off center, a wooden bowl filled with salad made a small tray of garlic bread its companion. "This looks great, babe." He pulled a chair out. "Have a seat, beautiful, and I'll serve us both. Rest your feet."

We talked, we laughed, and we sipped wine, enjoying our intimate dinner for two. After being so estranged from each other, it was like we'd peeled off the bad layers of our relationship, the ones that were dragging us down, allowing fresh new life to blossom between us.

And when Scott finished with his first helping, he most certainly went back for more.

"I like the smell of that diffuser Amy gave you. We should get another one for the family room," he said as he sat down with another plate full of food.

"Sounds good." I took my last bite of garlic bread, my stomach as full as full could get.

Scott filled our near-empty glasses and raised his in the air. "I want to make a toast to my lovely wife who, for some unknown reason, married me." He spoke as if there was a crowd in front of him. "I thank God every day for you. You are so beautiful inside and out."

I clinked my glass against his. "And I want to toast my wonderful husband, who would rather make himself sick with worry than burden me." I wagged a finger. "Although, that's not going to happen anymore, right?"

"Right." He sipped his wine, blinking sheepishly.

"I'm sorry game night didn't work out." I gazed back at the kitchen, where a very large pan of lasagna would have fed everyone and then some.

"I'm not." Scott wiggled his eyebrows. "We can still have game night. How about a game of strip poker." He gazed upward, his index finger tapping his chin. "I seem to remember you had a surprise to show me. If it's only one article of clothing, however, this will be a very short game." The grin that stretched across his gorgeous face was a welcome sight.

I smiled with a new spark in my heart. "Well, Mr. Williams, it just so happens that it is only one article." I stood. "How about we clean this mess up, and I'll show you."

Scott rose. "Let me clean this up. You've been working in the kitchen all afternoon." He took our plates into the other room.

I followed him in. "If you let me help, you can get to that surprise much faster." I leaned against the doorway, feeling desirable and ready to please.

Scott peered back at me, his gaze traveling from my head to my waist. "Deal."

* * *

Lasagna was for dinner, and *I* was for dessert. Scott took one look at me in my negligée and practically fell to his knees.

"Jesus Christ, you're gonna kill me, woman. Keep it on while I taste you."

Naked and fully erect, Scott licked my folds with a delicate tongue that quickly transformed into one meant to drive his wife wild. His hands roamed over the silk fabric finding my breasts, knowing just how to ramp up my sexual thirst on both ends of my body. The hunger in his eyes and the quality of his fingers and mouth had me arching my back in no time, screams of ecstasy flying from my lips. And then we played, fondled, and licked some more, my suggestive outfit there to witness it all.

As our encore, I straddled my hunky husband, my hips moving with the rhythm of Scott and his robust body, his massive erection finding all of my G-spots. By that point, I'd lost count of the orgasms and of the time. A quick shower and sheet change, and we wrapped up in each other's arms, tired and satisfied, Scott spooning me the way he always did. We were two pieces of a puzzle that fit together perfectly.

He kissed the back of my head and inhaled. "That was amazing, babe. Although, you may need to trash that negligée. I'm sure it's got some of *me* all over it. I started out being careful, but you drove me wild."

A sigh escaped from my lips as I reached behind me to lightly cup his muscular butt. "A small sacrifice. I think you may have torn it anyway during our last session." I chuckled, thinking of the slip sprawled out on the bathroom floor. She was my soldier, one who had done her due diligence for our marriage.

"I'll buy you a new one." He snuggled even closer. "Love you, babe."

"Love you, too, handsome."

And that was all I said before sleep overtook my mind, pulling me into dreamland.

* * *

The next morning, Scott hummed as he roamed around the kitchen, making us eggs and bacon for breakfast. I brewed our coffee and tea and set our plates near the stove, our utensils arranged on the table in the breakfast nook, holding ground until our meal arrived. Outside, billowy clouds floated across the sky, the sun peeking out every now and then to say hello. Since the snowstorm, the temperature had remained in the low thirties during the day and in the teens at night, preserving the snow and the feeling of winter. My weather app promised no new snowstorms for the next few days, other than maybe a dusting. Good news, considering Abigail had planned to drive south soon. Interestingly enough, they lived in Vermont where no snow had fallen yet this season. Not good for ski areas, who depended on the tourists for income.

"Do you still want to go to Ben's tonight?" Scott asked as he pulled the bacon out of the oven to sprinkle with maple sugar and flip. The room filled with a smoky flavor, my nose mesmerized, my stomach growling with anticipation.

I dropped two slices of bread into our toaster and pushed the handle down. "Sure. It will be fun. I made taco dip and brownies yesterday to bring with us." I grabbed some butter from the fridge, the scent of last night's lasagna dominating the confined space with aromas of garlic and various herbs.

Scott placed the bacon back in the oven and smirked. "I knew about the brownies. I got up in the night and had a couple." He widened his eyes for effect. "They were awesome."

"You did? You brat." I shook my head at him as my toast popped up, all brown and ready to butter.

"You know it, babe." He winked at me as he heated up the pan for the eggs while drizzling a thin layer of olive oil onto its surface. "I left plenty for the party." He went to the fridge to get the eggs, on his way, grabbing my butt with a gentle squeeze. "It's your fault. You wore me out. I needed the energy."

"Energy for what? Sleep?" I buttered our toast, the knife making a scraping sound against the surface of the cooked bread.

With a carton of eggs in his hand, Scott scooted up behind me, his lips finding the nape of my neck, my hair pulled up into a ponytail to allow him full access. "Well, how was I supposed to know whether or not my she-beast would want more lovin' in the night?" His free hand slid around my waist, making my insides tickle.

I nudged my butt into his front, not remotely surprised that he was hard already. "You are impossible."

As he leaned into me, I continued to work on the toast.

"And don't get any ideas, mister. I need a day to recover."

"Aw. You're breaking my heart, babe." He returned to his duties. Another wink told me he was doing just fine.

With a full belly, I wiped my mouth with my paper napkin and then sipped on my tea, the cinnamon, a nice complement to my meal. "Do you have more work today?" I rather enjoyed having my husband back and wasn't quite ready to see him go.

Scott sipped his coffee, scraping his plate clean with his last piece of toast. "I do have a few more things I need to take care of, but they can wait until tomorrow." He rubbed my thigh, his palm warm from the coffee mug. "Today is all about you." He sat sideways in his seat. "What would *you* like to do?"

I had to think about that as I slid my legs over to face him. "Play." I braced my hands on his shoulders. "But not the kind of play you're thinking of." Before his posture sagged too much, I continued. "We can fit that in, too, but I'd like to make a snowman and maybe have a snowball fight." I pondered that for a moment. "And we can take our sleds over to that hill at the edge of our property and go sledding." I clasped my hands together with excitement. "I can make us hot chocolate afterward." In my imagination, I was already living inside of a Hallmark movie, or maybe I was simply trying to recapture a memory from my youth.

Scott's eyes shined as he pushed his chair back and stood, taking our plates to the sink. "Well, then, we have a plan."

And what a plan it was. Mother Nature lifted the temperature just enough to allow a limited amount of melting to take place. The snow was sticky and perfect for outdoor activities, except for skiing, of course, but I was far too uncoordinated for *that* sport. Wearing hats bearing down on our brows, gloves, thick coats, and boots, Scott and I rolled a small ball of snow around the yard, gathering up friends, until the small mound grew into a much larger base for our snowman. The shape of the body was slightly smaller, and the head, even more so. Scott found several miniature pinecones that we used for the nose and for the mouth, while I grabbed an old scarf to wrap around the neck.

We stood back and assessed, our noses red, our smiles wide.

"What do you think, babe?" Scott's breath collided with the moisture in the air, creating his own fog bank, my breath contributing to the tiny weather system.

"I think he needs a hat?"

"He?" He quirked a brow. "How do you know it's not a woman?"

"No boobs."

That made Scott laugh. "In that case, I have the perfect hat." He trudged through the snow all the way to the barn, where he unlocked the door and disappeared inside. A few moments later, he appeared, carrying a yellow hard hat.

Of course, I thought to myself.

Scott plunked the hard hat onto our snowman and stood back admiring his work. "What should we call him?"

"I don't know." I searched my mind for a name. And then it came to me. "Olaf from *Frozen*, since my student Annabelle loves that movie." I nodded once with pride.

"Olaf it is." Scott stood next to me, his arm thick with GOR-TEX wrapped around my shoulders. Suddenly, an icy blast slid down my neck, making me yelp. "You brat." I grabbed my collar to stop the torture, which only seemed to make it worse, a handful of snow sliding down my back, leaving goose-bumps in its wake.

I chased Scott around the yard, grabbing mounds of snow to throw at him. "You got that right down my neck." Any effort to wiggle it free continued to make it worse, the frigidness sliding farther down.

And then, *thwack,* a snowball hit me straight in the chest.

"You're in trouble, mister." I ran through the snow, trying my best to catch my athlete of a husband whose aim was annoyingly accurate. It wasn't long before I grew tired of lifting my boots through the snow and slowed my pace, eventually stopping; my body bent over, my hands braced against my thighs.

Scott came jogging up. "Christ, woman. We need to get you into a gym. Are you tired out already?" He lowered his head to see me better. And that was when I got him. A snowball right in the face.

I laughed with abandon as he stood back and sputtered, trying to shake the snow from his mouth, nose, and forehead. "I'm not as out of shape as you think, *dude.*"

And the race was on. Our footprints scattered across the

snow-covered lawn, until we were lying side by side, our lungs ready for a break, our bodies covered in snow.

When Scott caught his breath, he took my hand. "You still want to go sledding? We've got enough time if we go now."

I sat up. "Yes!" I didn't know how long the snow planned to stick around and wanted to enjoy it while I could.

We grabbed two sleds that Scott had taken from his parents' garage, since they never used them, and plodded through our backyard and over to an area where the land slanted downward. Any farther and we'd be on the Andersons' property, although we had enough at our disposal to do the trick. I planted my sled next to Scott's, and together, we pushed ourselves closer to the hill's edge. To my delight, nothing stood at the bottom, no trees or vegetation to get in our way. When gravity allowed, our sleds took over. I grabbed hold of the outer lip of the sled and sailed down the hill, "whoo-hoos" flying from my lips. A small bump at the bottom of the hill threw me out of my sled, landing my butt, smack dab, into the snow.

Of course, Scott sailed through just fine.

I laughed, realizing how even sledding, I was a klutz.

"You okay, babe?" Scott called to me as he rolled off his sled at the bottom.

"Oh, yeah. I'm good." I also rolled over to get up on my hands and knees when something stopped me. Two some-things, if I counted both indentions. The smile I'd been wearing melted from my face. "Scott?" I motioned with my hands. "Come here quick."

Thump, thump, thump. He traipsed through the snow toward me. "What is it?"

I climbed to my feet and pointed just as he reached me. "Are those footprints?"

There, about twenty feet away, footprints came out of the woods and ran from our property, across a small ravine, and up onto our neighbor's land, a barbed wire fence either cut or broken to allow passage.

I shivered.

This was my fear all along. Randy roaming around nearby, trying to find a new place to hide out. Was this evidence of an escaped murderer or something perfectly innocent? Suddenly, I felt exposed, our house a million miles away. I gazed into the thicket, fear wrapping around my mind. Up in a tree, something dark and foreboding loomed over us. "What is *that*?" Once again, I pointed. It looked like a demon made of organic material. Like something you'd see in a horror movie.

"It's a tree stand for hunters," Scott said, his eyes gazing up into the woods. "And it's on Mr. Anderson's property." He motioned toward the footprints. "Those could be his too." His eyes tensed as though something had just occurred to him. "But I don't know why he'd be on our side."

Something else sparked in his eyes.

"Scott what's wrong?"

He exhaled. "If I'm not mistaken, Mr. Anderson is in Florida right now."

If Mr. Anderson is in Florida, who left those footprints?

Chapter Fourteen

"We better get back."

Scott didn't need to tell me twice. I grabbed my sled and took off toward our house, trying not to think about the sight of a gun pointed at the back of my head.

When we reached the pavement of our driveway, we kicked the snow off our boots before I punched in the code for the garage door to open.

Inside our mudroom, we peeled off our winter layers and entered the kitchen, where Scott grabbed his cell phone off the counter.

I collected a glass from the cupboard and filled it, using the separate spout delivering filtered water to the sink, another luxury of this house. "Are you calling Mr. Anderson?" I took several large sips, then refilled it for Scott.

He punched in some numbers and nodded. "Yeah, he asked me to keep an eye on the place."

I handed him the glass. "I didn't know he had asked you to

do that." Bart and his wife, Sandra, were a nice couple in their late sixties. The Andersons had a son who lived in Florida with their three grandkids, and a daughter who lived out in Arizona. Their nice old farmhouse sat on five acres of land that Scott's grandfather had sold to them many years ago when they were just starting out. I had only met them once when Scott and I were out for a walk last summer, but Scott had known them for years.

Scott blinked with meek eyes. "Yeah, I'm sorry I didn't tell you. Bart stopped by the other day when you and I weren't on the best of terms." He guzzled a few sips of water down and then exhaled with an *aah*. "Thanks, I was thirsty. It's possible he may not have left yet, though. I thought he was supposed to go yesterday but maybe it was today. I planned to stop by on our way to Ben's party to check on things." He waited for a few more seconds and then spoke. "Hey, Mr. Anderson, this is Scott Williams next door. I was just out back with Sara and spotted some footprints in the snow connecting your property and mine. Over near the tree stand. The fence there appears to be damaged as well. It could have been already like that, but I wanted to mention it. With Randy on the loose, I figured you can never be too cautious. Can you call me when you get a chance? Thanks." He pushed the End button and then placed his phone on the counter, finishing his water. When he was fully hydrated, he looked at me again, an unusual smirk riding all the way up to his eyes. "Nice hair, hon."

I rushed to the guest bath where I gazed into the mirror and laughed. As though someone had smeared grease all over my head, my hair had literally matted itself to my scalp, my cheeks rosy red. Hat hair at its best. In fact, I looked like a cartoon character.

Scott watched me from afar, his grin full of mockery.

"Well, your hair doesn't look any better."

He came into the bathroom. "What are you talking about?" he said with bogus indignation. "My hair is *always* perfect."

Normally, Scott's soft, golden curls were something to admire and equally fun to touch, but not at this moment, when those locks stuck to his head as though they'd been painted there with paper-mache, his cheeks rivaling that of Rudolph's nose.

Together, we resembled two of Santa's elves gone rogue. Not a pic for the Christmas album, that was for sure. The sound of Scott's ringtone interrupted our jocular moment. He rushed into the kitchen to get to his phone in time.

"Hello?" He waited. "Yes, Mr. Anderson." Then Scott chuckled. "Sorry, Bart. Did you get my message?" He paused. "Oh, okay. That's too bad. But I can't say as that I blame you." Another pause. "I hope so too." Scott stopped talking again to listen. "I figured it was something like that. If you want me to meet you out there, it's not a problem."

I watched Scott as he listened to more of what our neighbor had to say.

"Roger that, Bart. Give my best to Sandra. Yes, happy holidays to you too." Scott ended the call.

By now, I was standing right next to him. "What did he say?"

Scott set his phone back down on the counter. "He said that he and Sandra are gonna wait to go to Florida after this mess with Randy is cleared up. He doesn't want to be that far away from home in case something happens. If they catch Randy, he said they may go for New Year's."

"That's too bad. What about the footprints?"

"Well, he said his buddy Tom may have been out there scoping deer."

"May have?"

Scott gazed down at me from his six-foot-three frame. "Let's try not to worry. He said he'll take a look." His hand went up and down my back with comforting strides.

"Should he be going out there alone?"

"He's gonna check with Tom, first. If that doesn't pan out, he said his brother Roy lives just up the road. He'll take him out there with him. He also said he's pretty sure the fence was already like that, probably trampled by deer. I told him I'd meet them out there, too, if he wants me to. You don't mind, do you?"

I did mind, but I wasn't about to say so. Scott was doing the neighborly thing here, but selfish me didn't want him to risk it. Maybe Bart's friend would offer answers and put the entire matter to rest.

* * *

Dressed in a silvery sequined top with split cuffs and black dress pants, a long winter-white wool coat to keep me warm, and the same black suede ankle boots I'd worn at Amy's, I rode shotgun in my SUV, admiring my husband's beauty. The man certainly could fill out a slim-fit dress shirt, which tonight happened to be dark maroon, and a pair of brushed cotton tan pants, all hidden beneath his black wool overcoat, a pair of brown derby loafers on his feet. I watched him dress earlier in awe of his chiseled body and the way the fabric hugged his muscles.

"I won't take long." Scott pulled our car into Bart's gravel driveway, the car's headlights washing over the white farmhouse with black shutters. Their fat Christmas tree adorned with multicolored lights twinkled from what I assumed was their living room window. "It looks like he's home." Scott shifted the car into park and cut the engine right behind Bart's faded red Ford Bronco. "I'm sure he just forgot to call me back. Keep the doors locked and hang onto these." He handed me the keys. I watched as he climbed out of our vehicle and jogged over to Bart's front door, where he knocked. A few seconds later, he disappeared inside. When Bart hadn't called Scott back, of course, I started to fret about it. I hoped Scott was right, and he had just forgotten.

While my husband was gone, I peered out into the darkness with the same trepidation that I always felt when dipping my feet into murky waters. Just like a poisonous jellyfish could be right next me in the ocean, or even a shark, Randy could be standing only a few feet away, and I wouldn't know any different. I rechecked the door locks.

The six o'clock news reported that authorities were investigating the staff at the prison to determine whether Randy had had any help with his getaway. According to their sources, Randy had faked illness the day before the incident, which brought him to the infirmary. Somehow, between the time he was released from the infirmary and the time he was supposed to be returned to his cell, he had vanished. I couldn't imagine helping a murderer go free. If someone did, in fact, help him, they must've had a screw loose to do such a thing.

Hurry up, Scott.

As though he could hear my thoughts, Scott emerged from the front door, his hand on the knob. He said a few words, nodded, and then closed the door, jogging over to our car.

I unlocked the doors, allowing him to hop inside, carrying a frosty breeze with him. "Do you want the good news or the bad news?" He took the keys from my outstretched hand, latched his seatbelt, and then started the engine.

"Bad news first." I had always been a delayed-satisfaction kind of person. I preferred to get through the hard stuff with the promise of something better on the other side.

Scott turned the car around in an area just large enough to allow such maneuvering. "He couldn't get a hold of Tom, which is why he never called me back. So, he's not sure if those footprints belonged to him or not."

"And the good news?"

"The fence was already damaged, and he checked the area with his brother. He said they went pretty far into the woods. They didn't see anything that concerned them. He also called the local precinct and let them know, just in case."

He pulled onto the road, our destination Ben's house.

* * *

Lighted Christmas trees, live ones, sprouted across Ben's massive front yard, overlooking a small herd of gold reindeer, each one glittering as though Tinker Bell had blessed them with her wand.

We passed car after car until Ben's private drive expanded into a circular parking lot, crowded with cars, pavers extending over the ground. To our surprise, a spot sat vacant, which we immediately took for ourselves.

I grabbed my stuff, realizing I was missing something. "Crap. I forgot my purse." I was so focused on getting a bottle of wine ready for Ben's house, gift bag and all, plus my taco dip and the brownies packed up and ready to go, it had slipped my mind.

"No worries, babe. You should be fine without it."

He was right, but I still chastised myself internally. My mind never stopped, which was the reason I often forgot one thing or another. Most of the time, I was preoccupied with three more tasks that I still had to take care of.

Carrying my taco dip with a bag of tortilla chips, and Scott carrying the brownies, plus a very expensive bottle of wine—

everything in festive containers that would remain here—we climbed out of the car and onto a wide staircase made of brick. Thick swaths of garland, riddled with lights, weaved around each of the railings, illuminating our path forward. I gazed upward at three stories of windows, each embellished with chubby wreaths glowing with brilliance and bows.

Ben's skills as an architect reflected in the symmetry of the large pillars holding guard on the expansive front porch (also wrapped in garland and lights), the windows detailed with granite trim, and the rooflines that inspired the house to stand taller.

The arched-top, double-entry doors with stained glass were already opened wide when we arrived, Ben waiting on the threshold. Two large lighted wreaths chosen by Judy, I assumed, hung joyfully from each door to greet their guests.

"Happy holidays, you two." He half hugged me and then patted Scott on the shoulder since our hands were already full of treats. "So glad you could come." Ben ushered us inside, where I was sure *Better Homes and Gardens* had decorated for the occasion. Christmas came to life in the cluster of oversized poinsettias flanking the front door and along the base of an impressive curved staircase, its railing wrapped with even more garland and lights. The marble floors reflected it all from beneath our feet. "I have good news for you both. But let's get you a drink and find a place to put down your food." He guided us into his formal dining room, the table accented with mahogany and maple veneers, where I placed my dip by a crowd of other appetizers, and Scott placed my brownies near a matching buffet for desserts. I counted four Christmas trees throughout the house. Tall nutcrackers stood like wooden people in this corner or that, some of them holding trays with more snacks, even though Ben and Judy had hired a full wait-staff to attend to their guests.

Our hands weren't free for three seconds before Ben placed a flute of champagne in our grasp.

"Thanks." Scott handed him the wine. "I hope you like red. This is one of Sara's favorite blends."

Ben stared at the bottle with discerning eyes. "Judy loves red blends." He smiled. "Thank you. I'll put it away so we can share it another time." He greeted a few guests who passed by. "Okay, I got you a reservation at Bon Appétit for tomorrow night at eight o'clock." The spark in his eyes and the pitch of his voice told me he couldn't wait to share this news.

In all honesty, I had forgotten about the dinner, figuring we'd make it work for Valentine's Day. Not wanting to disappoint him, though, I ramped up my enthusiasm. "Wow. Thank you. That's great."

"Yeah, Ben, that's awesome." Scott's hand slid across my lower back. "You're gonna love this place, babe. And I was hoping you'd get to see it for the holidays." He tapped his glass of champagne against mine and then Ben's. "This deserves a toast. I should have known you'd make this happen."

Scott's compliment brought delight to Ben's smile. "Happy to help. Sorry about the short notice, but they just called me today. I hope it won't interfere with any of your plans." His gaze drifted over to me.

One thing about being angry at your spouse was that I'd been super productive with my meal planning, my mind and my hands needing a project. "Not at all. My family won't be here until the day after. Thank you, Ben." The idea of getting dressed up in my special gown was already pumping blood into my adventurous heart.

* * *

Scott worked most of the next day, but he promised he'd be free for all of Christmas Eve and Christmas Day. I spent *my* day cleaning, making beds, and anything else I could think of to prepare for Abigail's visit. I was over prepared for sure. Once again, I filled the house with Christmas music and essential oils as I worked. I also took out my dress to examine it and my shoes, locating the fancy purse I had saved for just such an event. It was small, and I wondered if it would hold all my stuff: a cell phone, lip gloss, and other essentials. A test run was needed. A few minutes later, I confirmed that everything fit just fine.

At lunchtime, Scott ran out to get the prime rib. I offered to go in his place, but he said he needed a break, and so I continued to work on my own. Knowing my family would be here tomorrow gave me all the energy I needed to do just about anything. Especially after a couple of weeks of nothing but stress and anxiety.

Within no time, my husband was back in our kitchen, delivering the goods. "Hey, babe." He planted a quick kiss on my lips. "Carl said he reserved the best cut for us. I'll fix the rub early in the morning." He placed the bag on the counter, pulled out the prime rib wrapped in brown parchment paper, and brought it to the spare fridge in the garage.

I had just approached the shopping bag on the counter when he appeared.

"I also got orange juice, almond milk (which I preferred to real), more ham, in case you want to make egg-a-muffins (my own nickname for the breakfast treat), eggs, and sausage just in case. Oh, and bread." Always a planner, my husband was.

"Perfect. I think we had enough of everything, but we'll be covered now for sure." I started unloading his two bags. "What time do you want me to be ready for dinner tonight?"

Scott seemed to ponder that. "Our reservation is at eight, right?"

I nodded. "Yup."

"It will take us about an hour to get there with no delays on the road. I think we should leave at six-thirty to give us extra time just in case we hit traffic. If we're early, we can have a drink at the bar." Behind his beautiful blue eyes, those wheels were turning. "I've gotta put in a full day today, so I already brought my outfit down to the barn on my way out to the gym this morning. I'll drive, so I'll bring your car down as well. Are you okay walking down at six-thirty? The road is clear, and there's no patches of ice or anything. I checked."

"Sure, I can do that." It was kind of cool that Scott wouldn't see my dress until the last minute. Silly, I knew, but this dress had a long history with us. She deserved a real introduction.

"Is there anything you want me to take with me, so you don't forget it?" He lowered his brow, staring up at me.

What could I say? The man knew me and my forgetful mind. "Yes, take my fancy purse. You can leave it in the car."

Scott went to the table in the breakfast nook where a gold-colored, glamour handbag glistened against the lunchtime sun. "You mean, this bag?"

"Yes. Thank you."

Scott approached with another kiss. "Okay, see you at six-thirty. Looking forward to tonight." As he backed away, the twinkle in his eyes told me how much.

At four o'clock, I decided to stop working around the house and get ready for our special night out. I wanted plenty of time to primp. And primp I did, to the nth degree. I even put curlers in my hair, hoping to promote long, lustrous waves.

My makeup was perfect, my hair behaving, when I decided to put on the dress and my shoes. As I stood in front of my full-length closet mirror, I was amazed with the results.

The halter top of the chiffon dress, its fabric shimmering in crab apple red, hugged my breasts, making them appear larger than reality—ample amounts of cleavage to support the illusion—and the long, flowing skirt with the generous slit down the front, brought elegance with a touch of sexy. But what really set this dress apart from anything else I owned was the exposed back that plunged all the way down to my waist. To accentuate this feature, I pulled my hair over my left shoulder, using a large barrette and a few bobby pins to keep it in place. I wanted Scott to see the entire dress, not hidden by long blond hair.

When I reached the kitchen, I was surprised to see 6:25 p.m. on the clock. I had five minutes to reach the barn in time. That was if we planned to leave by six-thirty. I grabbed my black, oversized faux fur shawl from the hall closet and headed for the door, giddiness pumping through my veins. Something about how this date was starting brought a feeling of newness to our relationship. I almost felt like a princess, going to meet her prince. Not a modern-day thought, I realized, but who cares?

I punched in the alarm code and reset it as I opened the door and stepped out into the winter landscape, half expecting a carriage made of a pumpkin and my entourage of mice to escort me to my destination. I stepped off the porch flooded with Christmas lights, realizing the moon wasn't as bright as I had hoped. In fact, a sky full of clouds forbid it. The lights from the porch would guide me part of the way on my short journey and the lights from the barn would finish the job. Only, the barn was cast in darkness. Not a glimmer in sight.

And then I realized I didn't have my phone, which would have certainly helped with the flashlight feature. Where was it? *In your fancy purse.* Oh, no.

Why was it so dark down there? Had Scott already left and was heading toward me? I *was* running a tad late. I squinted, my eyes trying their best to see him advancing, not picking up any movement in my direction.

And then I heard it. *Pop, pop.* I halted in my tracks. What was that?

I heard it again. *Pop, pop.*

A tremor rattled from my feet up to my heart. I knew what that sound was. It was a gun. And then questions hit me as cold as the air on my skin. Whose gun was it? And why were they shooting it?

Chapter Fifteen

I ran up to the house, punched the code back in, and dashed through the kitchen, my heels tapping down the hallway, my destination, Scott's nightstand. When I got there, I thrust the drawer open to discover no gun. *Of course, he keeps it with him at all times.*

Was that what I had heard? Him shooting or was it someone else? And why? Only one reason made sense: Randy. A terrifying scene played out in my mind's eye of Randy breaking into the barn, Scott confronting him, and the rest, too horrifying to imagine. I was beyond scared. I wasn't sure what to do next. It was like that night when we had thought Randy had broken in upstairs, only this was far worse. Back then, no one was shooting at anyone.

Dread, the strength of a bear trap, clamped around my lungs, making it difficult to breathe. My fears of what could happen were cropping up in real life. I had to do something. Scott was in danger.

With wobbly legs, I made my way through the house again and back to the front door. If only I had kept my phone, I could have called for help. How could I be so careless? I was too busy playing dress-up to pay attention to important details that could be the difference between life and death. I touched the doorknob. All at once, an eerie sensation crept over my skin, presenting a stark possibility. What if Scott was dead? What if Randy was on his way over here right now? And what would he do to me next?

My inner voice already knew the answer to that scenario. Whatever came at me, I'd fight to the death. If Scott was in fact gone, then what did it matter anyway? I didn't have a gun, but I did have a knife, which I grabbed from the knife block over by the stove.

Grip tight around the handle of the long knife, I slinked outside, stepped off the porch, and started down the driveway toward the barn, the shadows beckoning me forward. Danger lurked at every turn, the wind taunting my bare shoulders with its icy breath. Not a sound came from the barn. Not a word came from the trees as nature watched my walk of doom.

I was freezing, yet I was burning on the inside, unable to determine an accurate body temperature or how it was affecting my movements. The fact that my legs kept advancing was astonishing. Each step brought me closer to that dark structure, its walls and roof, staring down at me like a giant from another world. *Come to me, Sara. Meet your doom.*

I tried not to scuff my feet, wishing I'd had the wherewithal to put on boots. When faced with this kind of danger, the mind forgets, and mine had.

Another few steps drew me within reach of a situation that would change my life forever. I couldn't process, my lungs paralyzed, my head lighter than helium.

If Scott had won the gun fight, he'd be out here right now, making sure I was safe. I knew this just like I knew the sun would rise in the east and set in the west. And I also knew that

Scott would never allow anyone to hurt me, not without fighting with everything in him first. I would do the same—as ill equipped as I was.

My overactive imagination harassed my nervous system as I drew near. The light above the door—the one I referred to as the second sun—remained off. Only a switch would cause this to happen, another sign that Scott was not in control of the situation.

Was Randy watching me now? And here I was, dressed for the ball. Cinderella's ball. *Should I run? Should I hide?* I had to find Scott. I had to be with him. Nothing else mattered to me.

One step, and then two, I closed in on the front door. And then it opened, a dark figure looming not twenty feet away from me, something gripped in his hand—that *something* pointed right at me.

I froze. If I was still breathing, I had lost the ability to tell. Any second and I'd be dead, or worse. It was too late to run. My knuckles and fingers strained from my hold on the knife's handle. *Guns shoot at a distance, Sara. Knives need close proximity.* Once again, I had failed.

This was it. My final seconds before hell rose up and snatched me with its evil hand. And all I could think about was Scott. The love of my life. The man who changed who I was and gave me a family and a future. He was all I ever wanted in this world. *We'll be together soon, my love.*

"If you're going to shoot me, do it already." I heard the words fly from my lips, barely aware that I had spoken them. And then I let the knife drop to the ground. Would my heart bleed out like poor Arthur's had done behind his hunting cabin?

An alarmed voice rang out. "What is going on?"

At that moment, the second sun burst to life, its intense glow raining down on Scott, standing before me dressed in a tux, a small, clear-plastic box gripped in his hand. He wore a tie that matched the color of my dress.

Is that a corsage?

The emotional charge of the past few minutes tossed my head into the spin cycle, and I struggled to stand. Down I went, and right into Scott's arms, his musky scent welcoming my heart back to life.

"Are you all right? My God, Sara. What the hell is going on? Why did you think I was going to shoot you?" He glanced down at the ground. "Is that our kitchen knife?" Distress clouded his eyes as he held me close, giving my legs time to strengthen.

"I-I was ... I h-heard ..." An avalanche of thoughts overwhelmed my brain. I tried to make sense of it as I straightened up.

Scott was okay. Everything was fine. I saw this with my own eyes, yet it took my heart a few seconds to believe it.

And then I caught my breath. "When I left to come down here, I heard gunshots."

Scott's eyes narrowed with confusion. "Gunshots?" And then his face relaxed. "Oh, that wasn't a gun, babe. I'm so sorry I scared you."

I put a hand to my chest. "I thought Randy—"

He cradled my cheeks in his hands. "No, no. It's okay, babe, you don't have to be scared anymore. They caught him." Scott waited a moment to let the news sink into my confused brain. "He was hiding out at a woman's house who worked in the infirmary at the prison. She helped him escape. I guess they had suspected this for a couple of days now but wanted to make sure before they sent a SWAT team to her house." He placed his hands on my upper arms, the warmth from his skin salving my frozen muscles. "I texted you to tell you the news but—"

"You had my phone."

"Right. I realized I had your phone. I just figured I'd tell you when you got down here." And then he said it again, caressing my face. "They caught him, it's over."

I fell into his arms. "Oh, thank God."

Scott let a few seconds pass before he pulled back, his gaze examining me. "Wow." He shook his head. "I mean, wow. You look ..."—He rubbed his jaw—"incredible." He pivoted his body around and then bent over to pick up the transparent plastic box from the ground where it had landed when Scott had rushed over to catch me. "I got you a corsage ... for your wrist." He opened the box and placed the flowery bracelet on my wrist. He ushered me into his office. "You must be freezing. Where's your coat?"

Once inside, I gazed around the area, finding nothing new. It was the same tongue-and-groove pine walls, the same desk and chairs. "I must've dropped it in the house ..." I spent the next several minutes explaining what had happened. Again, Scott apologized for scaring the daylights out of me.

He got me water and stood close to make sure I was okay. He even retrieved my glamour purse from the kitchen counter, where he must've placed it. What he didn't do, however, was explain the noise.

My eyes found the clock on the wall, hands pointed at 6:55. "We better hurry or we'll be late." I made for the door, when he took my arm.

"We're not late." His face was bursting with anticipation, his eyes sparkling like two stars. In fact, I don't think I'd ever seen him this excited.

"What do you mean?"

"Before I tell you, I want to take one more look at you in that dress." He took my hand and twirled me around.

I watched as his brow rose, his jaw falling slightly open.

"Stunning. I get it now. That dress *is* special." As his gaze traveled over me and my outfit, his hand kept rubbing his mouth contemplatively. "I can't believe it took me nearly six years to finally see it, but it was worth the wait. And your hair." He ran his fingers along the wavy, blond swath running down the side of my chest. "Not to mention that back. It's sexy as hell." He turned me around again. "I want to kiss every inch of it." Using his finger, he ran a tender line from my waist to the nape of my neck, making me shiver. "Once again, I'm at your mercy, woman." And then he seemed to snap out of his reverie. He rubbed his jaw again in a thoughtful manner, reminding me of a college professor studying a problem, *hmm*, sounding from his lips. "But it's not complete." He went to his desk, where a red box with gold edging sat, one I hadn't noticed in all the confusion. It was the size of a five-by-seven-inch photo. "I got you something. An early Christmas present." He approached me and handed the box over to my outstretched hands.

I stood near the drafting table, appreciating its height as I set the box down and opened it. Inside a pear-shaped necklace beamed up at me, a ruby pendant dangling from its cut-glass chain. Not only was the ruby my birthstone, but it matched my dress perfectly. "I love it. It's beautiful. Thank you so much. Put it on me?" I handed him back the box, so he could take the necklace out and clasp it around my neck, which he did a moment later. First a corsage and now a necklace? He'd really gone all out for tonight.

I gazed over at the door, wondering when he was planning on leaving. We were definitely late *now*. "Shouldn't we get going?"

A funny expression washed over his face. "There's no need." Scott approached the sliding barn door and gripped its handle. "To answer your earlier question, we're not late because we're already here."

Chapter Sixteen

"**A**lready where?" What was he talking about? Had my husband suffered a bump on the head?

He pulled the door open. A dark room sparked to life with lights and activity. "Surprise," sounded off from various mouths around the large room.

I stepped closer, my lungs still trying to catch up to the adrenaline rush and then the sudden relief that all was well in my world. And now this. My brain wrestled to take it all in.

Scott's hand found my lower back, steadying me. "You've never been to a prom ... until now. This is your prom, babe." His lips were literally shaking with anticipation. He took my hand, walking me inside what used to be a large storage area, but not tonight.

If my eyes could have grown any wider, everyone would have thought I'd turned into a lemur. White swaths of tulle swung across the ceiling, coupled with strings of globe lights going right along for the ride, bringing elegance to the barn. Large lanterns—illuminated from within—hung from above, gathering the tulle at its peaks. Six round tables stood in formation around the room, smaller lanterns at the center of each, holiday greenery encircling them with a gentle hug. Some sort of white stretchy material covered each chair, much like the ones we had used at our wedding, and a very long train of banquet tables waited off to one side. One section displayed large chafing dishes with a few serving bowls intermixed, and drinks and a large punchbowl crowded others. Three caterers stood by ready to fulfill everyone's dietary needs.

Is that a photo booth?

At the back of the barn, a makeshift stage held, if my eyes didn't deceive me, Luke and all of his DJ equipment. *Luke?* "I see we've caught our guest of honor at a loss for words." Wearing a light-blue tux that looked like it came from the '70s, Luke fanned one hand out across the room, his voice amplified. "Welcome to your prom, Sara." And then the crowd came forward, Amy, Ben and his wife, Judy, Giselle from work with some guy by her side, Jason and Heather, Scott's parents, along with Kelsey and Stuart. Even Tanya and Andie had made the trip out. But what really threw me was when Abigail, Joel, and my little sister, Mel, emerged from the fray. Mel ran into my waist for a big hug.

Adding to the surreal moment, my bonus mother stepped up in a pink-and-black beaded dress with spaghetti straps and a straight skirt that reached all the way to the floor. Joel stood next to her, dressed in a nice-looking navy blue suit. Abigail secured the black velvet wrap around her shoulders as she moved forward, her shoulder-length, auburn hair shimmering under the lanterns.

Luke's voice bellowed throughout the large room. "I think it's time we get things rolling with the song 'Speechless' by Robin Schulz and Erika Sirola. Let's hope it helps Sara find her words." He chuckled, clearly enjoying my dazed expression.

The song played as everyone zeroed in on me, Scott

backing away a few steps to allow a plethora of greetings to unfold.

I started with Abigail, who had just hugged me—once Mel had loosened her grip on my waist. "How?"

I was reduced to one-word sentences, making Abigail laugh.

"Scott planned it all. In fact, he's been planning this for weeks. He asked us to come a day early." She touched my hair. "You look so beautiful, Sara. Did you do your own hair and makeup?"

I touched my hair, as well. "I did, thank you."

Her gaze took a journey over my dress, much like Scott's had. "And that dress." She shook her head in amazement. "I remember you showing it to me years ago, but the hanger didn't do it justice. That necklace is perfect too. Did Scott give that to you?"

I nodded as the pads of my fingers appreciated the smooth cut of the ruby. "Yup. He *just* gave it to me."

"You look like someone who should be posing for the cover of Vogue right now."

I shared a quick glance with my husband about her modeling observation, a smile pulling the corners of our lips upward.

"You look beautiful, too, Mom." Not only had she made the long trip, but she'd obviously put a great deal of effort into this night, and the outfit proved it. I touched some of the black beading, a stylish contrast to the swatch of pink satin, running diagonally across her bodice.

Abigail spun around, exposing the crisscross pattern of the dress's back. "It's my prom dress from back in the '90s." She brushed her hands down the waistline. "I'm just glad it still fits."

"Really? Wow, it looks great." I touched a hand to my lips,

my heart brimming over with love and gratitude. "I'm still freaked out that you all did this for me." And I was. This wasn't just a casual party for a birthday or an anniversary. This was a big deal, everyone taking time out of their busy holiday schedules to dress up and be here for me. I tried not to tear up.

"Don't you dare cry and smudge that mascara." Dressed in a metallic blue dress that reached mid-calf, the sleeves poufy, and a large bow adorning the front, Scott's mother approached. "Of course we did this for you. Every girl deserves her prom night." She made a face. "I wish I could say that *my* dress still fit, but I had to take out a few seams first." She lifted her chin, feigning arrogance, something that didn't come naturally to her kind heart. "I'm a little older than your mother, so that's my excuse. She was the '90s, and I was the '80s."

Abigail waved her off. "You're rocking it just as much as anyone, Beth. Don't sell yourself short." She offered a supportive grin.

I touched my mother-in-law's arm. "Yeah, Beth, you look beautiful. My mom had a dress like that one from her prom. Also, from the '80s." My gaze found Scott's father standing beside his wife in a tux, no less. "And you look pretty dapper, too, Theo." I kept my tone playful, knowing my father-in-law wasn't one for compliments or anything of the sort.

As expected, he shrugged me off. "Yeah, yeah. Took a very expensive bottle of bourbon from my son to get me into this monkey suit." He headed for the bar area. "Come along, my dear, we need drinks."

Beth fell in line. "Yes, I want to try that red blend I ordered." She picked up her pace.

"You look like a princess." Mel peered up at me with her youthful hazel eyes—the same hazel eyes that matched our mother to a T—pulling my attention away from the room. She tugged on the skirt of my dress. "Why is everyone so dressed up? It's not Christmas yet."

I squatted down to her level. "First of all, thank you for the compliment, sis." I touched the holiday tunic she was wearing with plaid edges that matched her plaid leggings and scarf. "You look pretty great yourself. And second of all, this is my prom. So that's why we are all so dressed up."

Mel seemed to contemplate that. "Prom?" She tipped her head this way and that. "What's a prom—"

"Okay, let's go get you something to eat, little one." Joel picked Mel up and pulled her away before one question turned into twenty, my mother tagging right along with them.

I thanked my stepfather with a nod and a smile.

Amy was the next in line to greet me. "Hey, Al. Pulled one over on ya, didn't we?" Wearing a dark-purple short coat with tails, a Gothic edge to it, over a pair of leather pants—black ankle boots with spiked heels on her feet—Amy's catlike grin spread across her face, her colorful hair flowing down to her shoulders, which always reminded me of a Skittles waterfall.

"As always, I love your outfit." I touched her lapel, enjoying the thick feel of the material. "You and Luke both look great."

Amy leaned in. "I wore this to *my* prom."

I was flabbergasted, my head flinching back. "*You* went to prom?" The surprise was hard to hide in my voice.

"Yeah, yeah. Don't start, Al. I only went because the girl I was seeing at the time wanted to go. Didn't last long. She ditched me for another girl, and I left before nine." She gazed up at Luke, who had switched to the song "Something Just Like This" by Coldplay. "That was when I decided women were too moody for me." Her green eyes, decorated heavily with makeup, shined. "I prefer tall, lanky men who I can pick on whenever I want."

I giggled. "Yes, I remember that about you." I nudged her

shoulder playfully. "How did Scott plan all of this without me knowing about it? And did you know about it when I was there for our visit?"

Amy planted one hand on her hip and made a *pfft* through her lips. "Why do you think Scott came up with that idea to come to Richmond? He wanted to check out Luke's DJ equipment and hire him for this."

I was glad Scott was paying Luke. That thought had also occurred to me, remembering the conversation I'd had with Amy about Luke's income.

"I'm blown away." I had to close my mouth from it hanging open. "I don't remember them discussing Luke's DJ business when we were there, do you? Wait. Was it when we left them at the bar?" A pang of guilt landed in my chest, but I tried to ignore it. Even when Scott and I were fighting, he was planning all of this. Yes, he'd made me madder than I'd ever thought possible, but I understood why now. It didn't excuse his behavior, but it did explain it. Still, it was pretty amazing that he could be in that much emotional turmoil and pull all of this off *for me*.

"I'm sure they talked about it then, too, but they scooted off once or twice when you weren't looking." Amy took a sip from the bottle of beer she was holding.

I crossed my arms. "You guys were all in on it? You brat." I lowered my voice as the song by Coldplay ended and another took over, this one by U2. I released my grip on Amy. "I'll have to tell you what was going on with Scott and why he was acting that way at the bar." I realized I had a lot to catch Amy up on, although I'd sent her a few texts explaining most of it, enough that she knew we were good now.

"Glad he came clean." Amy gave me that look, the one intended to pull me out of my obsessive mind. "Don't think any more about it tonight. We can discuss it later—"

"How'd you like my decoy of a dinner reservation at Bon Apétit?" Ben and Judy grinned from ear to ear. "I was so worried I was going to flub up and say the wrong thing." Decked out in another tux and gown, Ben and Judy were such a handsome couple. Everyone was, especially tonight.

"Oh, Ben, you did a great job. I had no idea." I smiled at Judy. "I love your dress, Judy, and your party was so much fun last night. Your house is gorgeous." I looked around for Scott who had moved away to mingle.

Donning a perfectly styled bob with chunky blond highlights, Judy bowed slightly as if in gratitude. Her off-the-shoulder, kelly-green dress with a drop waist (definitely from the '80s), didn't quite live up to the gold sequined mini dress she wore hosting her party the night before. "Thank you, Sara. Your house will be just as nice when it's completed. Ben brags all the time about how skilled Scott is at his job."

As I was thanking them, Scott's mom interrupted our conversation, plunking a glass of red wine in my hand. "Sorry, but you look like you could use a drink." She turned to take in the joyful room as Ben and Judy smiled, excusing themselves and departing for the buffet.

Amy remained in my peripheral, sipping her beer and listening to my conversations. Since her husband was preoccupied with the music, I enjoyed having her nearby.

"How do you like everything? The photo booth was Kelsey's idea." She pointed to the opposite side of the food area, where a sizable white-and-gold balloon arch loomed over a black backdrop, the words "Prom night" shimmering in over-sized gold letters. "Oh, my God, Beth, it's incredible. I owe you *and* Kelsey dinner. *Big time.*" As I spoke, my sister-in-law proceeded toward the booth, Stuart right by her side. A dark-maroon off-the-shoulder velvet gown graced her body, one with a full skirt and a slit down the front. Stuart wore a black suit. If that was her prom dress, Kelsey had made the right choice. Holding a beer in his hand, Scott meandered over, striking up a conversation with his sister, his free hand moving this way and that.

"I'm just in awe of all of this, Beth. This place looks amazing. We could have had our wedding here." I took a much-needed sip of wine, my taste buds enjoying its fruity hints, and gazed at my mother-in-law. "Was this all your idea?" I thought back to that evening in my kitchen—pizza night—when I had reminisced about my dress and mourned in front of Scott's mother and his sister about my lost prom days.

She shook her head. "Nah. I can't take credit. Kelsey mentioned our conversation to Scott, but he was the one who took the ball and ran with it. We just helped."

"I hope you and Kelsey didn't get stuck doing all of this decorating." Beth was the type of woman who would do anything for anyone and never complain about it, either.

"Oh, no. It was a group effort, and Scott did most of the work. In fact, he worked well into the night a couple of times to hang those lanterns with the tulle and the string lights. His father helped him." She took a sip of her wine while I thought about last week and how late Scott had been working. He was doing it all for me? And his father was here? I had no idea.

"You know how this family loves a party, Sara, and this one sounded extra special." She touched my cheek. "I hope you like it, dear."

"I love it." Making sure not to spill my wine all over her vintage dress, I gave her a side hug. "And I love *you*, Beth."

"I love you too."

"Aw," Amy said with a slight grin.

I made a funny face at my friend. "I love you, too, Amy."

She waved me off. "Don't get all sappy on me, Al."

Beth laughed at us before moving off toward the drink

table, making room for Andie and Tanya. Andie came dressed in black dress pants with a red blazer, Tanya, red dress pants with a black blazer, winter-white camisoles shimmering underneath, and four-inch black heels on their feet. Just like in life, these two women complemented each other well. "Sorry. We threw out our prom dresses. They were nothing great, anyway." Andie made a face, bordering on a grimace. "When Scott told us about this party, we were psyched to come." Tanya lifted her glass of white wine. "Once again, cheers to picking one of the good ones, Sara." She took a quick sip. "And cheers to you wearing that dress so well."

"Thanks, and you two look pretty great yourselves." I hooked Amy's arm before she had a chance to drift away. "This is my best friend, Amy." I motioned from Amy to my new friends. "This is Tanya and Andie. They own the yoga studio I was telling you about."

"Cool. Good to meet you." Amy gave Andie and Tanya a once-over. "Love the outfits."

Andie nodded at Amy. "Likewise. That jacket's lit."

Amy, Andie, and Tanya drifted into conversation at my side as Giselle appeared, wearing a one-shoulder hot pink foil print dress called an Anarkali if I wasn't mistaken. An attached drape flowed behind her. Her handsome date donned a black suit with perfect proportions.

"Giselle, thank you so much for coming. You look amazing."

Giselle smiled. "Thank you, so do you." She motioned toward her date. "This is my boyfriend, Rishi."

"Nice to meet you, Rishi." Taking his place by my side, Scott reached out and shook his hand before I had a chance to. "And Sara always says how much she likes working with you, Giselle." He smiled, and I swear, Giselle blushed. That was my charmer of a husband.

A few more greetings, and then we filled our plates with food, chatted some more—drank some more—and then danced the night away. Every now and then, a few people would jaunt over to the photo booth, me included. We posed for traditional prom photos, goofy photos, and everything in between. Having dabbled with photography in college, Stuart brought his expensive camera, along with his talent for using it. We supported his efforts by taking a gazillion cell phone pics. We laughed at the images we created, encouraging us to pose for more, one of them a human pyramid.

Another master of his craft, Luke revved up the crowd with just the right ratio of dance music versus ballads to either wind us up or slow us down.

Intermittently, I'd meander over to the buffet to sample goodies or take a sip of wine, Scott always by my side. "You have to try the punch," he said, pouring me a glass that tasted like fruit punch had collided with turpentine. I tried so hard not to grimace.

"I spiked it just for you."

I laughed. Scott had truly thought of everything. He only pressured me to take one sip. Thank God. I was happy with my wine, but I did appreciate the sentiment.

Scott leaned closer. "Sorry I wouldn't let you come into my office the other night. My mother had just dropped off a bunch of decorations, and I didn't want you to see them." He took a bite of chicken satay, made by a caterer his mother had hired, although, Scott assured me he had paid for everything. "I let her help decorate, but I wanted this night to be from me."

"Oh, that's why you wouldn't let me into your office." Another puzzle piece fit into place as I hugged my man and sipped my wine. "Well, I'm relieved. I thought maybe you'd stowed one of those horny women from the bar in the back of my SUV and brought her home." I smirked, quirking one brow.

He leaned in, his lips landing on mine, leaving a few of the spices from the chicken, savory on my tongue. "Not a chance." He pulled back and shook his head. "They were certainly horny, though. Christ, I wasn't sure they were going to let me leave with my clothes on." He held the chicken skewer near his mouth for another bite. "I can't imagine how men who strip for a living deal with that. You women are animals." He giggled. "I'll stick with my she-beast, thank you very much." He winked at me, his smile dazzling.

I just sipped my wine and enjoyed his teasing. The man was adorable.

Once he'd chewed all the chicken clean from the wooden skewer, he threw it in a nearby trash can and wiped his hands, the napkin also going in the trash. "And I'm also sorry I got so defensive in the car when you brought up the subject of proms on our way to Amy and Luke's place." His cheeks took on a bashful hue. "Truth be told, I was afraid I might slip up and tell you something about tonight."

"Okay, folks, let's slow things down again. Not my typical music, but I felt this song called 'Perfect' by Ed Sheeran was just right for this moment. Don't you all think so?" He motioned with his hands for people to respond, which they did with hoots and hollers. Everyone felt loose and ready to party, Amy the loudest of them all. "Let's get Sara and Scott back out on the dance floor. This song was popular back when I went to my prom." He winked at Amy just a few feet away.

Standing next to Andie and Tanya, Amy cupped her hands around her mouth and yelled, "Who'd you go with, dude?"

Luke shook his head. "No one special."

"Good answer. You might just get lucky tonight." The people around my bold friend laughed at her reply, including Scott's parents and Abigail. Luke just shook his head.

"May I have this dance?" Scott took my hand and led me to

the center of the dance floor, where his hands embraced my waist, my fingers lacing around his neck.

As Ed Sheeran serenaded us, Scott held me in his arms. Outside our little bubble, nothing else existed. It was just us. He took my hand and kissed it, then returned it to his shoulder, his eyes never breaking contact with mine. "I love you, babe. This is the best prom I've ever been to. Once again, you've upped the game for me."

"*I've* upped the game? I didn't do a thing. This was all on you, handsome." I tried not to cry. I really did, but sentimental tears had a mind of their own. "Oh, Scott. This is just amazing. I'm glad I never went to prom because this night is far more special than any other prom I could imagine." I rose up on my tiptoes and kissed his soft lips. "Except for maybe our wedding." I looked down and then up into the loveliness of his gaze, my heart starting to ache from all the turmoil we had just gone through. "I only wish—"

"Nope." He put his finger to my lips, his voice as tender as rose petals. "Not tonight. I could apologize every day for the rest of my life, and it wouldn't be enough, but this night isn't about any more sorrys. It's about us. And *our* prom. The first time we made love, I told you that it was a totally different experience for me back then. That's what tonight is. My proms pale in comparison to this one, where I get to hold the love of my life in my arms. You looking like an angel." He pulled me closer.

Our bodies matted together, my breasts pushed up against his strong chest, our hearts pitter-pattering their own version of Morse code. And then he sang into my ear, helping Ed Sheeran with the next set of lyrics, the ones that said everything his eyes told me he wanted to say. "You look perfect tonight." His hips swayed, his body encapsulating me in the cloak of his love and his heart.

By ten o'clock, my family was starting to fade, or Mel, anyway. Abigail, Joel, and my precious little sister drifted off to the house, while the rest of us partied with gusto. I loved not having to worry about house alarms or locked doors. Tonight, we were safe. Tonight, we were young. And tonight, I was with my soulmate.

One of many benefits of knowing the DJ was getting him to play until midnight, which he did without any argument, Scott promising me he'd include a very large tip. Luke even danced with his wife a few times, making sure she wasn't too lonely.

"You having a good time, Sara?" Luke asked from his microphone. "Is this prom all you hoped it would be?"

Still on the dance floor, I nodded and yelled, "The best ever!" letting Scott hold my waist as I leaned back and swayed side to side with delight.

"Well, it's not over yet. Your husband has one last surprise for you."

I stood upright, my eyes on alert. What could possibly top this party, I wondered. Was Ed Sheeran going to appear in the flesh?

Instead of playing another song, Luke hopped down from the small platform and strolled over to the back of the barn, where an extra-wide garage door stood ready for something to happen.

Without the help of amplification, Luke called out, "Would you all join me at the back of the barn, please?" He waited as the crowd did just that, most of them grabbing coats as they wandered close. And then, he hit the button for the garage door to open, cold air rushing in.

So, this is going to be outdoors? And here I was without a coat. But not for long.

All at once, my faux fur wrap enveloped my shoulders,

snuggling my upper body in warmth and softness. "Thank you, handsome." I ran my hand over the furry fabric.

Of course, Scott had gotten it for me. But when? I shook my head, deciding it wasn't worth sleuthing over. This was a special night, no need to question the details.

"I can't let you freeze at your prom." Scott spoke with protective indignation, his hand returning to my lower back.

God, I loved this man.

With everyone gathered, Luke signaled to someone I couldn't see, and then a small firework display lit up the dark sky, a few pops intermixed within the spectacle.

Pops? That was the noise I heard.

Scott leaned over, his mouth closing in on my ear. "There's your gun." He draped his arm around my shoulders as we all watched in awe of the show. If only Abigail and Joel were here to witness it.

A nudge from Scott had my eyes drifting to the right, where my mother and Joel stood off to the side in thick coats and wide smiles. Abigail waved at me.

I waved back.

Oohs and *ahhs* filled the night, and everyone's eyes glazed over from the overabundance of spirits and fun. Andie and Tanya, Amy and Luke, Beth and Theo, and everyone else stood together to capture this special night, the holidays supplying an extra dose of magical ambiance.

Eventually, the three fridges—two at the main house and one in the barn office—grew overstuffed with leftover food, the drinks left on the tables to be dealt with tomorrow. Even though I protested, no one would let me help. "You'll ruin your dress," being the most popular excuse. I couldn't argue with that one.

So, I used the time to waltz some more with my husband. Later, after everyone had left, taken home or to their hotel by a small bus, much like the shuttles at the airport—something Scott's father had scored from a connection with his business—Scott brought me to the back of the barn again, the echoes of the party lingering in the air.

"Are you sure you didn't know a thing about this?" He narrowed his eyes at me, his head tipped sideways. "Not even the bus dropping everyone off out back earlier? I was so afraid you were going to see them. I turned the light off above the barn door to make it less visible."

Another puzzle piece. I shook my head. "No! I must've been getting ready by then. I had no idea. How could you think any different? I thought Randy was here shooting you. Remember?"

His face relaxed. "That's true." He took my hand.

"Where are we going?"

He led me out back, where his truck awaited, its engine running idle. "No prom is complete without a good make-out session, don't you think? My back seat is all ready for us. The truck is nice and warm." He opened the back door to his twin cab. "Your chariot awaits."

That was something Scott had said to me on our first date. On our hike up the mountain.

"Don't worry. I have no intention of ruining that gorgeous gown like I did with your negligée. I just want some time with those pouty lips of yours for a few *very* long minutes. I'll bring you home to your parents' place soon." A twinkle in his eye brought a smile to my lips.

On the other side of Scott's truck, Abigail's minivan sat parked, its windows all frosty and cold, something I hadn't noticed during the firework display.

"Oh, you will, will you?" I approached the truck, letting him lift me up inside. And then I spoke with an artificial southern drawl. "Well, you better, kind sir. My family won't take kindly to you soiling my reputation, Mr. Williams." I stared down at him, loving this little game.

He kissed my hand, his voice all new and heavily southern. "Miss, Sara. I wouldn't dream of doing such a thing. Your virtue is safe with me."

* * *

The next few days were picture-perfect. With Randy securely behind bars, there was nothing to stop us from enjoying the holidays to the fullest, Mel's dazzled expression on Christmas morning bringing it all home.

Watching my family, I realized that none of us knew when our time would come. And for that reason, we had to live each day as though it could be our last. I had given and received more love than most people deserved.

Besides ... there was no point in worrying about tomorrow, not when today was so doggone awesome!

Tell me what you think ...

Authors are nothing without their readers. I would love to know what you think about *Bleeding Heart - A Holiday Romance*.

Please consider leaving me a review (a few words are plenty) on Amazon, Goodreads, and/or BookBub. For self-published authors, reviews are so important.

Thank you for reading, and keep an eye out for my next project *A Collision with Love* coming very soon.

Also by Tricia T. LaRochelle

Sara Browne Series Romantic Suspense:

Flickering Heart - Book 1

Revive - Book 2

Handfast - Book 3

Bleeding Heart - A Holiday Romance - Book 4

Stand alone Contemporary Romances:

Sun in My Heart

Coming soon ... A Collision with Love

Acknowledgments

This has always been my favorite page in a book. It's a place where authors get to thank those who have helped them along the way. And let's face it, authors need a lot of help!

My support system has dwindled over the years, which I believe is a good thing, since I don't need the same level of help as I used to need. Let's hope anyway (wink, wink).

I dedicated this book to two amazing women, one of them being Hattie LaRochelle. Hattie has been instrumental in helping me with all of my books. She proofs, she edits, and she offers valuable feedback that has helped bring my books to the next level. And she's never missed a launch, showing up at my door with a bottle of wine and a handwritten note of congratulations. Thank you, Hattie, from the bottom of my heart.

Next to Hattie, I want to thank my oldest son, Ryan. Like Hattie, Ryan has proofed, edited, and offered a male's perspective, which is always invaluable. And when I say he's proofed, I mean he's got the eyes of an eagle, catching everything most professionals would miss. He's a sweetie too. Gets it from his mother.

Melissa Shelton Harrison is my editor, proofer, and cheerleader. I rely on her expert opinion for so much these days and would be dead in the water without her spot-on advice. She never lets me down. And that is something I have grown to value more now than ever.

I always love those book bloggers, who go above and beyond

to help authors get their work exposed and reviewed. Laura from Reading in the Red Room is one in particular, who I value more than she knows. She's a master reader, who could most certainly win a contest by her level of speed and insightfulness.

Deborah Apodaca does PR but she also helps authors whenever she can. I called on both Laura and Deborah for some preliminary advice, and they both came to my aid. You ladies rock!

To Xuni.com and Indie Penn, you ladies (and gents) do such amazing work on my website and the PR for my launches. I am so fortunate to get to work with you all.

He didn't get to read this time, but my awesome husband, Bob, lives the experience of being an author. He's there when I need a boost and is great for bouncing ideas around, both creatively and with promotion. Love you.

And then there are you readers who I long to make a connection with. I would literally be nothing without you. Thank you from the bottom of my heart.

Tricia T. LaRochelle

Since she was a little girl, award-winning author Tricia T. LaRochelle has been obsessed with tragic love stories. No beach reads for her. In a true love story, it's the struggles and the sacrifices that two people endure *and* overcome to be together that make a romance interesting and compelling.

Growing up in central Vermont, she has seen her share of tragedy but remains a hopeful romantic. She now lives in central Virginia, where she continues to foster the possibilities of how love can conquer all.

Her Sara Browne Series has won multiple awards as well as her stand alone contemporary romance Sun in My Heart.

Sign up for her newsletter at TriciaLaRochelle.com for updates, announcements, and giveaways, or follow her on Facebook, Twitter, Instagram, Threads, or Pinterest.